# HARIYANA

by harvey meyers

illustrated by regina meyers

commenced as a written transcript
from memory, eighth year Śiva Kalpa

OMKARA PRESS
51 Scott Street
San Francisco, Ca. 94117

Orders for this book may be placed through the
publisher.

Library of Congress Catalog Card No.: 79-84779
ISBN: 0-934094-01-2

# Part One:

# The Yoga of Dejection

ॐ ऋतो स्मर कृतं स्मर
ऋतो स्मर कृतं स्मर

Omkrato smara kṛtam smara
Krato smara kṛtam smara

Om    O Will, remember that which was done
remember!

O Will, remember that which was done
remember!

Iśa Upaniṣad

"... by exclusive concentration on formal and material limitations, by negation of the very essence of existence until the critical departure from Truth touches off the recoil of a spontaneous reawakening in the divine light of Saccidananda."

from the Definition of Existence in the document entitled
*Śiva Kalpa*

AUM        ŚIVAYA        NAMAḤ

bow down to the supreme aspect of Lord Śiva. May He
continue to burn down the ignorance of my limited and
mortal imaginings...And may my sister, the Goddess
Saraswati, grace me with language commensurate to the tale I
wish to tell.

The thirteenth year in the cycle of divine consciousness
known as Śiva Kalpa having commenced, I celebrate the most
wondrous events occurring ten years ago when Śankara first
wooed Venus into His dance, when Gauri first enticed Jupiter
from the icy regions of His remote dispassion to take part in Her
game of phenomenal nature, when, in the terms of our past
contrivance, the divided hemispheres of our own mind, the East
and the West, came together...Ten years since in this form the
glory was perceived.

Praise, dear Goddess, that Union in Truth and Light which is
the wondrous beginning of all things, and permit me to reveal
that portion of the witnessing subjectivity I retain. To those
granted even partial understanding of the Truth herein conveyed all sorrow is removed; to those who plunge deeper within
Its meaning the Consciousness of a Blissful Existence becomes
the permanent result.

AUM        TAT        SAT

first met Father on October 29th, third year Śiva Kalpa, though I still called it 1968.

I had returned that morning to Calcutta. Stepping down from the painted lorry which had been my chariot for the past three days, I thanked the *Sardarji*[1] for his kindness in bringing me to my journey's end, and mused upon the cycle this completed. A little over twelve months before I had arrived for the first time in Calcutta. That time I had descended from the clouds, surprised to find that Dum Dum Airport was hardly part of the uniform decency of the international airways system; I was wearing a light green suit and I carried a huge pack just bulging with possessions, the prize of which was a 16 mm. movie camera with which I was going to film my impressions of this new experience. But by the end of my very first bus ride from Dum Dum to Calcutta, I was a changed man. I could no longer maintain any illusions of dealing with the world, as it now lay before me, based on my past understandings.

[1]term of respect applied to male Sikh.

Now, upon my second arrival, I had but one shoulder bag in which I kept my journal, passport, and the accumulated letters which had found their way to me. I carried my *yatra*[2] staff and stood bare except for a frayed maroon robe which had served me for many many months. But the change in my physicality was slight compared with the liberties India had taken with my mind.

This morning it had drizzled at daybreak when the Sardarji and I followed a turn in the Hooghly River by Dakshineshwar. As I looked out upon the widening arcs on the grimy surface of the Hooghly, I realized that since I had left Kashmir, I had for these last months unintentionally been following the course of the Ganga to its present degeneracy. Starting in Hrishikesh as a fierce gush of purity, its flow was regulated by a canal system in Hardwar where pilgrims prayed beside it, on to Benares where from the burning *ghats*[3] ashes of cremated dead drifted upon it, to this local indignity as the recipient of the industrial refuse of the modern India – an indignity great enough to warrant a change in name from the beloved Ganga of song and prayer to the ridiculous Hooghly. And there at its mouth stood the residue of all the waste of India – Calcutta.

Returning, I felt a kind of amnesia, somnambulism, if you will, that India had induced upon me, though certain facts announced themselves clear as *Diwali*[4] firecrackers. No matter how distant or to what extremity I had taken myself, I had never lost sense of time and place. It seemed it wasn't permitted, for I knew that in my terrestrial consciousness a great chronicle was unfolding. At first I thought it was mine and went through the vanity of trying to create a chronological, artistically ordered record of it until one day near the hills of Simla the voice in my own head just ran out, ceased, and in that brief silence I knew that I was a blank page upon which the hand of God was writing. For whatever purpose, time and space remained clear

[2]pilgrimage.

[3]series of steps leading down to a body of water.

[4]the "festival of lights."

to me no matter how far I wandered in other areas of confusion. It was October 29th – I knew that. Twelve thousand miles to the west, when the sun would come up there, my daughter Celia would be turning three years old.

That other life seemed discontinuous to me, however, and this one, for all its logical absurdities, seemed somehow regular. For coming to Calcutta a second time, I seemed to be returning home in some strange way just as I had returned home to Philadelphia and California in a former life. Everything in Calcutta felt intimate and familiar though it was not from any particular physicality that I recognized and remembered it. I knew this city now not so much by buildings as by feelings, a resonance of mood, a certain quality of light which told me all I needed to know and much more than I could comfortably use.

That was one of the things about India, the buildings and structures were palpably impermanent to begin with. Not like those of Philadelphia or California which had seemed so fixed, so imposingly inflexible. No, India had made it easier, visually, to dissolve the *maya*[5] in the first place.

That was the seduction through which she tempted us to take one step further, then one step further, only to disclose always at her very center a kind of chaotic joke. For all its passion and all of its variance, the center seemed constantly to elude revelation with a kind of contemptuous mockery. In the sincere hope that India's center would present its secret to me, I had surrendered many times only to have ashes put in my tea and to stand abuse from her infinite capacity for cunning. And yet I had remained sanguine throughout, knowing that I was destined, predetermined to win that burning grail, to stand again amongst those I had abandoned, and triumphantly for I would possess that which would make all things new. But at this moment my spirits were in the descendent, the nadir of my subconscient sojournings. I was easily depressed and at quarrel with the strange

[5]commonly defined as "illusion," the whole network of phenomenal projection.

4

destiny that had brought me again to this city of limitless delusion.

rom a random encounter seven months prior in a dirty and flea filled Bombay hotel, I had an address for someone in Calcutta. I remembered Ken Wilson proclaiming his musical ambitions there in that hotel room so small for his enthusiasm that his swift gestures put to shame the ceiling fan's half-hearted, sluggish efforts. The address on a scrap of paper nestled in the bottom of my bag, but I had much doubt that it would still be good since I fancied at that moment that I was one of the only western aspirants still left in India, the only one who hadn't yet come to his senses and been repatriated or, failing that legitimate if slightly disgraceful means of escape, flipped out and been deported to some less baffling and trying region on this earth, a place where the illusion of progress and accomplishment was easier to sustain.

At the Dharamtalla crossing I boarded a tram for south Calcutta. I'd be half way there before the fare-taker could get to me, so dense in human flesh was the conveyance. I had become quite expert at dodging ticketmen and conductors... insisting for miles on end that I didn't understand what they were talking about at all, that in my own country I always rode free, that it was their duty to allow me to ride, whatever would serve for the time to minimize my relationship with their physical, phenomenal-plane concerns. Early on, almost at the outset of my venture here, I had decided that I would have no part of the mundane matters of this strange and chaotic country, would decline involvement in the rules and regulations, call it the reality, which did not govern so much as herd and corral the lives of its inhabitants. That way madness lay. I knew it. I knew it instantly from the frenetic behaviour, from the strange balls of nervous energy that all Indians had seemed to me from the very second I encountered them.

South Calcutta. Rash Behari. Ballygunge. Less teeming, green swards, fewer cows, curd shops – a good district really.

At Ken Wilson's there was a gate. A boy of indeterminable age from 15 to 35, dressed in the ubiquitous khaki shorts, showed me in.

"Come, *sahib*,[1] yes, you just come," It felt distinctly as though I had been expected.

The flat was huge and luxurious and devoid of people. There was expensive recording equipment against one wall and beautiful, polished stringed instruments: serbahar, tamboura, sitar, sarod, ishraj and sad saranghi. A set of tablas also and other drums, and a *shenai*[2]... one of each, just like that. There was also a strange tone and pitch to that main room, unmistakably sharp and clear though unidentifiable and lasting but a moment.

The boy showed me the shower and left. After ablution I wandered into a bedroom, surprised to find a sandy-haired form asleep there. How could I have missed him at first? He was an Englishman, it turned out, very young, very sweet, quite flipped out. David Bray. From him I learned that Ken and the others who studied music there were off on a vacation and that I was welcome to stay, many did. He himself had arrived at Ken's quite some months back, just after leaving Benares where he

[1]term of deference for a white man; left over from British rule in India.

[2]reed instrument; close to an oboe in sound.

had resigned himself to a quiet insanity, and had just stayed on, being taken care of by Ken and his musician companions, Josh and Gayle. He was later repatriated, placed in a mental hospital in Sussex, and eventually I would hear that he died in an automobile accident.

By now the American Express office was open, and I hastened down there. Oddly enough there were three pieces of mail for me; I hadn't been in communication for almost two months.

There was a note from Sal Friscia, a painter I had known in Kashmir who had started his journey in Tunis and sort of painted his way around the middle east and wound up in India. In Kashmir he had hidden behind his miniatures and didn't want to get to know any of us. He was a bit older, almost forty. I had run into him recently in Benares where I had found myself in the position of justifying to him why I was staying on the road in the particular form I adopted – as a *sadhu*,[3] the would-be yogi, the messiah for the West. He had tried every argument that reserve, caution and compromise could muster. We seemed to have hit the prototypic enzyme of our relative positions in that round, for I felt in answering him that I was also responding to my elder brother Mel's form of censure in my pre-college days, my Dad's warnings about disappointment before that, and God only knows how many other influences for moderation. I loved Sal for having acted it out at its most absurd limit.

The note from him said that he was in Calcutta, that he'd like to see me should I come through, and that he had a show of his miniatures at the U.S.I.S. The other two pieces of mail were from my wife Alice and from my mother. Both were negative and reflected the hurt they had suffered due to the inexplicably long turn my absence had taken. Alice's earlier letters had been supportive, but it was inevitable that they would turn critical as time went on. From my mother there was a new apprehension: "Are you on drugs?" Both letters pled for my return.

They came at the right moment. *Bas*, enough, I said. I could hold out against most things, but not that my obviously fruitless quest could inflict pain in those quarters. I confess that in places

[3] literally "saint;" wandering holy man.

I'd been, wife, children, mother seemed vague fictions to me. But this hurt was real. I received it.

I quickly wrote two aerogrammes telling them I knew now I would be coming home. Lack of funds necessitated my return overland, which would take some time, I told Alice. Or if I were to fly back, should the means present themselves, the only stop I would care to make would be to locate my younger brother Rich who had left India four months before and was now somewhere in Europe, I thought. The answer to the letter would decide my next move. Meanwhile there was still my present existence to put up with and it was hungry.

I was walking along the Chowringhee – the mad main thoroughfare of Calcutta where under a great metal canopy every imaginable distortion of the human psyche parades itself in its own mental neighborhood of isolation. All this, only for the privilege, mind you, of witnessing the diversity, the erraticism, the fecundity of His omnipotent imagination. It expanded the mind mostly in the direction of seeing how obtuse, how dark, how suffering existence could be. And yet it always spared us in its vision by lifting us up, out of the person perceiving it, witnessing placidly, immutably, not being drawn into its terms of torture. Yes, walking on the Chowringhee when from its maze of phantom sorrows emerged a familiar form cutting through its mournful mass with a brisk stride and the westerner's inherent sense of purpose – John O'Shea, sadhu friend, fellow pilgrim.

I had last seen John in Kashmir. For the most part I had supported that particular scene, anxious to get rid of the responsibility of the last little bit of my money, impatient to be totally at the mercy of circumstance. I had been helped in this by all the vagabonds of the road: ripped off materially by the French, betrayed emotionally by the Italians, loving everyone through it, blaming only my impotence to help anyone. Just before I left Kashmir, I wanted to give each of the persons I had lived with some one small thing that I had heard them mention wanting. For John, who had often sat by my bed as I was recovering from hepatitis, I imagined a real brass water bowl, suitable for alms. I would really have liked to have given him a silver *trishula*, a shivite trident, to replace the one he had once and was so fond of recalling, but its expense placed it beyond consideration. John had been a proper sadhu, you see, keeping track of every *giti*[4] stone, carrying his own *safi*,[5] almost finicky within his pauperhood. It was probably his years in the Marine Corps that ironically prepared him for the unique role he enacted and the code of conduct he displayed along the road of spiritual seeking in India – our semper fidelis sadhu.

When I offered him the bowl, he thanked me for the intention but told me that he would be heading toward Europe. He had had it with India, then, when I was just about to strike out anew, invigorated by the thought of my incipient destitution. But here he was, two months later, walking along in smacking new white pyjamas, his shoulder-length copper hair nicely oiled. He looked a man of luxury and elegance to me, for now I stood in rags.

"Have you got a *bidi*,[6] man?" I asked. That had been our traditional opener with each other. I let him know I was hungry.

There were four other Americans with my friend at the time, two young men and two girls. I had barely noticed them until John whispered something to the paler-looking male, clean shaven, thinning hair, and thick eyeglasses. I took them all in quickly. The other young man was bearded, also with thinning hair, and he wore a tiger's claw necklace. One of the girls was very pretty. She seemed high strung and charged for her eyes darted everywhere very quickly, not so much looking at things as a little above them. She could not have been long in India and certainly had not come overland for she showed none of the scars that the glances of Muslim lust inevitably leave on road ladies; also she was still wearing western clothes. In fact, she might have just now stepped out from the pages of *Mademoiselle*

[4]small rounded or tapered stone dropped in bottom of smoking implement called chillum to block bottom of conical bore so only smoke and no matter passes through.

[5]cloth wetted and wrapped around bottom of chillum to cool smoke as it is inhaled.

[6]native non-tobacco cigarette; type of leaf in which the mixture is wrapped.

or something like that; I'd been away from the west too long to clearly place her. The other girl was not so striking, frizzy hair, and her electrical current much much slower. Whoever they were, my presence arrested their flow for a moment since I had emerged as stunningly in their vision as they had surprised me. It was always so when westerners passed in this seldom broken sea of Indian inertia; kindred energy systems of high intensity sensing each other over great distances, standing in mute awe and rare wonder before qualities considered mundane or pedestrian on their native grounds. We came back into ourselves from this frieze of Olympian recognition when the bespectacled traveller drew from his *kurta*[7] pocket a couple of rupee notes which he gave to John. These four floated back into the human traffic and John and I stalked off with our money to satisfy my hunger.

We took a booth in Nizam's, dirty and greasy, and the service rude and sloppy. The Muslim waiters ran around in what seemed to be their underwear, slapping plates down in front of you, pouring water from a bladder bag and coarsely shouting out the orders – *do paratha, ek kabob*. Somehow it came to pass as efficiency, and simple pleasures took on the aspect of catered comforts; some anise seed served up with the bill, an after-dinner bidi to smoke or *pan*[8] to chew, and one felt a veritable gentleman.

In this momentary glow of content I surveyed the surroundings with supreme satisfaction. I had eaten here often with my brother Rich the year before, and it was at these very tables that he had shown me the proper way to eat with my fingers and initiated me into his more subtle mysteries of survival in the shock of the tropics. Rich had loved the labyrinth of tile booths in Nizam's and the way they were reflected in the wall mirrors, giving the impression of more rooms than were actually there, and he had found the setting a proper metaphor for what he was telling me of the hysterical complexity of his year's experience there prior to my coming. I was sort of telling John this when I

[7]shirt of light cotton (khadi).

[8]betel nut, small pieces of silver, tobacco, sweet bits, coconut sometimes, wrapped in a moist green leaf.

noticed in one of those mirrors that Sal Friscia was sitting alone at a booth suspiciously eyeing the glass of water that had just been placed before him.

We three had last been together that summer in Kashmir, and when he joined us a moment later, we naturally fell to talking now of what had occurred in between for each. As it turned out, all three of us had fairly recently been in Benares where Sal had seen John in passing once or twice before I came and had seen me quite a bit (mostly for those sessions counselling me to forsake my yogi ways) after John had left. It seemed John had slipped out of Benares just moments before a bust had taken place on one of the houseboats. Arrests of westerners were still pretty uncommon in India, and this one had set up something of a shock wave amongst the mobile international community for it foretold that the time of the indulgent finding of self at the expense of local customs and feelings would soon come to its end. I had come into Benares just in the wake of this bust.

Since that time, John had been here in Calcutta where he had found a kind of benefactor in the person of a Dr. Śivamurti Prasad. This man was encouraging John O'Shea to do a tour with him as a western sadhu. He would show John all the holy sights of Mother India and foot the expense for the story of John's quest. Perhaps he had in mind starting an *ashram*[9] with John as the resident yogi; it wasn't quite clear. John, however, was hoping that this Dr. Prasad could unravel some of the secrets of the chemical composition of the legendary *soma*. [10]

Sal had gone to Kathmandu where he had put together a show of his watercolors and ink drawings. He was bound back to the U.S.A. and he thought a credit or two for having had a show in India could not help but advance his artistic career. I was amused that both Sal and John could entertain the notion that anyone's experience in India could possibly result in pragmatic benefit. Yet I realized that the two of them, through vastly divergent channels, were still somehow on the threshold of

[9]a monastery for Hindu holymen; originally from "ashrama," meaning stage of life.

[10]ancient libation reputed to have mystical properties.

having their dreams fulfilled, and they shared an anticipatory enthusiasm. Was it only I, then, whose hopes had suffered a reversal in these last months, whose journey seemed to move away from that certainty and sureness? I shall always be grateful to John O'Shea for picking up on my moment of depression and for trying in his sweet feelingness to allay it.

"Hey, man, it's still good," he said. "It's still good."

He pointed out that many toiled for untold years and never earned the sights we had already seen, that we were essentially free in each moment to create the next while nearly everyone else was bound to actions not of their choosing. It did not turn my mood, but it reminded me of how recently I held the exuberant assurance that my present privilege was the reward of many lifetimes of earnest endeavor, that it would purchase redemption not only for me but for unimaginable scores of others who had invested their lives in petty concerns so that Truth could be attained in my form. What bothered me was that such peaks of assurance were almost always followed by the nagging nihilistic doubt that there was, in fact, nothing to be found, that I would return before my patient stockholders with nothing but incoherent mutterings as the sum total of my indulgence and privilege and their investment.

"Besides," John continued, "just around the corner from here are some people who just came from California, and they still have some Mexican weed which I am sure will make things look rosier. Shall we?"

*Allak Naranjan Sabadu Kabhajan* – Never deny an offering. So we three went past the New Market and through the alley of *dhobis*[11] and on to Sudder Street where stood the Astoria Hotel, a dive but still above my recent standards, and we ascended to the second floor where in a room along with some other people sat Father.

---

[11]people who wash clothes as an economic occupation.

"**R**emember the first time you met me," I have heard him say a thousand times since that moment, sometimes as a question, more often as a command. Indeed, it would be impossible to forget your first encounter with Father, easier to forget your own name, as you will see. What is difficult is to re-imagine the relative puniness, mediocrity, mundanity of the world before he announced his presence. A hundred times I have walked through those doors in my memory, drawn aside those green curtains and there he is, yes there he is along with the others in the room, and could it be possible that at that moment I was more interested in the others?

He was lean, with a beautiful white beard, benign smile, humbly magnificent. Beside him in striking contrast sat a middle class Indian, pressed-slacks variety, pen-in-shirt-pocket type, wearing tinted glasses, Dr. Śivamurti Praṣad, my friend John's patron. I was mostly interested in the westerners, two of whom I had already seen on the Chowringhee. One, the young man with the tiger's claw necklace, was now reclining on the bed, wasted with dysentery yet somehow gracious and sporting;

he smiled as we entered. On the bed beside him was a tall giant of a man, red-bearded, gaunt, wearing a leather head band, Don McCoy. The pretty girl from the street below was pacing about nervously, wringing her hands – Charlotte Partridge Wallace, nicknamed Shotsy, her parents' endearment meaning "darling," from the German "schaatz," I learned. "Darling" she was and is, sweetheart of the western world. The other woman, new to my vision, though extremely young-looking, had the way about her of an older, more seasoned matron. Her name was Sheila McKendrick, and the most notable thing about her in this moment was her unexplained nakedness. She was completely composed, acting the hostess, greeting us. It was from her that I first heard the term "Father" used in reference to the Bengali beggar who sat before us.

"Yes, six days ago . . . Spiritual Summit Conference," she began muttering.

"Sheila, you must remember," came gently from the beggar, "it was Shotsy who saw me first."

As for Shotsy, she just kept pacing nervously with a sort of "Oh God, spare me" look, glancing fiery at us all the time, where to begin?, where to begin?, where to begin? The relationships were not clear. For about a week prior, they had all had an intense experience together revolving around this beggar character, this "Father." That much was immediately obvious. Yet some of them had known each other before, it seemed, in California – at least three of them: the boy on the bed, Buz Rowell, and Don McCoy, and Sheila; Shotsy was sort of the maverick. As it turned out, Shotsy was the only one who was an actual, legal, bona fide delegate or representative to the Spiritual Summit Conference, which, I gleaned, was an actual occurrence and not just a metaphor for their individual meeting; it took quite a while to sort that out, and I am leaping ahead of myself.

The air was crackling with intensity. They were in great agitation, trying to tell us of their meeting with this beggar, yet there was composure too, mostly on the part of Sheila who, despite her nudity and possible insanity, was doing quite a good job at her somehow-delegated role as hostess.

"He has come," she said in the sweetest voice imaginable, "to liberate us, to liberate the entire planet, in fact. He is your Father, your own true father who was in Heaven and now is here."

No sooner would she start in that strain when the giant of a man, Don McCoy, would jump up and change the energy. Sheila took Sal Friscia's hand and started talking to him privately in a corner. Shotsy started pacing frantically. Buz resigned himself to his dysentery and I to my musing.

One thing was obvious, and I let it all rest on that for the moment. These westerners were undergoing disintegration and shock which exposure to India would inevitably generate, only somehow they were doing it all at once and together. They had found what I assumed to be their guru in record short time, and I was both envious and contemptuous of them for that. I was interested primarily that they should be here at all, that my imagination should suddenly be peopled with so many Californians, for I'd be going there soon and these were people who, though not really fellow voyagers of mine, had at least been to India and were thereby possible future solace, people I could retreat with to imaginary Indian rooms when resignation with the west would grow tedious again.

But really my marking them for a future comfort had little chance of endurance against their insistence that I, or rather we (for there were still John and Sal), come into their present. There was Sheila trying to convince Sal, who couldn't possibly get beyond her nudity at that moment, that he was a divine angel while Don McCoy was threatening to break the whole thing up into blood and thunder, and Buz, struggling through his own physical discomforture, was trying to make us feel at home and at ease, for Shotsy was on the verge of dismissing all of us out of hand immediately; and above it all, what we didn't need was the droning voice of Dr. Praṣad going on and on in that whiney educated Indian inanity, "Oh, it is so good that you have come, so good to see the beauty of our Mother India," whirling round and round, getting nowhere close to sense or matter or even a joint to smoke when crack! the energy centered, focused, changed.

Father was chanting:

yadā-yadā hi dharmasya
glanir bhavati bhārata
abhyutthanam adharmasya
tadā 'tmanam sṛjāmy aham

growing deeper, bellowing, full, filling every crevice and dimension of that room, enveloping it in a smooth, liquid, sweet, amber-glossed fluid in which we slid and swam in eternal suspension...

paritranāya sadhūnaṃ
vināśaya ca duskṛtām
dharmasamsthāpanarthāya
sambhavāmi yuge-yuge[1]

It was the most beautiful voice I had ever heard, and it came out of that scantily clad, fiercely thin, beggarly form sitting on the settee. It had command and authority. It was not the cant monotony or ranting of rote or ritual piety. It grew out of the very atmosphere, virile and sentient. It was at once both awesome and familiar.

"Whenever you have reached the critical departure from Truth, almost as a mechanism, inevitably, I am there. Through the agency of my beloved *yogamaya*[2] I incarnate Myself to my friends, my lovers, my children, my gods and goddesses. I have always been with you, you have always been with me. I have been waiting for you for two and a half years. I incarnate Myself into your collective cognition as the image before you, a slave to your love and understanding."

He bowed his head, long, low, in sweeping introduction. Why? I thought.

"Why? you ask. To teach you right from wrong once again. To show you in my own person how easy, how joyous, how graceful is the ascent into Truth. To be with you always as a guide and a friend because I love you and you love me. In short, to resurrect

---

[1]*Bhagavad Gita*, Chapter IV shloka (or verse) 8; the one preceding is verse 7.
[2]the power to control or arrange the circumstances of phenomenal nature.

your own remembrance of your immortal nature. Call me
Panchu. I love you so much. I love you so much."

He went on like this for about an hour, not interpreting but
creating, using his own authority, speaking to my very essence.
It reverberated within me. I could feel it. I cannot recall much of
what he said. He spoke of things that would unfold in thousands
of years. He brought me into an eternal moment. He had always
been with me. He was instantly familiar, speaking, lulling me to
sleep, waking me up, shouting at times, punctuating things he
said with a *Bom Shankar Bholenath*[3]...Shankar, Shankar,
Śiva, Śiva, Bom, Bom...Yes, it moved, everything I had
thought began to circle around, and it came, and he struck the
very chord of my being with his speaking. It was real. It was

*Yes, loving us, more than anything else, that was it. We were
wrapped in his love. We were warm. It was what all of us had
yearned for.*

[3]mantra and prayer invoking the Lord of Synthesis and beseeching that His
Knowledge be realized in one's own form. Father translates it as "Wake up, my
self-oblivious gods and goddesses!"

true. I believed him. I could hold on to nothing he said. I only knew that I was in that room for ever and ever and that it would go on, that I would re-enter that room over and over again. How it had happened I did not know. It did not matter. He went on and on. I could only take in very little, bit by bit. On and on, hypnotizing us, speaking to us, reassuring us, loving us. Yes, loving us, more than anything else, that was it. We were wrapped in his love. We were warm. It was what all of us had yearned for. Who were we anyhow? We did not know each other before. It would all be told. It would all be told.

escending one flight of stairs dropped us light years into relativity; I asked Sal on the way down what he had made of the scene we had just witnessed.

"I've been so long in this sexually repressed wasteland that it seemed to me the greatest sight I've seen since I was weaned."

"Not Sheila, you fool," I said, "I meant the old man."

"I know what you meant. I'll let you get turned on by what you like if you let me get off in my way. O.K.?"

"No, really, Sal, what did you think?"

"Look, in Kashmir you were hot to tell me that this Ganesh Baba had secrets that he could unfold to you that were just marvellous mysteries. Later, in Benares, you bombard me with equal assurance that there is no such thing as a guru, that nobody can impart knowledge to you, that it's a single, lone journey."

"I know, Sal, but this man was different. He was really beautiful."

"I know he's beautiful. I'd like to paint his eyes. All the same, leave me alone to my cynical denials, as you'd call it. At least

I'm consistent."

John paused before a room directly below the one we had just come from. Friends of his were staying there, he said, and there was good chance that they had some hash. Were we with him? I was, but Sal had a few things to do before his show and left us.

Within this dimly lit room, feeling as empty of life as the one above had seemed full, I could discern the contours of four forms. As detail entered my perspective, I realized I was already slightly familiar with three of the people here. One couple I had seen a few hours before when I first ran into John. The fellow with the thick glasses who had given us the money for our meal was named Richard Horne, and he was from New York. His girl friend of the dark frizzy hair was named Lynne, and she was from New Jersey. The name of the girl I hadn't seen before was Annalise. She had stringy dirty blonde hair, was Dutch, and never smiled. Her boy friend, Chris Jagger, was someone I had seen very briefly in Kashmir. He was the brother of a superstar in the musical scene in England, and his arrival in Kashmir in a Volkswagen bus had had, I recalled, a faintly lavish note.

The appearance of John was enough to signal his desire without any accompanying verbal request. Richard dipped into his stash box and produced a *gooly*[1] of rich black *charas*.[2] A *chillum*[3] was made and we smoked.

I was introduced as a travelling sadhu friend of John's "from way back," veteran even of the now legendary Amarnath pilgrimage. Their eyes widened in respect. John and I were discovering that by the mere longevity of our endurance in the subcontinent we were becoming notorious.

Richard told me that he and Lynne had arrived about two months before in Kathmandu. They had flown there directly for the hash harvest.

"I thought that would be a good time to catch the road hippies at a peak. You see I'm a writer. I have one book published with Grove Press, and I'm doing a series of articles for the *Evergreen*

[1] a small quantity, rounded ball of [2] hashish (approximately $\frac{1}{2}$ to 1 gram in weight).

[3] ancient smoking implement; conical pipe; usually made of clay.

*Review,* I hope."

So in one year of my experience it had come to this already. The road, which if it had any pattern at all was discovered only after many seemingly random encounters with one's fellow pilgrims, now had become a fixed concept with almost routine expectations and certain key calendar goals, like hash harvest, to structure it. The circumambulatory map was no longer determined by the fifty-two way stations, holy spots upon which had fallen the remnants of Sati's body, severed step after step from the groaning weight of Śiva's sorrow by the relieving grace of Vishnu's discus, but was rather an itinerary which ran something like this: Easter in Kathmandu, summer in Kashmir, Christmas in Goa. After the Aryans and the Mughals and the British, was India to become now a plaything of the leisure and boredom of the children of materialism? Not really, I was sure (with the inevitable duality of an "on the other hand"); India could defend herself from our idle curiosity with her enormous passivity alone; she could absorb the probings of the west's desperation for purpose, just as she had the enterprise of the Empire, and reduce it all to her only known denominator, India's listless indifference to change. And in the end perhaps, as my friend Marc had been fond of hypothesizing, we westerners would make as poor sadhus as the Indians would make engineers, with the loss or at least mongrelization of all culture as the inevitable result.

"It seems to me pretty obvious," Richard went on, "that mass enlightenment is going to be the phenomenon of our time and that the hippies who are now here in the East are the vanguard of this occurrence. I hope to pursue it in Benares and Goa and all the places where everyone's been getting high."

"It's the same thing," Lynne added, "that's happening in Mexico. I was there last summer. Only there it's mushrooms and here a hash diet."

"Just imagine," Richard continued, "what with all the western energy about, and the tools that the East can provide like Mahayanism, and all the specific disciplines, the planet's going to enjoy an awakening the likes of which we haven't even dreamt."

*...could defend herself from our idle curiosity with her enormous passivity alone...and reduce it all to her only known denominator, India's listless indifference to change.*

"You're probably right," I said, not telling him that the only tenet of my faith was not to preconceive in any manner whatsoever the form that the spirit was taking in its movement. "But one thing I'll wager you is that in whatever corner you track it down, the definition of it, and the answer, will elude you like so much quicksilver down the cracks. Unless, of course, you personally embrace those cliché Buddhist concepts you mention. In which case, you'll come up with so many answers that you'll forget the question."

"Don't you think," Richard went on, half-offended, "that the Tibetans have kept their machinery the cleanest over all these centuries, and that Buddhism will at least give a way for all these western seekers to realize themselves?"

"Give a way!" I went on. "It will give an eight-fold way. Look, as far as I'm concerned, Buddhism gives you nothing but a logic.

Outside this room there are hundreds of millions of Hindus. Every one of them would be insane by anybody's standards but his own. No two of them pray alike. Some, as well as dipping at the knee, catch hold of their earlobes with their fingers. Others, kind of overzealous types, wander around with little spears through their cheeks or tongue.

"Also there are millions of Muslims out there. No two of them will deviate one iota in the way they pray. Some may dye their beards red to lord it over the others socially, but they'll pray the same. I was in a hospital in Kashmir, and when the sun's last ray was dying on that opaque window, the Doctor who was examining a patient in the next bed stops then and there and gets down on a rug on the floor. The patient, who I had thought was dying, gets down on the rug with him and the two of them facing Mecca go through the exact same calisthenic routine of prayer.

"Anyhow, what they all have in common, erratic Hindus and predictable Muslims, and they share this in common with your – do I detect Jewish? – ancestors, the same ancestors you and I turned our backs on, is that when it comes to knowing God, they approach it with their heart."

"And the Buddhists don't? Is that what you mean to say?"

"Buddhists are too busy distinguishing between the right hand and the left hand paths and the greater and the lesser vehicles... Just like our friend O'Shea here's ancestors, Aquinas and that ilk, too busy finding out who sits on the right and who on the left, and what the place looks like and who gets in and who gets out, too busy to even consult their heart. It's all just so many distinctions... well, so much bullshit. What I don't get is, look, any westerner here figured out for himself years ago, whatever religion he was born into or raised in, that the whole thing was nonsense, that isms didn't work, couldn't possibly work. Yet bring him over here and his mind gets blown a little bit and for sure the thing he's going to take cover under is Buddhism. I just don't understand it."

"Well, what do you think it's like? Where do you think it's going?"

"Really, I don't know. I just know one thing. God is simple, like a baby." I stopped at this last utterance. It wasn't mine. I had always kept from personalizing any concept of deity, kept from notions of what God is or is not like. It had just popped out. How had it come to me? Was it something I had heard or felt in my hour transfixed upstairs? I could almost feel that old man Father breathing upon my neck, blowing on my hair, smiling the length of my spine.

"Look, I'm sorry," I went on. "I don't mean to put down anyone's belief. Tibetan Buddhism, all right. Lots of my friends have wound up there. It's just that I think it's kind of a betrayal of the integrity of the way this thing really goes on and feels. I think you'll see what I mean. I've gone through all the scenes, man; I've gotten really high, I've hit peaks, and . . . well, it's always eluded me. I guess that's all I'm telling you. I'm just speaking for myself, and I'm kind of down now. I'm going to be going to the States and I don't know what I'd give for one thing to blow my mind and keep me there once and for all."

"I thought most of that stuff you said," Richard picked up, "was pretty good. And look, man, I have some LSD with me. To tell you the truth, I've been afraid to take it here in India, afraid of where I'd come back, but if you wanted to take it with us . . . well, we're planning a trip this full moon."

"Thanks a lot," I said, and then our talk drifted on into other things. Richard told me about the novel he had already written and of the ideas he had as to what was happening with the road travellers. I told him that I had chronicled a good bit of the saga in my head and had even written some stuff in a journal. I knew who had gotten his first fix on the Bosphorous, why a certain party had o.d.'d in the Crown Hotel, when and whom enlightenment struck on Juhu Beach, who was the first American arrested for hashish in Delhi. Yes, I was a veritable encyclopaedia of road trivia. I told Richard he was welcome to anything my literary ego had come up with to date, that, indeed, I'd consider myself getting the best of the deal swapping him everything I knew for one tab of acid.

We talked on in that instant intimacy which chance encounters afford. Shyness and suspicion suspended, perhaps the heart opens easier on unfamiliar turf. Annalise did not speak though. She never smiled. Chris giggled boyish things. He half expected a bobby to barge in and blow the whistle on us. John acted as one who took natural pleasure in presiding over council, respect for form having come to him in Japan during his Marine Corps stint. Lynne was buoyant that her beau had found, in this flyblown byway, a bookish peer. And I, seeing everyone set and fixed in the approaching dusk, fell to my old habit of pacing.

On a table in a corner I saw a pamphlet. Some bold type struck me immediately: "Seized by the divine will of self-revelation the world is being consciously evolved by the immortal self-awareness of Ciranjiva, beginning ŚIVA KALPA on the nineteenth day of September One thousand nine hundred and sixty-six years after death of Jesus Christ." And then further on were some definitions of divine terms, beautiful definitions they seemed at once, pure in feeling, although I couldn't say that I literally comprehended them word by word. Then, some more bold type fairly shot out at me:

### Absolute Existence
### is Beauty of Truth Consciousness

### Truth is the Beginning
### Truth is the Middle and Truth is the End

Because

### God is Truth – Truth is Light – Light is Life

Because

Truth is Knowledge, Knowledge is Light,
Light is Power, Power is Existence,
Existence is Life, Life is Beauty, Beauty
is Love, Love is Man, THE MENTAL BEING.

Because

Mental Being is Self Consciousness, Self
Consciousness is Self Respect and SELF
RESPECT IS THE WAY TO THE LIFE OF TRUTH,
KNOWLEDGE, POWER AND LOVE.

There followed some paragraphs which I only quickly glanced over. None of it was in the usually lame promotional type language which advertised some specific method or discipline, promising immediate or even long range utilitarian effects. It seemed rather a proclamation for its own sake with no hint of a compromising motive. At the end of the pamphlet under the title of "Re Evolution" appeared this rather remarkable poem:

> The journey that never was made
> Amid hopes and perils the trail was laid
> Through adventures that never took place.
>
> Mission lost in passions transient
> Seeking pleasures always in pain
> Desire-moments fettered time thru' space
>
> Path blazed by desires in flame
> Journey awakes to its joyous game
> Guided in darkness, now in light
> Motion becomes its own delight
>
> The end is ever in the source inscribed
> Around the circle never described
> Time and space and motion sublime
> Rhythm of Stillness signs the hymn.
>
> All is yet an intense Reality
> A moment in Conscious luminosity.
>             om tat sat.

"It's pretty interesting, isn't it?" Richard said, noticing that I had become engrossed in reading the pamphlet.

"Yes," I said.

"I got it from those people upstairs. The ones with – uhh – Ciranjiva."

"Is that the name of the man up there?" I asked. "The one they call 'Father'?" Richard nodded. So, the world is being consciously evolved by the immortal self-awareness of Ciranjiva, I thought: heavier and heavier.

"I meant to ask you about those people when I came in."

"I don't know too much about them," Richard went on. "They're here with some Spiritual Summit Conference. As a matter of fact, do you know who's around the corner there? There are still a few people hanging around the Grand Hotel. The conference itself is over. Thomas Merton. He was there. We could go and talk to him. He might have a few ideas about the direction it's all going to take."

"Yeah, he might at that," I said.

"They met this Ciranjiva there a couple of days ago. He lives with his family in some village in the country somewhere around here. They went to his village the first night they met him. Sheila was telling me. It sounded quite interesting."

"What do you make of those people upstairs?" I asked. "What do you think they're going through?"

"That Don McCoy's kind of a strange brute," Lynne volunteered. "They say he's a millionaire."

"It's my idea," Richard claimed, "that that Don McCoy is here to buy not just Ciranjiva but half a dozen holy men and take them back to the States."

"Really!" I said.

"Yeah! Don't you know, man, that gurus are this country's biggest exportable item right now. It's not just you and I who know about this mass enlightenment, you know."

The sign on the door of the U.S.I.S. exhibition hall said:

October 25th to 31st – 6 to 9 p.m.
Drawings and Watercolors
by Salvatore Friscia

It was dark now. John O'Shea and I had parted company. The city was well into its evening rhythm. The air hung heavy with the smoke from the bucket fires of the pavement dwellers. Shawls appeared now about the shoulders of the homeward, and the edges of sarees were clutched against the delicate nostrils of Hindu femininity, wary not only of the visible soot of the night but also fearful of the less tangible jostling of caste and the pollution of social integration which the encroaching dark threatened. With evening, too, the rush of reflection would enthrall me completely.

In this day's unfolding I could sense that India was about to rob me again of my resolve to be quit of her. Not that my sadness had cooled with the evening. There was still a nagging tinge of despair somewhere, a dry sorrow in my throat. But fascination for the next unpredictable turn of events had definitely taken hold and, more than that, the perennial conviction that I was being led somewhere special, that I was about to stumble upon the elusive and coveted master-plot was beginning once more to command my instinct. No sooner, it seems, had I resigned myself to calling off this particular journey, to ending the Indian chapter of my life's narrative, than the great chronicle resumed its parade with gusto, populating this maleable landscape with the pilgrims and principles my year's quest produced.

Following this day's drift, acting not at all under direction of my own volition, I now found myself before one of the haunts of my early attempts to come to terms with India: the United States Information Service, Calcutta. My brother Rich and I had played here often. I understand now that the reason my brother and I ducked into the U.S.I.S. library almost daily was not so much to check the movie schedules in the Amrita Bazaar Patrika and other local papers but more that in the surroundings of those well-lined bookshelves I might for a moment catch respite from the siege Calcutta was to my senses and preconceptions. If through the familiar company of Marx, Darwin, and Samuel Langhorne Clemens I could gain contact with the me who so recently was certain that he permitted and measured experience as it struck his cognition, then, like taking a deep breath, I could gauge the degree to which I would submit to the murk of Indian madness.

Small assurance it was fated to be; instantly upon my re-emerging into Calcutta's streets, India would assault my vision with enormous contradictions. What chance did literary companionship have for stabilization when the sight of a cow with a fifth leg grafted upon its hump could set me spinning, when I was sure to encounter at any moment not only lepers but beggars so badly bent they evoked more disbelief than pity or a face so swollen and blown it comprised one half the unfortunate's body! No, there was no way that my first awakening to find myself in India could seem logical or predictable or the result really of one rather routine airplane ride. Despite my brother's sensitive and energetic attempts to balance my exposure to the bizarre and unexpected with things familiar to my past or consonant with my future expectations, India could never appear anything but a radical wrenching from the normal course my existence had pursued up to that point.

Rich himself had undergone the same shock a year before. He had come to India under the guise of a volunteer for the Peace Corps, popular then because it had caught America's idealistic youth in a rut of indecision. They had trained him to expect that he could serve India's physical basis with a touch of American organization and an inspiration, however slight, towards self-determination and independence. He hadn't even reached the place of his first assignment when that particular illusion was completely dispelled. Rich and his two friends, Jack Bell and Jim Russell, were to undergo their first metamorphoses in the relative quiet and serenity of the villages of southern India, Madras state.

During that first year, aided by the local *ganja*,[1] they filled with their rampant imaginings that dreamy stretch of time in which rural India sleeps. Those who supposedly supervised them from their cantonment offices in Bangalore overlooked the smoking of ganja and even the increasingly frequent ingestion of opium but decided to act when Jim Russell married a teenaged village girl. All three were flown up to Delhi where they were officially drummed out of the Corps, and their return to the United States was vigorously suggested. Instead they discovered while in Delhi that a whole network of western travellers was beginning to emerge upon the face of this continent, and they decided to become part of it.

Immediately upon rejection of the notion that he could possibly be of any benefit to India, Rich became deliriously happy in the realization of the benefit that India was to become to him. His mind ran riot in the freedom that anonymity afforded. It had been confined too long in academic pursuits to which he was temperamentally unsuited. He drank *arrak*[2] and toddy at the

[1]cannabis; marijuana.

[2]country liquor.

wild festivals on the tea plantations where the performance of fire-walkers wiped out once and for all the limits that had been placed upon his conception of the possible.

His letters conveyed quite a bit of his enthusiasm and something of his nascent liberation when they came before my eyes, which were then viewing my present constricted Berkeley circumstances with increasing depression. So he had prepared for my coming to join him, with love and exuberance and concern that he find in this new environment something familiar to our past association to cushion the inevitable shock India would be to my perceptual system.

Rich himself was his own most familiar and reassuring offering. He placed himself entirely at my disposal, answering any questions he could, dispensing riddles, paradoxes, and the knowledge his own fertile mind had gleaned through a year's observation. In those early first months of my travels we were inseparable, as indeed we had been through most of our lives. We became known throughout the circuit of travellers simply as the brothers.

Before our respective individual demands of American adulthood had separated us, we had nurtured, Rich and I, our tandem fantasies through thousands of hours at the movies. Now, coming together again, we indulged considerably in this old comfortable ritual. We became great frequenters of the English-language matinees in the Calcutta movie houses. Psychic survival in India had taught Rich to delight in the incongruous, to draw stimulation and energy from even the forceful juxtaposition of extremes; that delight he gave me through so simple and available a pleasure as juggling the banal of Hollywood with the surreal of Calcutta, the well-worn clichés of past fantasy with the surprise of present reality, a predictable gesture with a random response. The relative merits of detailed observation became lost in the sweep of vision as love of content gave way to process. The fruits of recent maturity, called judgment, discrimination, and taste, fell away before a faculty which saw any movie, tasted any food, sensed any pleasure with equal appreciation.

Just as at that time we made contact with our American past through movies, so too India had employed earlier the same medium to beckon and influence our future. Some years back a group of films from Bengal were well-received in the artistic quarters of the U.S., and they found no enthusiasts greater than Rich and myself. Satyajit Ray's *Apu Trilogy* entered our lives at a time when our aesthetic tastes and artistic ideals were ripe for inspiration. As we saw them over and over again, they became a measure for the depths of our feeling and a touchstone of our own purity. I am certain that they helped guide Rich out of his then usual indecision; on the Peace Corps application under the directive "List your first three choices of countries to serve in order of preference," he wrote and underlined "India, India, India." Rich's special treat and welcome for me as our lives joined again here in Calcutta was the arranging of a meeting for us with the great director Satyajit Ray; the name we already held in reverence, and now we were anxious to honor the man.

Ray lived in south Calcutta on Lake Temple Road in a flat which, though comfortable by Calcutta standards, was hardly a tribute commensurate with the man's stature and accomplishment. More than courteous, he took a friendly and paternal interest in us. He did not disappoint any of our expectations of a great man. Urbane and sophisticated, he was a reassuring proof against a mass of Indian confusion that such things as logic, conversation, and an aspiration for universal feeling did indeed exist even in these parts and were not merely indulgences of a western sensibility. There was, however, something tremendously sad in his very exceptionalness. Even to our admiring eyes, it was painfully obvious that he was completely out of context in the rush of modern Calcutta. He seemed of the time and spirit of Rabindranath Tagore, more out of place even than we scraggly travellers, oblivous pilgrims, astonished voyagers. He was paid lip service by many but understood by none of his contemporaries. He was quoted and referred to, cited as though he were a national monument, but hardly anyone went to see him. The more he became known, the more intense his isolation. In our repeated visits, we probably wound up as much consolation to him, that spheres did exist in which he was understood and aprreciated, as he was comfort to us, that our fate in India was not devoid totally of parents, guides, or concerned overseers.

Rich and I would often of an afternoon take a tram to its last stop in a suburb of Calcutta called Tolleygunge. There we would follow a lane as it curved and narrowed between walls encrusted with numerous cow dung patties. At its end stood a small complex of buildings which, looking more like barracks than anything else, were actually the studios of the small but, thanks to Satyajit Ray, prestigious film industry of Calcutta. Here Ray would show many of his films to us and sometimes we were joined by other westerners paying homage and respects to the great director. One time we met James Ivory there. He was an American who had spent quite a bit of time in India and had made a few of what I thought were mediocre films exploring the mixture of east and west. Later when we were down and out in Bombay, Rich picked up a little money appearing as an extra in a film Ivory was making called *The Guru*. Another time, a fellow viewer of ours was the French director Louis Malle who was interested in doing a *cinéma vérité* type film on Calcutta and India in general if he could negotiate the financing when he got back to France. Ray had a project on his mind. He was to film a musical fantasy from a story his father had written. An old fortress in Rajasthan was to be the set and Ray suggested that if Rich's and my travels should converge there at the right time, we might enjoy watching and helping him.

The year Rich had spent in the Peace Corps I had utilized in teaching myself something of the craft of filmmaking. Along with the 16 mm. Bolex camera, I had brought with me to India prints of the four short films I had made. I intended to show Rich the beginnings of my accomplishment in this field, and I introduced myself to the assistant director of the U.S.I.S. in hopes that through him I might have the use of a projector on which to show them. He was a young man whose name escapes my memory though I recall that he was from Oklahoma, and though he had no access to a 16 mm. projector, he invited Rich and myself to a gathering at his residence where some travelling film buff was bringing a projector and some films from the Museum of Modern Art. This traveller turned out to be the film critic Donald Ritchie who, after spending several years living in Japan, was returning to the States where he was to become curator of the Museum of Modern Art's film library. He was carrying with him a series of short experimental films, which he was exhibiting in different countries on his route home. Satyajit Ray, his art director, Bansi Chandragupta, and cameraman, Subrato Mitra, were also part of the party. The next day Ray and my brother, Donald Ritchie, Bansi, and I took a look at my four films. Mr. Ritchie was very encouraging and said that if I submitted the films to the Museum of Modern Art, he could almost guarantee that they would be accepted as part of that library.

This was very flattering. These were offers and contacts beyond all my recent film ambitions. They almost argued that the unforeseen purpose in my coming to India might be to speed up the advancement of my film career . . . .

I had initially conceived my tenure in India to be three months, possibly six, but whatever its purpose beyond the immediate reunion with my brother I did not know. Certainly I had no intention of drifting for over a year in search of something I had argued most of my life did not exist, or of finding myself penniless in some of the planet's darkest spots. The whole key to the incredible saga which came to possess my Being was that I had been drawn into this journey of consciousness through no intention of my own, beyond my ability to preconceive or control it.

If it could have been otherwise, if resistance to India's seductive stream of surrender were to be maintained, it could only have been accomplished through the agency of my own ego, my own film aspirations. I would have had to focus myself solely on those aims, surround myself completely with these associates in film, just as the young Oklahoma-born assistant director of the U.S.I.S. and his wife surrounded themselves exclusively with friends from the diplomatic service. It would be necessary for me to look upon India merely as a colorful background or eccentric study or hobby against which or through which my individual goals were being attained, much as the young Oklahoma-born assistant director and his wife kept a caged mongoose in the foyer of their residence. A set of very opaque blinders would have been necessary to keep my attention from being drawn towards the immense anguish or crazy comedy being played at the periphery of my vision. Even then, however intense or singular a beam of purpose I employed to ignore the panorama of ambiguity, uncertainty, lack of comprehension, India would still have torn away at my defenses.

Some people like the young Oklahoma-born assistant director and his wife could possibly do it. When Rich and I went to their place for a traditional Thanksgiving dinner, we were amazed at how successfully they transported us back to the suburban feeling of any part of the U.S. He spoke only of the subjects in *Time* magazine and commiserated with me upon a loss which was already not a loss to me but a blessing glimpsed. Yes, he and his wife were able to keep India at abeyance just as the beggars were physically kept away from the government compound in which they lived, but Rich and I could never have succeeded in attempting to do so even had we desired it.

Our visits to Satyajit Ray, which in a way became routine, had opened a door to a surprising quarter. During one of our early soirees, a young Englishman named Peter Roberts had come to see Ray. He was a seasoned vagabond, having travelled in India and Ceylon for sometime now. His head had been shaved, and he wore an earring. He was well-educated and a natural storyteller, using language replete with irony and an emphatic rhetoric. The tale he told fascinated me. In Benares, the holy city Ray had used for the setting of the second film in his famed trilogy (and the most orthodox and conservative spot of Hindu propriety), there had formed a band of western seekers who had voluntarily abandoned their native identities in hopes of acheiving rebirth into eastern vehicles of enlightenment. He described the costumes and habits that had come about with this crew and their exploits of cultural collision.

The name of an American, Eight-Fingered Eddy, caught my

fancy as did the story of an aristocratic Englishman named Jasper who had gone completely savage or sadhu and now stalked the ghats with his hair matted and dressed in nothing but a loin cloth.

Later, Rich and I went with Peter Roberts and had some Chinese food at Lee Johnson's where he told us more. Then, after we scored some hashish for a chillum at Horace's in the Anglo-Indian section, the story took on greater depth, penetrating more than my curiosity and stimulating glands and responses deeper than artistic. By the end of our encounter my surrender to the lure of the road was a foregone conclusion. It's odd that for all the crossings and re-crossings of my path with the paths of other Americans and Europeans, I never did see Peter Roberts again after that night, although years later my brother became great friends with him in England. That one encounter was enough, however, to impress me greatly. I must have had something of the same effect on Richard Horne, only in that case he had prior knowledge of and definite intentions toward the road community whereas Peter had captured in me a complete innocent.

It was almost instantaneous with my arrival that India's rape of my sensate being robbed my ego of its capacity to limit, control, or even indulge the vanity of thinking it knew what was happening. Even the supposedly familiar presented itself through an angle of vision so weird that in effect it too hastened the cause of my surrender to the unknown: At Dum Dum Airport I had failed to recognize my own brother. One year had wrought such change in him that even looking directly at him in that dilapidated lounge wherein he awaited my arrival, I mistook him for an Indian. It was not the *dhoti*[3] he was wearing, or the kurta, or even his wild hair so much as a certain ease and sense of belonging he emitted. Later that evening while visiting Jim Russell and his child bride Rukmuni, who busied herself as we talked by carefully pasting sea shells into the lid of a cardboard box, I saw a suffused orange light, tending towards

[3]several meters of white cotton draped around the legs and waist; proper dress for a man.

golden, about my brother Rich's head. It was the first time I had clearly perceived an aura. It made him appear ancient and holy, almost rabbinical, and it impelled silent surrender on my part to whatever it was that had happened to him.

Rich had arranged accommodations for us in a Sikh *gurdwara*[4] where any traveller was welcome to at least three days of free room and board. I stowed my camera and its attachments under Jim and Rukmuni's bed, and Rich and I went on to the gurdwara near the Kalighat and slept on a stone floor in the company of numerous wheezy and grouchy old Indians from all parts of the continent.

It was really an act of particular capriciousness, which I claim was the hand and character of India herself, that furthered me on my route to sadhudom. Going to see Jim and Rukmuni one night, I was informed that my camera and everything with it had been stolen. In the front room of the building in which they lived dwelt in exile and begrudging poverty a family who claimed to be Ranas, the deposed royalty of Nepal. Their daughter Lakshmi had become friends with Rukmuni, and the latter had shown her my camera with the same pride and interest she took in displaying her seashell collection. That afternoon Jim and Rukmuni, returning home from a Tamil-language film, discovered that the camera was gone and so were the Ranas. They had not given notice nor left any forwarding address with the landlady who was angry because they had been in arrears on their rent.

The next day I went to the local police station there in the Entally district and filed a report on the theft and a complaint against the suspects. The fat mustachioed officer in charge told me that there was little likelihood of finding it even under the best of conditions, and at that particular time they had a *hartal* to contend with. A *hartal* was a general strike closing down much of the city, and it had just come into effect the night before. Legions of variously clothed police officers and soldiers began patrolling the streets.

It was in this atmosphere that I conducted my fruitless search,

[4]temple and refuge, spiritual hostel maintained as part of Sikh charity.

*It was in this atmosphere that I conducted my fruitless search . . .*

making inquiries at several branch stations of the police and talking to runners at the New Market. I undertook this search more as ritual than in any real hopes of recovering the camera.

I returned to a concerned Jim and Rukmuni who felt a little guilty, and I assured them that it was all right, that I had already reconciled myself to the loss. Hindi film music blared outside. We took a walk across the square in Entally where a cyclist, Muhammed Lateef from Lucknow, was engaged in his claim that he would ride his bicycle for seventy-two consecutive hours. He was attempting this in a small circle whose circumference kept slowly decreasing as the spectators pushed in. A man ran beside the cyclist and squirted water into his face to refresh him. He was now, we were told, approaching his thirtieth hour. Jim and I laughed at yet another presentation of the meaninglessly outrageous spectacle of which India seemed inexhaustably capable. I told Jim that however I seemed to be acting about the stolen camera, that I myself was actually witnessing myself going through the motions and was viewing it from as removed and unconcerned and even amused a vantage point as that from which I now beheld the cyclist.

Later that evening we went to see Satyajit Ray, and I told him the story of the camera. He clucked his tongue and felt bad about it but was emphatic in telling me that there was no possibility of its being regained. Ray explained the *hartal* to us. It seemed that the Congress party of Indira Ghandi had just dissolved the United Front, something of a leftist coalition that for the last four years had held the power in the government in West Bengal, and had imposed President's rule on the area until new elections could be held. In support of the United Front the *hartal* had been called, and now in retaliation for that a curfew was being imposed. This curfew did not place a time limit on movement outdoors but restricted the number of persons able to gather in any one place to twenty-five. This seemed impossible in Calcutta's density where every tram stop had three times that number fighting for space. Ray hinted that things might get nasty and that Rich and I would do well to leave Calcutta. The next day was Thanksgiving, and we had been invited by the assistant director of the U.S.I.S. to his home in celebration of it, but we assured Ray that after that we would leave Bengal.

As we walked the streets on Thanksgiving morning, we heard occasional gun shots in the distance and once or twice sounds which seemed like home made bombs exploding. It was eerie how deserted the streets and neighborhoods were in fact. Where did that huge population, which seemed to have no home but the streets, go, I wondered.

We said goodbye to Jim and Rukmuni. As Rich and Jim embraced, I felt the enormity of the journey that had taken them from the programmed existence of the Peace Corps to this moment where each had to pursue, unadvised, his separate calling in India. Suddenly the music from outside which had been blaring the popular "Ja-pan, love in Tokee-yo" stopped. We went out in time to see an unfortunate Muhammed Lateef, collared by some soldiers, being carted off under protest. The cyclist had been stopped in his fifty-third hour and arrested for violation of the curfew in that the crowd about him exceeded by far the permitted number. They were half dragging him as though he were resisting, but I think he was merely stunned. Also his legs probably hadn't yet shifted back into linear use after all that pedalling.

At dinner with the assistant director and his wife we got a bit drunk. They were not too concerned about the *hartal* because there was nothing in it that suggested any anti-American sentiment. They were more concerned with the unfortunate theft of my camera, and the husband went on and on bemoaning the "loss."

The a.m. found us on a train north towards Raxaul, our departure point from India for Kathmandu.

As time and my travels moved on, I came to appreciate the cunning and irony that induced India to strip me first of the one possession which could have kept me from seeing her clearly. The loss of the camera, like the loss of an ego, removed from me the possibility of hiding from the moment; no longer could I imagine that I was merely a recorder of experience. It had come as a shock at first, losing the filter, literally the lens, actually the posture that could brace me with specific purpose against the overwhelming flux. Yet, after the shock came relief. I was subject to enough suspicion and attention just walking anywhere, and I could imagine the extra harassment toting a camera would create. It was valuable too as my first lesson in non-attachment. I became grateful in having the weight and responsibility of that possession lifted from me. Total vulnerability became my secret goal, and I never relaxed in India until all possessions were removed. I knew that I should have to stand virtually naked and would have to reduce the necessities of my formal, mobile, material game to that which could fit in one small shoulder bag.

This was now the case as I stood before the exhibition hall of the United States Information Service, Calcutta, where on the door was a sign which read:

October 25th to 31st – 6 to 9 p.m.
Drawings and Watercolors
by Salvatore Friscia

istinctly Muslim were the faces and figures Sal had arrested and displayed through graphic transposition. The ladies wearing their heavy silver fortunes like harnesses were probably originally spotted in Shrinagar. The workers in the fields were reminiscent of the rural area where we had lived in Kashmir. Women in purdah making ghostly figures as they walked along the road could have come from any part of the Mohammedan world. The heavy lidded eyes, the bend of the backs, the sullen lips, the masculine figures huddled around coal braziers – it was all Muslim. I did not realize this when I had seen Sal's work piece by piece and stretched over a period of time, but displayed all at once, the predominence of things Muslim became obvious.

When we had been in Benares, I knew that Sal was fascinated by the tense energy of the Hindu, their riot of color, and the natural contrariety exposed in almost any inch of that human landscape. I suppose that he was not successful in capturing these more subtle properties for there was no representation of any of that here in this show.

"The Muslim" – the thought came full upon me as though such sociological observation were my natural bent – "has a heavily physicalized orientation towards existence, while your Hindu" – if such a creature could be said to exist – "seems always somehow in conflict with his physical environment, seems to be fighting against it in all his efforts, pretending he is fairer of complexion than such a climate would permit, cleaner than his primitive sanitation conditions would allow, and infinitely more particular and finicky than the dearth of food or matter would seem to warrant."

Was it because Sal's own journey had begun in Tunis, in the midst of the Arab world, that he moved so readily and worked so proficiently upon that particular inspiration or was it suggesting something of Sal's own reluctance to abandon a primarily physical vision of the world?

It seemed to me that most of us travellers had spent a good bit of our resources attempting to escape the Hindu. Rich and I, though, had been drawn by something in those more rarified mysteries. We found Hindu confusion, though ridiculous, compelling.

When we had made it to Kathmandu that year, it was pleasant to relax for a moment amidst Asians who had enough respect for their own doings to pleasantly ignore yours, who were not constantly probing, comparing, or encountering you. Most of the travellers found this relief paradise enough and were continually scheming and plotting to extend their Nepalese visas. Rich and I too found the handsome pagoda structures, the dramatically varied terrain, the availability of hash, and, above all, the luxury of privacy a wonderful oasis from the discomfiture of India. Yet, we hankered after Hindusthan, sought again and soon the dubious delights of the Deccan Plain.

Besides myself, there were about six or seven Indians looking at the various watercolors and another three or four down the end of the room clustered about Sal. The artist himself was dressed in pressed pyjamas and sported a new *jeeba*[1] of raw silk.

---

[1] vest with a high collar.

This and the manner with which he gesticulated towards his admirers told me that he was enjoying this moment with a degree of seriousness not usual with him. I averted my eyes so that he would not grow self-conscious at my witnessing this moment which belied his ardently affected air of cynicism and insouciance. It confirmed the presence of a lurking earnestness that I had always suspected was there despite Sal's posings to the contrary. In an ironically reverse appropriateness, Sal was using the U.S.I.S. much as I had a year before. He was practicing there the postures and attitudes he thought necessary for resumption of his American existence. He was rehearsing here for his exit from India just as I had used the same set to stage my entrance. It seemed ages since such considerations of time or purpose had fostered in me so idle, futile, and inappropriate a practice as calculation or planning. I turned back to his drawings and paintings.

Sal was an artist all right and a good one. It seemed I could understand him perfectly. I too had entered this Indian dream with an identity as an artist, but I had lost or sacrificed it somewhere in the vortex of change. Perhaps, having invested at least ten years more than I in his art, Sal could not afford to do so. Perhaps too, fear of losing this one certain achievement made him such a dogged realist, so determined an adversary to my spiritual turn. I somehow knew that art for him was a redemption for life unsuccessfully or inconclusively lived. I'd have to confess that part of my own aspiration for artistic expression was justification for some inexplicable and even undiscoverable failure in some ignored or unexamined area of my life. Like myself, Sal had bolted from family commitment. He had an estranged wife and daughter back in the States, and he had more than once confided to me his hopes for domestic reunion. I guess that's why Sal sought approval and admiration enough to bother having this show in so desolate and distant a spot, in so weightless an artistic sphere as Calcutta.

Sal's eye was good and his hand prolix, and to me that was really purpose enough. I had long envied the graphic artist his possibility of instant measure of genius in a line or flash of color.

My own literary and cinematic loomings did not permit of so tangible and ready a scrutiny. My elder brother Mel was a painter though, unlike Sal, the form or line or tone was never enough for him. He was overwhelmingly serious and sought monumental themes. We were all like that, we three brothers. We never dreamed but in titanic dimensions. Our reverence for art bordered on the idolatrous, and our smallest artistic schemes always demanded no less than a Michaelangelo or Tolstoy. I had long thought such grandiose promptings natural and universal if man would but face his unabashed ambition, but I'd come in time to allow the possibility that such traits were my own particular family's delusion. I had no right, at any rate, to project such serious propensity upon Sal who had worked hard no doubt to develop so studied an off-handedness, so determined a levity.

I had circled the wall of paintings by this time, and when I looked up the scene had completely changed. There were no Indians at all in the hall. Besides Sal and myself there was now only one other person present. It was Sheila. Dressed in a neat shirtwaist print dress and carrying a woven handbag, she seemed somehow much more petite than she had this afternoon in the contained atmosphere of that room in the Astoria.

She was engaged in what seemed deep conversation with Sal. I made a move towards them, but as I did they pulled apart. It seemed she was just leaving. She paused a moment on her way out and then turned to me.

"You know something," she said again in that sweet melodic voice, "I know Salvatore. I know him very well. I know who he is, and I know who you are . . . and most importantly, I know who and what Father is, and I know that you do too."

She took my hand, looked directly into my eyes, and crinkled her nose as she smiled.

"It's because you know who Father is that you won't be able to resist, so don't waste any time about it. Let's not lose him now that we've found him after all these years."

I was taken aback by the directness and the intensity of her plea, and the moment for response passed. In an instant she was gone, disappeared amongst the buildings and their shadows, amidst the veiled and cloth-wrapped strangers in their nocturnal driftings.

Returning to Ken Wilson's flat, I found David Bray seated at the kitchen table, staring vacantly ahead and stirring a cup of coffee that probably had been cold for hours. He got up and showed me in the corner of the main room a neatly arranged pack and a bedroll wrapped in a dark blue and yellow plaid blanket. I had shared space with these things and their owner before, but I couldn't recall the person that went with them at the moment.

I hadn't long to wonder for the door to the stairwell opened, and a tall, lean, red-haired figure entered. Of course, the blue and yellow tartan should have told me instantly: Robin Brown, regimental son of the Highland Pipers. He had never really been a close friend of mine. I had first seen him emerging from Lloyd's Bank, down on the fashionable end of the boarded promenade in Shrinagar. He had stayed that summer in David Lawrence's house, down the road from our garden paradise in Nishat Bagh. Also, he was one of the eleven westerners to undertake the Amarnath yatra, but I was soon to remember that his sharing that sacred physical effort did not make him fellow to our sacred urge.

I was genuinely glad to see him and told him so and asked how fate had directed him to this particular spot. It seemed he had run into David Lawrence some weeks ago in Delhi, and David, who was staying in a monastery off Connaught Circus, passed Ken's address on to him.

"Did David seem well?" I asked.

"Reasonably, if reason has anything to do with it," Robin replied. "He's shaved his head again and has probably achieved some degree of happiness through strict and regular resort to flagellation."

Ah yes, I remembered again the quick cynicism, the barely concealed edge of temper, the irascibility which shot through Robin. He was a pure son of British relativity, impressed by nothing, ruffled only by resistance to what he found blatantly obvious and practical.

"Well, I'm glad to hear that David is still around," I said. "You know I had thought just a little while ago that everyone had left. Ever since I found out that Marc went back to the States I've been somewhat depressed, thinking that our karma group had been scattered to the four winds and that nobody was here left to make it."

"Make what?" he asked. "Oh, yes, your blessed search, the brotherhood of eternal beseeching! You know you're mad, don't you? As for me, I'm just waiting for enough bread to come through to get a visa and plane to Bangkok. I'm off for Bali, man."

Often I had made the mistake of assuming that all westerners who travelled here sought, the Spirit let's call it, the meaning by which and upon which It all, in Its immense riddledom, turns, hangs, is. But Robin was a breed apart, he fancied: not a seeker, nor pilgrim, but a traveller. What excited him was the breadth of geography, the suggested and implied adventure in hybrid names like Dehra Dun, McCloudgunj, Khyber Pass, the Kush, contemplation of large areas on the map ostensibly closed to the white man, the hope of crossing rivers his fathers had known, the Irrawaddy and the Yangtze. His own father had, in fact, been a soldier of the Raj, and his grandfather before that too, I believe. Robin was the cast-off son of the Empire's collapse, but he too was destined to drift in that same groove, to perpetually astonish dark-skinned peoples with his shocking red hair. For his grandfather, the efficient cause had probably been the opening of new trade routes, the lure of a phantom spice or wondrous metal, and for his father, maintenance of an already established empire was undoubtedly sufficient cause not to be questioned; but for Robin himself, the same ground had to be covered without the shelter and sanction of any institutional blessing. His *raison d'etre* was more obscure: his own pursuit of dope, pleasure, and perhaps most of all, the vain hope of cessation of a genetic ennui. He was not a seeker, though. Definitely not! He maintained a separate existence through some undisclosed but regular and (by road standards) substantial source of income. There was a note of exclusive secrecy about his belongings, always neatly packed and arranged, and most emblematic of his isolation was a collapsible drinking cup I saw him brandish by our garden pump.

"You Americans," he said "you always think everybody is after the same purpose you perceive. Not realizing that your own trip is one big neurosis, you put it on everybody else. David's the same way. He's come to the end of his own tether so he hides in a damned monastery convincing himself that he's a *sinnyasin*."[1]

In part I agreed with him. I too saw capitulation to a formal institution, religious or otherwise, a surrendering of one's own authority for the journey.

"I'm sure you're right," I said. "Everybody is. But where do you see it as neurosis?"

"You Americans are basically provincial for a start," he said. "You have no business wandering off your ample continent, but let that go. Let's say you get to some Asian spot. At the sight of the first beggar, you freak out. You feel guilty. Americans are great at that. It's their specialty, feeling guilty. Then you realize

[1] the fourth ashrama or stage of life, that of a renunciate.

that there is not a goddamned thing you can do about all the suffering you see, so you conceive some notion of God's will and you try to understand that by sympathy with the most wretched. That's the best of you, the others just throw money and run. You can't just look at a man and see that he's a wog and that's all there is to it, and there's nothing to be done about it and nothing to be thought about it. It's all here just to move along, move through it!"

That morning I would have welcomed his comments as reinforcement to my indulged depression, but now for some reason I countered them. The upsurge had begun again.

"Move through it!" I said. "For what? What purpose? You mean that there isn't purpose or particular reason that you suddenly find yourself in these incredible circumstances, that as you and the others do move along your terms and whole spheres of reference change, that you're thinking things and feeling things that you never dreamt possible awhile ago; that's not leading towards anything, that has no purpose?"

"Look," Robin said, "that's where you're the worst of the lot. You always think everything has meaning or a reason. For one thing, you turned on too late. You were already used to taking school and crap like that seriously. You married really early and finally couldn't hack that so you left your wife and kids, which by the bye gives you a delicious bit of added guilt, so to make up for it, you've got to take the whole mess as purposeful. There's no purpose. It just is; it's just doing what you want, what you feel like. No one is really watching you or keeping score, you know, so why make such a muck about it?"

Robin at age twenty-two was six years my junior, and he had already been drifting for four years. But our difference was not age or national character but something deeper in the process of vision. Robin did not do justice to my own reserve of relativity if he imagined that I did not question and doubt the whole thing, test my feelings and actions along the same lines myself.

"The French hippie at least is comprehensible to me," Robin continued. "His total purpose is the flash. All he seeks is the fix. At least he knows his needs and deals with them cold. But you,

you are a lover of abstractions."

"Again, you may be right," I said, "but I think you've got to do another round, Robin. Round-Robin, that's kind of funny. You've just come to the point, you see, where they're all national archetypes to you. I passed that a while ago. Beyond that, we begin to merge. You'll see. What can I say? The real journey isn't an eccentric indulgence, you know. What you're doing, what happens to you, what you learn, for God's sake, it affects everyone."

Robin had stayed on in Kashmir after I had left, and when our talk now drifted into other modes, he told me something of the rather sad denouement of our scene there.

"Finally, you know that big Sikh police officer had had enough of being flagrantly ignored by 'those hippies' and sexually denied by their women, so he got tough about visas and this and that and finally ordered everyone out. It was beginning to get rather cold up there anyhow, so everyone took it as time to go and started preparing to leave. Well, Colombino resisted, so old Singh came back with some brute and they beat the shit out of him."

Colombino, Xavier Betincourt: somehow he had made it to India from his native South America, in the meantime marrying and separating from an Italian girl named Gina, who during this Kashmiri period was my friend Marc's love. I was not completely surprised that in the end Colombino would insist on making the terms physical. He, who was usually so light and ethereal, who would have seemed to have danced through all difficulties with a graceful shrug of his shoulders, housed a deep political streak that would, if given opportunity, court a physical encounter with the muscle of Sikhdom.

"And Mary Helen," Robin went on, "something weird happened to her. It's not quite certain what. First we heard that she really flipped out and was in the mental wing of Shrinagar Hospital, but someone went in to see her but couldn't find her. She just sort of disappeared, leaving a lot of her personal stuff scattered about the few houses and boats still occupied by any of us. I'm sure those Muslims she was buttering up must have raped her. Probably sold her afterwards to some slaver and maybe she's now working her way up some minor potentate's harem in Kuwait or something equally delicious."

And Mary Helen, what did she really want? She was a blonde beauty, originally from the mid-west, I think, but had travelled Europe some, come to India with a boy friend who split when she got hepatitis. We nursed her through that. She fixed morphine when she could. The strange thing about her was a game she had going with some Muslim houseboat owner. She would go and spend time with the man and his wife, sometimes stay for days on end there, and then come and tell us about all the jewelry the man had offered her and promises of lavish security, all of which she refused. I remember once taking a *shikara*[2] ride with her across Dal Lake. As the oars stabbed the silver water I saw something transient and fragile in her sky blue eyes, and I nearly ached with love of her.

I wrote her not so long ago, on the morning of the day I left Benares. I don't know why, I just suddenly felt compelled to write her. I wrote c/o Post Restante, Shrinagar. I told her in that moment not to despair, that the cycle was building up again, relief was at hand, the signs were good, something great was soon to happen. But there again I had acted on the assumption that she was a seeker. I don't know, however, what it was she sought.

"I'm off to Bali," Robin repeated, "that's for certain. And you? What are you up to?"

"I don't really know," I said. I told him about the letters I'd received that morning, that I was probably going back to the States soon, but that I was just here for the moment, not certain what would happen. I was tempted to tell him something of the fascinating encounter I had had today at the Astoria, but I checked myself. I was not yet certain enough about what I was feeling to subject it to the inevitable ridicule of this Scottish spark.

Robin removed an aerogramme from his pack and started writing a letter. I looked about the room and decided to avail

[2]like a small gondola.

myself of some of the diversions it offered. On a small bookshelf was a copy of Maugham's *The Razor's Edge*. It was one of the first really serious, grown-up books I had read. I was about twelve at the time. I remembered it with great fondness.

Of course, it occurred to me now, the search, India, the whole damned thing had been imprinted upon me. I had somehow been predetermined to make this journey from way back. It was reflected in the way I had fallen in love with the novel's hero, Larry Darrell. I had felt a great affinity with him and I remembered that somehwere in the book his eyes were described with irises so dark that the pupil could hardly be distinguished; similarly, as a boy my eyes were that dark, and this just secured my romantic infatuation and identity with him.

I quickly glanced over the first few pages. It was impossible for me to read. It seemed stilted and part of a definitely past impression. I remembered anyhow that Maugham had chosen not to deal with what had actually happened to the American Larry in India, what precisely were the mysteries that had opened his heart and mind, how they had been communicated, but had focussed on Larry's impact, basically viewed socially, his effect on his friends when he returned to the west.

There was a record already out upon the turntable so I played it. I had never heard it before. The cover told me it was something new. *Music from Big Pink* by a group called The Band. Some of the songs were written by Dylan. I heard clearly the refrain:

> I see my light come shining
> From the west unto the east.
> Any day now, any day now,
> I shall be released.

The words burned in and seemed to describe the feelings of my present moment with uncanny precision. That was what we valued in music from home out here on the road, its ability to anchor, place in native cultural context the changes we otherwise seemed to be going through in isolation. When our repetitive need to know this mounted, it was always answered by the arrival of new travellers with tapedecks and the latest material.

Of the messengers that made it through, Dylan was easily my favorite. My friend Marc had always said that in reading his own present moment of transition, to hear a Dylan song at random was as effective for him as the *I Ching*. I know that "Sad Eyed Lady of the Lowlands," when I heard it on the Goan beaches, epitomized all the poignant melancholic love for my homeland I had realized in my absence from her. Once in a darkened hut at night as we nodded slowly in tune with a well worn tape, his words that somewhere seven people were being born jumped out and proclaimed themselves to us, and Rich, Marc, myself, and the other four present all made silent count in that moment and looked across at each other in the candlelight and nodded recognition. "Queen Jane," "Visions of Joanna," and "Just Like a Woman" had the power to haunt us and strike home our often unavowed loneliness. They told us that we were both vagabond and outlaw, expelled by a culture that could no longer accommodate us and also that we were that same psychic culture's most refined, sensitive, and heroic explorers. We were bound to our home and culture and she to us inextricably through multiple subtle umbilical sutures. Our journey was for everyone.

> They say ev'rything can be replaced,
> Yet ev'ry distance is not near.
> So I remember ev'ry face
> Of ev'ry man who put me here.
>
> I see my light come shining
> From the west unto the east.
> Any day now, any day now,
> I shall be released.

When the door opened again a veritable carnival troupe was ushered in on the winds of its own energy. This group of three was most definitely dominated by a tall black man.

"Shaw's the name," he said, extending a large beefy hand. "Shaw, Jim Shaw, my friends call me James." He introduced the short, rather nervous young white boy, "This here fellow, my skinny partner, is Harry Glaum. I call him Glum," and also the girl who was with them. "Yeah, we just met her on the plane. We're gone up to Kathmandu. I understand there's some real good black hash there," he went on, and in a matter of moments revealed that the three of them were on a hash deal, having talked the girl on the flight up into carrying it for them on the way out. He was totally open, this big black man, though his partners seemed victims of a cautionary paranoia.

Jim Shaw could not stop talking. "Yeah, I run into this, uhhh, cat a couple of months back, in Hong Kong it was. Ken, Ken Wilson, and he give me the address for this place. This is quite a lay-out, quite a pad he's got here."

I wondered for a moment how he could have run into Ken in Hong Kong a few months ago when I had seen him further back than that in Bombay and thought he was still somewhere in India. But I let it go.

"Hong Kong! Now that's one hell of a place. You can get anything you want there. Anything! Why, man, the whole show is crumbling. I mean it's just coming apart at the seams. But what am I talking? Get a load of some of this stuff. This here's Vietnamese weed."

He drew out a bag with a large quantity of grass in it and started stuffing it into a large bamboo pipe.

"Now this here's the way they smoke it in Vientiane. This is heavy stuff. I'll bet you never had nothing like this."

We smoked. It was good grass. We talked. It seemed Jim had been travelling out of the United States for about a year, and six months of that time had been spent in a prison in Tokyo.

"For this much," he said indicating a small digit of a finger, "this much mary jane, man, and they slapped me in the clinker for six long months, baby. If I ever catch up with that son of a bitch who put the finger on me . . . Oh well, what the hell, it goes round."

It also turned out that before travelling Jim had been in California and had gone to San Jose State where he had studied mathematics and engineering. Prior to that he had been in City College in San Francisco where he might have crossed paths with my brother Rich for all I knew – the time corresponded.

His last year in the States he had been peripherally involved with the psychedelic movement, and he liked to recite the names of people he knew, recall the concerts he'd been to, and recount the happenings he had witnessed, participated in, and helped to organize.

"But wait a minute," he said "how long *you* been here?"

"A little over a year," I said.

This made him look hard at me, as though taking me in for the first time. I was sitting on the floor in my usual position, a sort of half lotus. That and squatting had become comfortable to me.

"This is a far out place, ain't it?" he asked.

"Further out than I ever imagined," I said.

"Yeah, I can dig what you mean."

He looked up and saw David Bray wandering around the apartment. "What's with him?" he asked and tapped his finger on the side of his temple.

"Yes," I said and nodded, "just too much India."

"No guts," he said "no guts. Man, if I wanted to go that way, I would have had plenty excuse there in that cell for six months. Those Japanese are mean-ass jailers too, I can tell you.

"Whoooweee! This grass is good. You know somethin'? You know where I got this grass? In Viet Nam. I got it off an army guy right in the airport, right at the Saigon airport! Can you imagine that? I mean those medics over there, they're sendin' home heroin and opium and all that stuff in silver supply containers. Just like that. I tell you the whole thing is just coming apart. It's coming apart. That's what excites me. Man, when this old show hits its bottom, then we're going to see some changes. Then we going to see it happen."

"Yes," I said, "whatever it is will certainly happen."

"They'll be some changes made," Robin sang, scratched his sparse rust moustache, and handed me a gooly of hash. I started working it in my palm for a chillum.

"Is that what they got up in Nepal?"

"No, this looks from around Lahore," I said. "Nepalese has a richer look and smell."

After we smoked, Big Jim was completely dazed. The white

girl and Harry Glaum had already lain back.

"Wheew! That is stuff! You guys been on this all along?"

"Pretty much," I said. "As much as possible that is."

"Wow! You been seeing all those crazy cats out there, running up and down half naked, watchin' cows wanderin' around the streets, and you been on this stuff too, huh?"

"That's pretty much it."

"Damn!" I could feel his eyes looking hard at me, singling me out for curiosity and a bit of admiration too.

"We just goin' to be here two or three days," Jim said, "but you think you could show me a few things around here while I'm here?"

"With pleasure. 'It is my duty,'" I said, mocking an Indian. "Calcutta's the place," I went on "to see it all at once, the hub of Muslim madness, the motherlode of Hindu insanity."

I was appreciating that Jim was having his mind blown and that for all he had claimed to have seen, he was giving India, and specifically Calcutta, her due. It was all, as he put it, "something else."

We talked more and Jim finally said, "Hey, man, you're small but you're a heavy dude."

"Thank you," I said.

"Yeah, I mean, I can see that you got the stuff. Somethin's happened to you. You been through a few trips here, right?"

"That I have, Mr. Shaw, that I have."

And then he again repeated his request, "You think you can show me some stuff around here? I mean something really far out?"

"I can try."

I found myself instantly drawn to this huge crude madman. He was open-spirited, obviously fast and intelligent, yet chose to play himself like just plain folks, a big buck nigger. Above all, he was honest about the fact that he was being blown. I enjoyed and respected anybody who let down their guard and just told you right out that the changes that were going on about them were overwhelming. I found his overt expressiveness refreshing in contrast with his companions' mistrustful secretiveness and

Robin's preserved balance.

We talked on late, long after everyone else had fallen asleep, and then it was time for us too to retire. I sat on a little balcony for awhile. It overlooked one of the park squares that could be so pretty in that end of south Calcutta. A dog was yelping in the distance, and I could hear a train not too far off. It must be a train running out of Sealdah station, I thought. I knew it couldn't be part of the main line running out of Howrah. I wondered where it ran, that train, probably through villages southeast of here. I would come to know. That same train would carry me soon, literally, to glory, but now its whistle was a vague undercurrent in my musings. Where on this sweet earth would I come to rest?

The stars hung extremely large in the heavens, and the heavens themselves seemed exceptionally close. A tremendous peace settled upon me. "Now I lay me down to sleep, I pray the Lord my soul to . . ." why, "release," of course, release. I was stoned. Thoughts and visions whirled about merging motion and moment in one sweet caress, levelling care and concern in one manly embrace. Yes, Arjuna, you are stoned, and whenever you are stoned, I come to you. Of course, that was not pure Gita; allow me a little vernacular, it feels something like that. How was it, I wondered, that the Old Man had put it? "I incarnate Myself to my friends, my lovers" – yes, that was it – "my children, my gods and goddesses." I fell asleep.

"Let me tell you about *bhang*,[1]" I started in on Jim.
Our taxi swung out upon a broad avenue of flesh in movement. The old Sikh driver steered straight into the heart of chaos, sped up even as the cross-currents of activity and the bustle of commerce intensified.

"Jesus, did you see that!" Jim fairly screamed.

Four coolies, with a flatbed dollie heaped high with sundry forms of oft-recycled matter, shifting their weight in unison, swerved it to the right upon its axis. The cow to their left would not budge mid-meal. Our taxi slid through almost on a diagonal.

"Sardarji, *kitna dur*[2] Berebazaar?" I asked with no interest in the stream of incomprehensible utterances which seemed to gurgle up direct from the old Sikh's throat without mediation of lips. I was showing off before Jim how seasoned and accustomed I had become, though in fact no Indian street scene ever struck me as commonplace or without surprise.

[1]cannabis ground with pepper into a paste.
[2]"how far to . . . ?"

The boulevard before us was one long arcade of animal and vehicular obstacles. Rickshaws drawn by barefoot and tattered boys, bullock carts, electric trams, double decker busses tilted and sagging with the overload of passengers, cattle of all sorts, runners transporting goods upon their heads or on wheeled pallettes, occasionally an entire herd of goats, limitless numbers of random pedestrians, and motor cars, the great majority of which were indeed taxis, all seemed constantly to compete for their place in the flow. Like so many stringed puppets, they would jerk aside, leap apart, vanish somehow from our sight; wave upon wave parting miraculously before the indomitable taxi, the elephant of modern India.

"Notice," I proclaimed, "that at no time does our venerable driver's elbow ever leave the horn; nor sway and swerve though he might will he be caught making an actual or a complete stop."

"I thought they were nuts in Tokyo," Jim said, "but you can see the pavement there. This is something else. Man, I don't believe it!"

"It's a treat, moving through it this way," I said, resting my head upon the cushion. "And I thank you for it."

My brother Rich had escorted me on this same expedition, in one of those seemingly infinite initiations of those days. Now, more than a year worn with observation and some merging into the phenomenal background, I could evince many distinct strains and patterns in what had before appeared an indistinguishable mass of crushing and frenetic humanity. Wirey Muslims, goatbearded, tended pyjama and *lungi*[3] stalls; rotund *Mewaris*[4] sat calm and complacent on the matted fronts of amply stocked fabric shops; squatting and tense bidi wallahs and other small-time salesmen guarded their limited supplies of rusted nails, piles of bone ends, dyed yarn, plastic and glass

[3]worn around men's waists; shorter width, less elaborate and formal than dhotis.

[4]Indians from an eastern district north of Bombay, known for their success in mercantile ventures.

bangles. Flakes of cotton and other packing matter floated about.

The streets gave way to the crowd-blocked and frantic alleys of north Calcutta, and we had to abandon the taxi to seek our objective on foot. We sought a temple at the center. Above and at the end of one of these trade caverns, I spotted Śiva's trident flying a red streamer. I could find it from there. At the front of the temple there would be a small railed park with sadhus and other loitering mendicants. Across from that, between utensil stalls and silver smiths, nestled a few bhang shops.

The one I had in mind had a silver bell hanging above the squatting wallah who both pounds and dispenses the sopping bhang. Wetted and pulverized, ground with peppers, the cannabis is prepared for ingestion. During my short stint in an ashram in Ujjain I had watched this preparation. It was laborious and demanding. With patience and a sort of petty propriety, finicky hours were spent upon the grindstone.

Our wallah dropped two generous portions into tumblers of lassi, a curd drink. We were seated on benches in the small shop which was raised a few feet above the street. The shop itself became a spare but comfortable sanctuary above and without the thrall of busy-ness.

"Well, Jim," I said as we held aloft in toast-like fashion our green drinks, "the first thing you want to know about Mother India, bless her, is that though niggardly with most comforts and pleasures she does generously offer her pilgrims frequent refuge like this. Physical privacy is unknown, not permitted, a luxury which can not be purchased at any price. You need lots of moments aside to endure it. They abound, of necessity. In any chai shop, under any tree, no matter how pressing or large the crowd around, you are completely alone. You find yourself stepping out of the action all the time. Bhang, grass, hash, chewing pan, opium, snuff, even a bidi will do the trick. India is opulent in offering ways out. It's been going on for God knows how long. You begin to live there, outside the whirl, within yourself. You don't have to seek it; comtemplation is forced upon you. Yoga is endemic to this place. You can hardly avoid it. And you know, it all becomes compelling and addictive."

We began to drink, and as we did so, the wallah rang the silver bell twice. He, or one like him, had done that a year before. I was listening for it.

"What do you make of that, Jim? Is that a sacred or commercial gesture, his doing that? There's a temple across the street, a silversmith next door. No separation of church and state here. No separation of anything. All the lines merge. You must pick your way through it without guide or instruction."

"Whatever it is, it must be good," Jim replied. "Here's to ringing all the bells all the time, and to blowing our minds."

I seconded the motion with a "Once again." We drained our drinks.

"All that seemingly human suffering and confusing stuff we passed on our way here," I continued, "is the tangle and jumble of past lives. It has to be the same everywhere; it's just not so evident anywhere else. The scope, variety or extreme range of it all here, or something, forces you to see it. You witness everything, a whole gallery of human, infra-human even, possibilities. What you see is mostly pathetic and kind of painful to watch, yet the witnessing of it itself or the contemplation of it is pleasurable. But that's not the point. Pleasure and pain do tend to cease to exist here, just as the scriptures say. What does matter after all is the compulsion to see and know it all. The only way to do that is to go through it without being in it, if you know what I mean. The more you do that, the more you encounter other travellers, seekers, passers-by who are all doing the same thing, and in moments like this you are struck in mutual awe of it. You hip each other to what you think it is all about. I don't think at this point that one can really know, though I have felt that too. You see all stages of evolution right there on the street, all at once, all pasts, superstitious or sophisticated, all out there co-existing, prancing before you, and what you feel inside mostly is an inkling of a future knowledge that will put it all together. You can almost taste it sometimes. Where I'm hung up at the moment is in trying to find some viable or even tangential present in the scheme of it. To feel or create the

illusion of doing anything or being anyone amidst this now
completely escapes me. Does that make sense, Mr. Shaw?"

"I think I know where you're coming from, man."

The bhang began to take effect. The bell rung, the journey
launched, spirals of thought felt, feelings cogitated, enveloped
and swept me along. Spirals, cycles interlapped; one could never
find the beginning, though a definite and precise end seemed
always to beckon. I became aware anew, though hardly for the
first time (the beginning could never be settled upon), of presiding deity. After all, He advertised Himself everywhere. Every
barber shop and chemist's counter displayed some representation or familiar portraiture of the Benefactor. Particularly popular in the places I had come to hang out was poster art of a
dreamy, almost sensually self-bemused Śiva. There were several
aspects upon the wall of this very shop. My eyes were riveted
upon his almond eyes, heavy lidded, almost sealed in distant,
silent thought. The Dreamer and the dreamed. Above him, a
sort of protective umbrella to the meditation, his trident is stuck

*...she does generously offer her pilgrims frequent refuge like
this...India is opulent in offering ways out.*

upended in the ground. We had literally found this spot by following such a trident. His *dhameru*, drum of *pralaya*,[5] lay at rest beside Him upon the tigerskin. The street noises seemed to recede even further.

"Well, what do we do now?" Jim asked, smacking his lips in exaggerated satisfaction. "We sit here awhile," I said, "and then we mingle with the crowd."

Once stoned, Rich and I always loved the plunge back into mankind. It was like the rush of sensation and sunshine one received upon emerging from a movie matinee. Still half-immersed in the movie, reality would present its energy complete and intense all at once, to be enjoyed in its brief-glimpsed fullness and not to be suffered as usual through the limited perceptions of participation. Such relished moments were more and more often, almost constant now. Almost invisible, we could move through the crowds easily. The paths and waves we carved through it in our personal vehicles were much smoother and subtler and more efficient by far than even the most adept chauffering sardarji could provide. We slid, jogged, and floated amidst the throng with a delicious lack of encumbrance, a slight taste of omnipotence perhaps.

Big Jim Shaw loomed over the crowd. True African black man, strutting through the dissolving maya tickled his fancy.

"Look at the size of that cat's head over there," he laughed. "Uncle Toby, I do believe, it's been years. Wait a minute! What the hell are these cows doing in the middle of Harlem anyhow? Speak up, baby brothers."

Riding both the tram and bhang waves a year before, Rich and I had dissolved in hysterical laughter from just the look a passing Sikh driver shot us. He had round cheeks and a chin band over his beard, and perhaps he was a distant cousin for surely we'd known him somewhere. And his look and nod too had been one of recognition. Was he in league with us or privy to our illicit mental orgy of dissolve? He was certainly amused and pleased to

[5]the dissolution of existence, destructive half of Śiva's dance. While dancing the pralaya, Śiva is referred to as Nataraja.

see us float, however briefly, by his day and life. Yes, from the almost unbroken wall of peering and inquisitive eyes, blank and dumbfounded, would sometimes twinkle a spark of tantalizing recognition. That look, shining almost subliminally from the ceaseless current of indifference, demanded attention. Was it a friend, a relative, or your own self, bizarrely disguised, amused to find you here? Whatever it was, it suggested a fraternity, or rather a patriarchy (for one never felt of age in India), seldom visible but always present, watching and taking pleasure in your performing presence. Even invisible, you were always watched; alone, you were never without company.

"I have a boy, you know," Jim said as we turned upon the more open, tram-tracked by-ways. "He must be about eight or nine now. Ohio. Long before I hit California. What beats me is that I married this Japanese chick, Kaiko, got her pregnant, see, and I had to leave her in the Phillipines to do this deal. Probably won't go back to her. You know how things turn around, twist a bit. It all piles up and you can't see your way back anywhere. But I hadn't ought to do that again; I mean a second time around is bad news."

"Hey, Jim, everything comes around of its own accord. You don't have to decide or make anything happen. Look, you can't ever be at this moment other than where you are, right? So the best way to always see it is that you have the most purpose to be where you are...exactly when you are. Nothing changes the fact that you're here and not there...and where you are... must be where you are supposed to be. I'm certain I'm supposed to be here, India, I mean, Calcutta, with you. I know I'm meant to be here, have even been held here without, if not against, my will, but what I want to know, Mother India," I almost shouted, "is why you won't accommodate me with a semblance of reason or vague relationship to my purpose here. Come out of the shadows, watchful ones, announce yourselves." The mosque on Chitpur road emptied a flood of pious, satisfied Mussulmen upon us. We whirled amidst the veiled ghostly matrons and fathers and sons in white ice cream hats.

"Jesus, let's get out of here," Jim shouted. "Taxi!"

"I can dig," Jim said as we slid into the vehicle, "that's what's groovey about living here or hanging around or whatever you've been doing here is that you're always a kind of superman here, a big dude amongst these cats. None of them seem real enough to take seriously."

"*Rich, brother, teacher, tell me what it is that holds it all in place.*" Questions constantly pushed forward then with a kind of nervous pricking; my own ignorance came at me from all sides with an almost angry insistence. We'd be walking along, enjoying some sweets, say, when we'd stumble upon an old and withered man lying there in the open, plain broadside, wrapped in a tunic of barbed wire. His tight skin was pierced in a hundred places, but little blood was drawn. Perhaps there was hardly any left, or perhaps it was not really his earthly skin that was punctured. His eyes rolled within their sockets seeking neither relief, nor approval, nor pity.

"*Most often,*" Rich said, "*it seems to be some kind of pervasive and mass penance, doesn't it? Neither judge nor suffer it.*"

The music shops of Rabindra Sarani fairly flew by. All manner of stringed, wind, and percussion instruments were available here. The subcontinent was a repository of music. All was accepted; every tradition flowed into it and enriched the melody. But what was the eternal note sounded . . . was it sorrow? Once, crossing at Raxaul into Nepal, Rich and I were passed by a solitary, heavily bejeweled woman. She wailed uninterrupted. No one or thing was visible on that plain either in the direction she was coming from or to which she journeyed. Her sound filled the air all about, a loud, long mournful whine. I could not tell whether she sang or sobbed. "*Why?*" again the question stabbed, "*What is the meaning of our being here at all? Who is amused? Do harmonics or dissonances result from these encounters between such disparate balls of sensate energy?*"

"*The cosmic laughter is equally apparent, brother.*" Rich always steered me towards balance in those days. "*The jokes are plentiful. There is not exactly mirth here but a superflux of ridiculousness. There is always a cow pie to step in, if you beat the local fuel merchant to it. You just can't look at any of this through your accustomed judgment: none of that works any-more."* Rich always insisted on that from the outset.

Chittaranjan Avenue opened up to receive the Dharamtalla. Strings of electric trolleys turned around to head back along the Maidan. The canopy over the Grand Hotel plaza of Chow-ringhee came in view, and yesterday's adventure popped into my head.

"The Astoria Hotel," I told the driver, "Sudder Street."

The taxi wheeled the corner, and Jim shouted out, "What's that?"

A *Baul*[6] muscian was strolling along with his *ektar*[7] shoul-dered. He passed the national museum and was before the brick wall of the Red Shield Guest House.

"Where are we going?" Jim asked.

"I don't know, perhaps to understanding."

"Can we take him along?"

The Baul hopped in and the taxi proceeded to the Astoria, and my second meeting with Father.

---

[6]a practitioner of the traditional folk music of Bengal.

[7]one-stringed muscial instrument.

I t is common in hotels such as the Astoria that the doors to
the rooms are split vertically and open out onto the corridor. Either a bolt or a chain will run across both halves
of the door, and this would be crudely padlocked if the occupants were out. The doors to this room stood open as they had
the day before, and the green curtain which hung just within
was waving slightly, in response, perhaps, to an intense energy
within. These curtains seemed to part of their own accord as we
approached, beckoning us in. Neither a knock upon the door
frame nor any sort of introduction seemed necessary. We made
the transition from the hallway without effort and found ourselves within the room, comfortable and familiar in an instant,
as though we had indeed been expected.

"For Thine is the kingdom and the glory forever," came the
bass of Don McCoy's voice, and I saw him at the head of the bed
close a book and place it upon a nightstand.

"And are these the toilers of the field?" Shotsy asked as we
entered. She stood to one side at the foot of the bed and was
clasping her hands as she began to pace. Though obviously high

strung, she did not seem as tense as she had yesterday, for she did
not seem so much to be wringing her hands as merely keeping a
good grip upon herself. Never fully relaxed, she struck me as an
operatic singer about to step on stage; an after dinner speaker,
perhaps, who no matter how prepared or well-rehearsed could
not quite take the address as a matter of course.

"Are these the troops passing for review?" she continued.
"Thank you, foot soldiers and volunteers, shock waves of consciousness: thanks for absorbing all this. What a heavy duty to
draw. Really, I don't know how you've done it out here. I'd have
gone mad for sure . . . Oh, my goodness!" She began to laugh,
taking note, I assumed, of the incongruity of our party and the
absurd costuming in which we seemed to present ourselves
before her. I wore a faded maroon robe, actually just a cotton
kurta I had had made extra long like a nightshirt when I foresaw
my wardrobe dwindling to a single all-purpose garment. Jim
Shaw was dressed western, a short sleeved tailored shirt and
plaid slacks. Also, his wire framed glasses made him appear a
touch out of place in our company. The Baul was in ochre-dyed
rags, and his wild hair was done up with crimson ribbons that
fairly screamed with an eccentricity bordering on madness.

The party already assembled in the room was pretty much
what it had been the day before. John O'Shea was there, seated
on the floor beyond the bed. Long strands of his pale-orange hair
lay over a naked shoulder. He was partly wrapped in a beige
shawl, and the upper edge of his marine corps tattoo was just
visible. His attitude was one of extreme absorption, but there
was nothing tense or taut about him. Dr. Prasad too was present,
seated upon a chair to our left. His pose was not relaxed. He
fidgeted with impatience, possibly boredom. Both he and John
were looking towards Father who was seated this time at the
foot of the bed. His back was towards us, and he was facing Don
McCoy. This giant was sprawled over the center and monopo-
lized the greater part of the bed. There was something in Don
McCoy that suggested he believed the show to be his, and that
the rest of us were welcome to witness it, even participate, but
the intensity of his attitude, the concentration of his iron-fixed

gaze, seemed to demand all Father's attention of the moment and to permit the others only peripheral roles. Buz, who looked a bit recovered from his dysentery, or less pale at any rate, sat upright on a small edge of bed to Don's left. Sheila stood between Praṣad and Father like a dancer poised briefly between measured movements, and Shotsy paced the area of floor between Father's back and the doorway through which we had just entered.

The moment I am now describing appears to me, not only in memory but at the time of its actual transpiring, to be a sort of single frame extracted from my movie of life. Everyone seemed frozen in their actions, arrested from movement, presenting themselves as a group portrait for my leisurely and even static consideration. Sound too seemed to cease; breath, pulse, even time itself were suspended. I felt that a lot more than myself had entered the room with me. My brother Rich was present some-how, perhaps peering through the windows of my eyes in assured anticipation that a significant encounter, indeed even one of his cherished epiphanic moments, was about to ensue. This same expansion of my perception, this same dissolution of my rational cognition, this implied transfiguration of my very identity I had experienced in this same room the day before, and now it was happening again. I felt embarrassed to have blun-dered into this precious moment in so rag-tag a manner, ashamed to have stumbled upon it yet a second time so ill-prepared. Perhaps I could adjust myself before the action would again resume, strike a more fitting devotional posture, before time, pulse, sound and breath would all proceed to unreel them-selves towards the inexorable conclusion of this extended moment.

I would pay my respects to Father. That was the key. A sincere *praṇam*, an obeisance of some sort seemed appropriate. In order to *namaskar* Father then, I had to move around Shotsy and step in front of Sheila. I barely saw his face as I bowed my head and pressed the palms of my hands together. "I have brought a friend with me," I thought I would say, in way of introducing Jim, and faltered for a moment to figure out a way to account for the Baul's presence. An apology hovered, a hope that we had not disturbed . . . what? I was not sure . . . a communion that I, having often sought myself, should not have taken for granted, or disregarded, or . . . Words are not necessary in the presence of a Master.

Next I felt a strong urge to touch his feet. My hands were already temptingly close, since Father was seated cross-legged upon that end of the bed. To touch an elder's feet is both the most elementary and cardinal sign of respect, a show of regard and reverence that is assumed as the basic ingredient of manners and good breeding. Every Hindu does it at least ten times a day – to his father, mother, eldest brother, to a host of aunts and uncles, schoolmasters, and to a guru, certainly, should he be blessed enough to have found one. I had stayed some months in an ashram in Ujjain, and the monks there were always requesting that I greet them so. Yet I could never bring myself to do it, perhaps because I had not mastered my western rebellious streak that made me shun what I thought was petty and pompous. And more than that, I did not feel that I had the right to do it.

"Leave them something," I had thought. "We wear their clothes, eat their food, invoke the names of their gods; leave them something." There was a part of me that yearned to do it, imagined myself a fine brahmin boy with sacred thread, but balked at cheapening, as I imagined, the unarguable ancientness and fragile dignity of their lives with this final imitative gesture. But with Father and in that moment it was altogether different. I felt compelled to touch his feet in a genuine surrender and awe which I fervently prayed would ripen into love.

Instantly his hands caught mine and stopped me from completing the genuflection. It all occurred quite quickly but in no manner was it rough. No, it was rather one of the most gentle and tender actions I have ever remembered. My face was drawn upwards so that my gaze passed over his hands and arms and up towards his shoulders, to become absorbed in the celestial clouds of beard that seemed to float like mist about the large *rudraxa*[1] beads of his *mala*.[2] Above that I remember a pair of

[1]the seed pod of a plant sacred to Śiva.

[2]a necklace with holy significance; something akin to a rosary.

lips, softly pursed, the umbered tone of skin about his cheeks which seemed to me to shine like burnished gold, and finally I was looking directly into his eyes.

It all happened for me in that moment. I understood everything in that instant, though to comprehend in truth that understanding and to make it active and viable in the reflexes of my own existence has become the work of my years since, and I can conceive no end to it. All sages and *rishis*[3] say that mind can not truly comprehend It and that thought and voice can never adequately express It; yet once felt and understood, there is nothing else worth expressing, and this very account and recollection is but an attempt to justify the perception of It in my form. Such moments are grace-granted and can not be commanded at will, and what I wish to tell you is that in that blessed moment I saw in the wave lengths between his eyes and mine the entire warp and woof of my world.

It was as though a single thread had been pulled at the center of the intricately embroidered carpet of my vision. I saw the entire pattern of my perceptions pull itself into nothingness upon that single thread, and from the edges of that cosmic loom working centerward I saw it all reconstruct itself with an impalpable but distinctly divine variation upon the theme. Maya danced and revealed so many aspects to me. This dissolve and reconstruction was circular in the extended peripheries of my vision, which broke into more and more disparate particles further from and nearer to the center of sight between us, which was at least a magnetic field, force current, call it what you will, this intense beam of recognition which had drawn me through innumerable circuitous and random-seeming routes from time immemorial to this very moment which was, and is, and ever shall be the eternal moment of existence.

Overwhelmed, I sank back, knelt for a moment, and finally sat upon the floor.

"What is it," Father asked, "that distinguishes this moment in reality from a dream? The past is now a dream, the future is but a dream to come, so what is now? It also is a dream, but a dream

[3] a seer.

which we contract to call and feel as real within our collective cognition of it. Right? You see, you have a dream, and while you are dreaming, you are not aware that it is but a dream. You see so many inconsistencies and absurdities in it that it seems preposterous that even while dreaming you could have been foolish enough to take it as real. So is the life you have just led. As you look upon it now, you will see that there was nothing to enjoy or suffer in that really ridiculous dream. What was it really but a dream of ignorance, petty strife, small incongruous pleasures, enormous and persistent pain – but I don't have to tell you or you wouldn't be here to awaken from it.

"To wake from that life into this life is so easy and so glorious, but takes again a contract in collective cognition, a conscious one this time, to make it real. We must agree to enjoy this reality together. Believe me, I have seen it all; I have done it alone, but it is so lonely!

"How could I wake you? You were each of you – and so was myself, more than anybody; please do not think it is this form that is speaking – so caught up in those dreams, and one dream just led into another, so that there was no way of getting in touch with each other. So, we made that dream so hard to endure, so insufferable, a nightmare even... is that what it became, a nightmare? Say 'no'? You know when you have a nightmare, how you sort of force yourself to wake up. Well, that's what we did. Thank you, *Kali*.[4] You did well, Kali, but the nightmare is over."

His eyes closed a moment, and he himself seemed to drift in the remembrance of it.

"When the nightmare has become apprehensive enough to shake us from that lethal slumber and we wish to dream it no more, what then are we to dream? Why, the eternal dream of bliss, of course. But how to keep from dreaming that mortal dream of self-denial once again? Well, in truth, you cannot cease from dreaming it for all time. There are only mortal and immortal dreams to be dreamt. They complement each other in

[4]the last age, the darkest period of the involution of consciousness is ruled by the goddess Kali, a frightening and destructive aspect of Śiva's consort.

truth and each must have their sway upon the dreamer according to the time. The power to break that cycle will not be
granted you. But you have just emerged from the nightmare of
mortality into the self-conscious blissful existence of immortal
gods and goddesses.

"Lend me your forms," he pled in a half whisper "and I will
make them glorious. Your job" – his voice returned to its full
authoritative tone – "is to make real the existence of gods and
goddesses upon this planet. This reality, let us call it a dream
no longer, you will enjoy for 164,000 years. Bom Shankar
Bholenath!"

The green curtains parted, and Richard Horne, Lynne, Annalise, and Chris from downstairs all entered.

"More grist for the mill," Shotsy giggled. "Fuel for the fire."

"Isn't it wonderful," Sheila began "that we are all here in this
room together once again?"

"Whoowee!!" Don McCoy shouted, "Are you washed in the
blood of the lamb, brother?"

Jim Shaw in his vulnerable and suggestive state began to
babble aloud his rambling thoughts as the energy swept him up.
"Burn it down! That's right. It's all a burn down or a rip off, right
padre?" He'd gasp and blurt these expressions without any obvious context; he seemed particularly anxious to maintain communion with me and for me to share his cryptic insights. "Did
you catch that red beam he just threw out? Can you dig the
destruction of that beam? Burn down! But that green ray she's
putting out might cool it. That's thought. The red is action."

John O'Shea grinned broadly. He offered a sincere namaskar
in my direction and then winked. He was taking a connoisseur's
delight in the exchange. "Hey Buz," he motioned and rolled his
fingers rapidly. Buz took a good-sized gooly of hash out of a
pouch and handed it to John who began to lovingly work it in
the palm of his left hand with the thumb of his right.

Richard and his party nodded various recognitions and began
to settle on the side of the room opposite me. Lynne, spotting
me, came over.

"Hey, that was really a hell of a rap you got into yesterday," she said. She continued speaking, but I could not grasp or follow. The cadence and accent of her voice was heavily east coast, U.S.A., and it seemed rude and unwarranted for this reminder of mundanity to hound me in so remote a place, in so inaccessible and tenuously ecstatic a moment. If I could, I would banish it from my thoughts; I tried to motion her to be silent. "Be still," I wished to say, "I can't hear you. Listen to Father," but there was too great a distance between my thoughts and any motor mechanism of expression. The bhang had slowed me down for sure, but more than that, Father's voice had lifted me out of body, and I seemed to float in an ether not of this room nor world. Lynne's voice and its unintended threat to the trance faded and receded as if on fly's wings the moment Father began to speak again.

"Every level of conscious and subconscious energy through which we perceive ourselves carries with it a whole legion of corresponding images and associations. As we came to accept mortality and our own death as an inevitable and incontrovertible fact, all our circumstances became proof and reminder of our own ephemerality. Everything died; like moths our ancestors vanished from our phenomenal cognition. If they died then so must we, we reasoned. The very first syllogism of any logic class taught anywhere in the English-speaking world begins, 'All men are mortal.' Yet, what has logic and reason to do with life and death. Life is not a matter of the intellect but an experience primarily of your feelings. You can no more stop your feeling of life than you could command your eyes not to see or your ears not to hear. It is nature that sees through your eyes and hears through your ears, and it is also nature that lives and experiences through your formal existence, so where do you come in? You enter the scene only and indispensably as a witness; and if life in some form or any form or even formlessly is eternal, then your witnessing of it must also be eternal, no matter in what form. Have you ever died, really? Can you imagine an existence without your cognition or witnessing of it? No, nor a time when you were not. What lives and dies then in the phenomenal existence? Only an incarnated thought, a materialized idea that, reaching the limits of its conclusion, kicks the bucket, no matter how. What dies is your limited conception of yourself. The old world has already died in you without your noticing it. You may die once or a thousand times more before you are completely dead to your own mortality. The trick is to do that and retain a vision of your form too."

Father laughed, and after a pause Don McCoy did too. It seemed to ring some truth in Don which I could not yet comprehend. "If you can do that," Father continued, "then you will have achieved the purpose for which we entered mortal forms to begin with."

In the momentary silence that ensued I could feel our hearts beat in unison. The room itself seemed to throb in anticipation of a collective affirmation, independent of any individually accumulated understanding. "Go on," our united will urged.

*The room itself seemed to throb in anticipation of a collective affirmation.. "Go on," our united will urged.*

"Our imagination, you see, creates our circumstances, negative or positive. Long before this present moment, we imagined this room and our meeting here. I could tell you exactly when we did that but the recollection of it would blow you away. I will tell you sometime, don't bother. It is not my purpose to hold anything back. I will tell you everything, you may be sure. It is my duty and pleasure to do so, and even a bit of a compulsion too. You will pardon me if from time to time I tease you with hints of a knowledge that I will not reveal just now; I do it only to keep you on your toes, to give you something to aspire to. It will not be much that I withhold from you, a mere ten paise extra to give me an edge in the game. How else could we tell each other apart? If we all knew everything in the same moment, we would merge together and time would cease to exist.

"But what is the agency that enacts our imagination and translates it into the apparent reality of circumstances? Why, maya, of course. Maya is nothing but that, a projection and mirror of our collective will in time. Man will go to the moon very soon, you will see. It has been imagined and willed long enough now to materialize. It is so simple to understand. You could not go to the moon if you did not imagine it first. The method and experience of it will be different than you might have imagined, but it will be through the imagination that it is done. Maya must always surprise the individual imagination or else she would give her own game away too easily. You see, it is not the individual imagination of ego that is fulfilled but the collective imagination of time's will in us.

"Where we get into trouble is in forgetting that it is Time and Nature that is doing the imagining and acting through us and getting caught up in the individual ego's preoccupation that it is doing everything alone. The more we forget the collective urge of the existence and the more we live in the illusion of a limited individual experience the more our maya becomes harder and harder to bear. This we translate into negative associations and the more fearful and painful become our circumstances. Ego sees itself everywhere, so the negativity increases in geometric proportion. But God is so merciful, you know, that He has placed a limit upon this spiral of negativity. There is a mechanism of truth in every expression of the Self that will endure just so much obfuscation, illusion, and falsification before it recoils against the distortion and responds with an invincible energy to assert right vision and true perception. That moment of recoil follows the limit of contradiction the existence can bear in an individual, and the Self begins to shout 'I am the same in all forms' in answer to this critical departure from truth. We reached this point – and by 'we' I mean the entire existence as we have known it on this planet – reached this critical departure point in 1966 and what happened is that I woke up.

"What I awakened to was my Self in everyone. Believe me I worship everybody and everything. There is nothing that I do not worship because there is nothing that is not me. When you awaken to this realization there is only one thing more to be done in the whole universe and that is to spread that realization from the individual to the whole of creation. How could I myself enjoy being awake if you did not awaken to enjoy it with me? And if we, say the handful of us that are in this room, enjoy together this awakening, do you think we could be content to stop there and enjoy it by ourselves? No, for we would still know our enjoyment to be partial, and we could not rest until it became total, and so it will. Everyone will come to enjoy this same recognition – in time. You cannot rule out Time's play in your or any other form of understanding. You see, if our individual awakening were not supported by a universal recognition, then it too, in time, would come to seem and feel as illusory as a dream once again. Remember, it takes our collective cognition to make it real. So how to do that, how to emerge from that world into this? We must constantly and persistently apply our will so that the maya of our circumstances becomes more and more blissful and increasingly pleasant to bear. It is so beautiful, I tell you, and easy too. Really, we have to do nothing. Time will do it through our forms. It is Time and our perception of it, individually and collectively, that dies and is born again. And, believe me, a new time was born in 1966."

Certainly there could be no better moment for the lighting of the chillum which John O'Shea had by now finished preparing. *Hara hara mahadev, śambu!!!*[5] We added then, together for the

---

[5]But three of the countless names of Śiva, invoked before smoking.

first time, the mantra that would ever afterward punctuate our agreement, the contract in collective cognition that would make it real: Bom Shankar Bholenath!

The chillum was passed to the right, counter-clockwise, but hardly made it all the way around in good orthodox *dhuni*[6] fashion as we were not arranged in a smooth simple circle nor on the same level but scattered about with some seated on the floor and some on chairs and the bed. The smoke curled and circled about and between each dhuni member, finally forming a huge serpentine wreath around Father, whose pull upon the pipe was the largest I had ever seen, and I had smoked with sadhus and chillum babas whose renown rested upon the quantity of their inhalations. Awesome was the billowing column of smoke which he exhaled.

A short, rough-looking fellow entered the room as the smoke cleared. He was a friendly, out-going sort and introduced himself in a kind of cockney accent: Dan, an Englishman, just recently returned to India where he had travelled before, glad to be back. Somehow, in our meeting, it was communicated that he knew who I was, had had my name from David Lawrence whom he had just seen in Delhi and somehow or other he had fancied he might meet me or come to travel with me.

"What are you supposed to be anyhow?" Shotsy, hand on hip and head cocked to one side, exclaimed of the Baul quite loudly.

"He is a folk musician of our Bengal," Dr. Prasad volunteered. "Their way of life you know has remained unchanged for hundreds of our years. Very, very fascinating! You know, our Tagore listened to these Bauls for so many the hours, and they are said to have inspired much of his simpler but most potent eloquence. You have heard perhaps the name of one Rabindranath Tagore? His writing is of so much beauty...the heart...you know..."

"Why speak of Tagore?" Father asked softly. He shrugged his bare shoulders and looked about at each of us. "Tagore was great, it is true, but he is dead. If we worship only and speak of the dead, don't you see that we will become dead ourselves. Don't you see that we have been doing that for so long? It is to

---

[6] a smoking fellowship, association; the circle of communication.

wake up to our own glory in this present moment in time that we have been called together."

"Still and all," Dr. Praṣad continued, "one must admit that Tagore had so much heart, much fame he has brought Bengal, and he was honored with your Nobel Prize too. We are in his debt for much cultural reappraisal. Why Shantineketan alone..."

"Of course," Sheila said taking and patting his hand, "but that hour is passed. We must all listen to Father now."

"Sheila, your hands are very beautful," Dr. Praṣad responded, "and do you know that these Bauls are also reputed to be versed in the reading of palms? I can tell you that there is much yet in India that is mysterious and wonderful, and I could with pleasure show you much that would astound."

"Can that dude really read palms?" Jim Shaw asked. "Here," he continued, reaching into his pocket, "how much would he take to read the palms of everyone in this room, say, or at least the palm of that babe over there" – indicating Shotsy. "Now what's that word for 'how much' again? 'Kitna,' right? Kitna, uncle, kitna?"

"It is not necessary," Dr. Praṣad said, taking Shotsy's hands and placing them palm upwards in the thin attenuated hands of the Baul. "It is his duty."

"Not that I couldn't tell you some things about her right off," Jim said. "Half her story is written in every movement she makes with that high class body. Aristrocratic hussy, aren't you? You're so wired and tense, you must be thoroughbred. Hey, I don't mean no harm. You're beautiful, baby, you're really beautiful. I mean it. Hey, ladies and gentlemen, you are... You are all beautiful people, I hope to tell you."

"Why thank you," Sheila said, coming forward and taking Jim's hand. "Beauty is in the eye of the beholder. You yourself must be beautiful to see it in others."

She patted him kind of condescendingly on the back and guided him to the edge of the bed which Buz had vacated at their approach. The Baul had begun and was muttering in a sort of sing-song monotone. Dr. Praṣad attempted a translation.

"He says you have had and will continue to have a most good life though you have in the past suffered some hurts and mishaps too deep and, uhh . . . painful to mention."

"Don't you see that the rascal knows nothing?" Father laughed lightly. "He is out of his element and really only confused by your presence. That is why, Don, I told you that you really do no service to give those beggars so many rupees. I understand that you have a good and tender heart, but it only increases their greed at worst and confuses their sense of proportion and reality at best. You must be careful. If you act so irresponsibly and indiscriminately with the small amount of power you now possess, how can I invest you with more? You would only use it to oppress. Grand gesture never helped. Only knowledge can help, but knowledge demands discernment."

Father spoke very tenderly in a lyric Bengali to the Baul. This latter indulged an imagined affront to his pride when Father spoke to Don and was just working up to really seething with it. I guessed this from the tell-tale flare to his nostrils. Bengalis always seemed to me blatant in their display of indignation, more demonstrative than with almost any other emotion that I could tell. His features relaxed as Father spoke. He then said something softly to Father in Bengali. Father sincerely offered his hands, and the Baul began to trace the lines upon the palms. He was slow and deliberate in this, pausing often and gazing from one palm to the other.

"Baba,[7] baba," he began to mutter, almost sobbing. "Bhagawan, bhagawan,"[8] he whined. "Baba, ama bappi, baba . . . dayakuri, Baba, ama kalmakuru, Baba."[9]

Father's Bangali almost imperceptibly drifted back into English. I could not hear or understand what he said as clearly as I had before. I had hit the heavy and drowsy stage of the bhang. I had to struggle to induce concentration. I knew my crash could not be put off much longer. I strained to bring the words into audible focus, but I was drifting. The room began to undulate in

[7]Father.
[8]Lord.
[9]expression of guilt and unworthiness; a Bengali "mea culpa."

waves and became definitely distorted. It was a bit elongated, and the people within it appeared foreshortened for the most part. And then some of the people present just vanished from my vision. Praṣad was the first to go. He just sort of eased out of the frame. Richard Horne, Lynne, Chris, and Annalise also disappeared from the periphery of my consciousness. The Baul was gone; and Dan the cockney, who I swear had just been right beside me breathing heavily on my left, also was no longer there. Then I heard Father clearly once again, though his voice did not seem to emanate from his form so much as to surround and encompass it.

"Although we have always been together, you know, it has never yet happened within the cycles of His-story upon this Earth that we have chosen to assume so many forms at one time. The *yajñaḥ*[10] that we shall undertake has never before been performed on so grand a scale. This creation is so new and so unique that I must beg you all to suspend for the duration of our eternal association all reflexes and preconceptions that you carry from your recent past and involved and limited existence. Otherwise, remembering the suffering we so recently endured, we would stop content with what in fact would be only partial relief, a mere fraction of what is in store for us.

"You see the vision that took possession of this form in 1966 is so vast that no mere age can express it. It is an entire *kalpa*[11] that begins with us. I knew and saw it all within an instant, the zero hour of creative destruction, the midnight of June 14th-15th. For this form to be able to express it, it took three months of wild phenomenal meanderings on the earth plane and tremendous astral projections. There I spoke with everyone, you know, even your Jesus Christ. I worshipped him first of all. He was the doorway in.

*Iśāvāsyamidaṃ sarvaṃ*
   *Yat kiñca jagatyāṃ jagat.*

[10]great sacrificial performance, requires participation of many.

[11]vast period of imagination, containing ages.

*Tena tyaktena bhuñjithā*
*mā gṛdhaḥ kasya sviddhanam* [12]

Jesus and Moses, Buddha, Ramakrishna and rishis and sages too numerous to relate, all bowed down with tears in their eyes and blessings upon their lips, bowed down and prayed that this vision would at last find fulfillment in my, and now, our forms. Vyasa only would not surrender. He laughed, I guess, at the audacity of what had been prayed for and is now attempted in fruition.

"I knew that you would come, that the small village in which I live would become the yogic seat of knowledge for the entire planet at the commencement of this great kalpa. I told the villagers that; I told them over and over again that gods and goddesses born in the west, and mostly from America to begin with, oblivious of their divine nature, were coming and would claim us. And now it has begun! I am so grateful, Mother, thank you. Thank you, Yogamaya, and thank you, my gods and goddesses, for understanding me and surrendering your forms to this understanding.

"As it took three months for this instantly comprehended knowledge to stabilize itself in this terrestrial form, so it will take you some time to stablize the feelings you are now passing through in your own forms, say five years. That is not very long, is it? It could be shorter, depending on your powers of concentration and your aspiration. I wanted to tell the delegates at the Spiritual Summit Conference, 'Listen to me, fifteen hours to Supermanhood.' Supermanhood would have been more than enough for them. They cannot conceive beyond that as yet. But no one would listen, not even fifteen minutes. So how are we to measure the completion of fifteen divine hours? I say five years because that is when, according to your western science, Freud said five years, that is when it is said the child's makeup is complete for a life of mortal ignorance. So five years to prepare us for the life divine is not too long an apprenticeship. You are

[12]opening shlokas (verses) of Iśa Upanisad.

born into your infancy now, and infants are always impatient to stretch their limbs. But think of the thousands of generations and the years that it took us to achieve our recently depraved state. Divine intelligence works infinitely faster. It is difficult, you see, to create darkness from total light. We did that too. It is infinitely easier to bring about total light out of darkness for the light is never completely covered. That is the condition of the existence, divine or demonic, the light can never be totally eclipsed. This light has been carried in men of vision during every age to remind the rest of humanity of the eternal and vast aspiration, the *satyam ṛtam vrat*[13] – to know God in a human form, in this mortal craft to enter the luminous and immortal regions.

"Each of those forms of light in each age only flickered and died without progeny for the will of the time was still to plunge the earth into further darkness. In order to stabilize itself this light must reproduce itself in more than just one form, ultimately in enough forms to overcome the objections of an apparently darkening existence. That is why my constant prayer since my awakening has been for you. I told you that I have been praying to you and waiting for you for two and a half years."

Don McCoy's huge body suddenly leapt off the bed. He threw his arms in the air and stamped his feet. Charging about, he shouted. "Father, make them see! The light is upon us! Father is the light! Make them see!"

Speech came to me for the first and only time during this interview, and I blurted out "For God's sake, let none of us leave the room this time until we have figured it out." I fell back against the wall totally unconscious.

---

[13]the Real and Vast Truth.

I woke to the empty cawing of the crows. Something in that grating chatter warned me that I had not yet finished my bout with melancholy.

Somehow we had managed to return last night to Ken's flat. Dan, my new-found English friend, was there in the Ballygunge flat upon my awakening, and he and Jim Shaw assured me that I had led them back here without hesitation or problem; I could recall nothing of the sort. The sun was well up when I stepped out upon the balcony, and I felt a bit groggy and let down from the bhang. The square below that I had imagined so charming the night before last now appeared to me an undistinguished patch of burnt out grass where screaming scavengers hopped about and pecked at each other over refuse and scraps. The long stretch of afternoon was just about upon us, and futile seemed any efforts of vision to exceed the dust and dreariness. Once again, it all seemed a sad and insurmountable wasteland to me, picked over at least once too often. Spent and exhausted, what treasure could this fallow landscape yield the expenditure of spirit? The shrieking of those birds mocked the memory of hope, and their wings blackened the sky as they sought the noon shelter of the trees. I feared a resurgence of despair, so despite the threatening heat, I headed downtown.

It felt different to me, and I knew something had changed long before I entered the small office and passageway at the rear of the Astoria. Whatever force had guided me with ease past this threshold on the other two occasions was not present this time, and, unaided, it seemed only with great effort at each step that my volition could move me through the sluggish and drowsy atmosphere surrounding me now. I could sense that what I sought had already slipped away, and that I now retraced but worn and vain footsteps towards an oasis that offered considerably less than yesterday's promise of paradise. The key to the padlock of their room was hanging on the board at the unoccupied office, and the whole scene emitted a sense of abandonment.

From his nap on a stringed *charpoy*[1] in the hallway, a bearer grumbled: "Big sahib and company, they go. Left this morning gone. Other sahibs and memsahibs still here. They already send me for Coca Cola and chai." I went down the hall towards Richard Horne's room, and the bearer added, drifting back into sleep, "What make big sahib shout so much last night?"

John O'Shea was there as I entered, and he greeted me with a quick "Bom, bom." On the cheap bureau Richard had set up his typewriter, and I could see that he had about half a medium-sized paragraph started on the sheet.

"Some scene last night, huh?" Lynne said to me. "You know they left this morning. I think they went over to the Grand Hotel."

John and I glanced at each other with an "Oh, well" expression as though we understood everything. We communicated quickly and telepathically with a kind of shorthand camaraderie of road veterandom. How could we expect any more from them, we empathized: they were so new to the road that it would be surprising if they had not opted for some comfort.

[1]wooden bed frame with ropes woven between.

"I feel kind of bad and sorry," John said, "for Father . . . uhh, Ciranjiva, you know. He probably went through a lot of hassle to come in from that village every day. I'll bet he was disappointed to find that they checked out on him. He was really getting off on rapping it down to them."

"No doubt, he wasn't overjoyed," Richard put in, "to find his birds had flown the coop. I'm sure he saw a ticket to America in Don McCoy. They all want to go to the west, you know, ever since the Maharishi made it big."

That was true, I had to agree. Last spring a fairly large group of us had gone up from Bombay to the small town of Ujjain along the Śipra River to attend the *Kumbamela*[2] there. After that insane week and after the sadhus and pilgrims were gone, I and a few of the Italians decided to stay on in that sleep-encrusted small town on the hot plains, and we lived in an ashram there until the swelter of summer drove us north to Kashmir. I loved the quiet of that place, and I was fond of the guru there who was a sweet man and quite adept at physical yoga. I surrendered to him somewhat, and he brought me quickly along from a remedial physicality to a fairly good hatha yogin who could boast the full lotus from a headstand. He was less successful in his attempts at Sanskrit, mostly because his English was so poor and also because he really didn't know Sanskrit himself, other than a few memorized verses. His imagination ran a bit wild for my tastes, and his ambition got completely out of hand. The presence of western "disciples" in his ashram stimulated such grandiose and inappropriate schemes of grandeur that he became progressively more idiotic in his pride and demands, and eventually, insufferable. Upon learning that Mario came from a landed family outside of Parma, the guru laid plans for the first Italian ashram. Later I noticed the same effect at the Amarnath yatra. Our presence on that pilgrimage inspired swarms of sadhus and visiting *vedantins*[3] to more readily than not display

[2]mela-gathering (melange) of holy men and pilgrims every four years; Kumbamela-grand, climactic, gathering every twelve years.

[3]proponent of Vedanta – philosophical involution of the Veda (Truth in scriptures).

the proud results of their spiritual *tapasya*,[4] and they even competed with one another for our attention. I'm sure many a *siddhi*[5] was shown and esoteric doctrine confided to us gratis that would have required enormous signs of devotion before being communicated to any Indian aspirant.

I was just cynical enough in this train of thought to think that the Bengali show of spiritualism and the lure that Calcutta could concoct would have to be more wild and fascinating than any other. Since my Indian journey had begun here, I held that this state and city was the soul, source, and finest example of all the contrariety and madness that had so plagued and inspired my wanderings. No doubt, the Bengali rap would exceed all others. You see, I had forgotten already Father's warning, and succumbing again to cynicism and disappointment, I had begun to measure him by preconceptions from my recent past.

"At any rate, gentlemen," Lynne said cheerily "there is always acid this full moon."

The ancient temple of Konarak was suggested as the scene and setting in which we might experience the sacrament. There followed a session of planning and excitement. Chris had a movie camera. We would make a film. Richard wished only to "knock off a few pages" on his article on Kathmandu, and then we'd depart. We aimed for the next evening. I quickly calculated the past full moons in my head. The full moon that climaxed the Amarnath yatra in August was on the 8th, I knew. September's I'd passed at Dalhousie where I ran into Mario and Mirella again. In October I was in Benares and had met Andy and James, and I watched her moon from the terrace of their comfortable flat. November's full moon would then fall on the 5th, and the prospect of witnessing it from Konarak was fine indeed; far more than I would have settled for in way of consolation when I had entered depressed but a half hour before.

When I returned to the flat that evening, my enthusiastic communication about this trip made Dan and Robin wish to

[4]merit or energy acquired by austerity; successful result of yoga.

[5]supernatural power acquirable by practice; a fruit which could be reaped by means of ascetic severities.

join us. Like myself, Robin was hanging around Cacutta awaiting mail, so the Konarak plan appealed to him as a means of biding time. He was expecting money that would put him on the Bangkok leg of his journey to Bali. Though I couldn't realistically expect the mail I awaited for a couple of weeks yet, it would determine the speed and necessity of my return home; meanwhile, I was in limbo. Dan, however, just returned to India, was eager for an adventure which would launch another round, an extensive one, he hoped, of travel in the subcontinent.

"There was no way I could live back there, man," Dan was telling us, "not once I'd been out here. Look, just for teasers, at the way we pop into each other last night, and here we are already snug mates and bound off south together. No way at home, man! It's all cutthroat there. Takes months to shy up to anyone and nothing ever moves or happens at all. Even in jail I didn't get to know no one, and we was forced together, you know what I mean. I'd have never gone back at all, but I got myself strung out on morph. Went back there to kick and couldn't do that either there. Not until jail and cold turkey. 'Petty theft' and 'social maladjustment' they call it but I name it 'just plain boring.' Did this tattoo here just out of boredom."

He rolled up his sleeve and showed us a crudely inked Bugs Bunny caricature on his forearm. Behind it was a rough-drawn knife.

"What I need," he went on, "is some quiet scene here like Goa used to be, you know, man, to get my head together. I'm still jangled from London. Don't try to go home, man. I wouldn't even think about it."

The next day Jim Shaw, Harry Glaum, and the girl left for their business in Kathmandu. I didn't let Jim get off without a quick trip downtown together, whereupon he purchased for me a new set of white dress pyjamas and a pair of sandals. I was ready now to travel on a bit. I thanked Jim and wished him well, and I told him in all sincerity that it had been a real pleasure and treat running into him.

"Likewise, I'm sure," he said. "Take care, brother, and keep the faith."

John and I hit the Astoria at about the same time. We found Richard Horne no further along on that same paragraph. Chris was sitting on the bed shaking his head over a beautiful Beaulieu camera. He had just blown out the rechargeable battery in it on the erratic 220 volt electrical current of the country. John and I took a look around the room and were struck by the large number of things spread about. "Never happen," we thought, "they won't make that train tonight," and it did not take much telepathy between us to reach the conclusion that we had better not hitch our quick exit plans too tightly upon theirs. It was agreed that John and I would go ahead and catch this evening's train along with Dan, Robin, and a Scottish John whom I hadn't met as yet but who had been John O'Shea's roommate of late. Richard, Lynne, Chris, and Annalise were to join us in a day or two at the tourist bungalow at Konarak. John tried to get enough LSD to get us stoned should their plans miscarry, but Richard was firm on the point of his holding the dope and assured us they'd make it there.

In my new white pyjamas and wearing sandals, I felt respectable enough to enter the Grand Hotel and make inquiries after Don McCoy, Shotsy, Sheila, and Buz. I was told by the saree-clad hostess at the front desk that the Wallace girl and the others I asked about had checked out that morning. The bulk of the Spiritual Summit Conference delegates had left the day before that for Delhi and a return west. "I believe I heard Mr. McCoy and the other gentleman and ladies say that they were next to visit Pondicherry," she volunteered. Pondicherry would mean that they were headed for the international Aurobindo ashram there. "So they were only tourists of India's spiritual institutions after all," I assumed, dismissing them from my mind with that thought. I don't believe I gave any thought whatsoever to Father as I blithely stepped back upon the road and went about my arrangements to catch the Puri Express Down.

From the Calcutta side of the bridge and in the gathering

gloom of dusk, Howrah Station appears like a long low mauso-
leum, sombre, dark, and apparently desolate. It is anything but
abondoned, however, for at any hour of the day, Howrah Bridge
teems with human traffic in the scores of thousands, moving to
and from the station. All mannner of transient persons, carried
there on missions of varied purpose, obvious or elusive, merge
for moments beneath the arched portals, stream through the
vaulted and catacombed corridors, and disperse upon the laby-
rinthian platforms of this vast terminus of the Indian railway
system.

It is just as much with a trembling heart and in trepidation
that I approach Howrah Station, now in my efforts to describe
it, as I did then on my exit from Calcutta. The intense spectacle
and experience of it both exhilarated and frightened me. Its very
walls reverberated with the roar and plea of humanity in a
moment of, and urge for, change and transition. The earnest or
indulgent, the desperate and vagrant, all converge upon this
nexus of energy, passengers all within the same process of time,
sojourners all through a common body in space. Point of congregation for such an enormous range of striving souls, Howrah
Station is for me as awesome as any temple or pilgrimage spot
and presided over surely by a most potent deity, fierce and
wrathful in aspect.

The privileged, like myself, pass through it quickly, but its
halls and floors are always cluttered with legions of others for
whom, lacking fortune's blessing of a speedy exit, it has become
a refugee encampment. Under the guise of awaiting delayed or
nonexistent trains, countless shadowy and wraithlike forms,
huddled on mats and newspaper, find temporary shelter here.
This sudden show of poverty and misery is to me more horrible
than the persistent pawing beggary of the streets. For one thing,
it takes you by complete surprise, and for another, there can be
no question of its awful sincerity, for it is not there to seek your
attention. It is as complete and integral a vision of hell as India
has to offer.

In such an atmosphere, what should be a routine maneuver,
the inquiry after a time schedule of departures and arrivals, the

procuring of tickets, and the locating of the correct platform and train becomes a harrowing experience. It makes the entire complex and ingenious railway system seem less a generous asset and more a treacherous legacy of colonialism. No doubt, the construction of this mammoth network was the greatest endeavour of the British Raj in India; its arteries and capillaries reach everywhere, connecting remote and inaccessible regions, arid with tropical districts, transporting caste and custom along a single vein of track. One wonders, however, if the overall effect has been at all beneficial or benevolent. If the intent and earlier effects of the creation of a railroad were to unify the country and to facilitate an orderly administration of it, the present reality and results are but poor arguments for it. They suggest rather that it contributed to the spreading and intensifying of confusion. One can imagine in the youth of empire what dreams travelled these iron rails, what hopes for commercial exchange and cultrual advance sped along the newly laid track. Calcutta must have flourished with the pulse of life that shot through the magnificent and virgin nervous system. It is easy now, however, to see that for all its promise, what the railroad actually accelerated in India was the process and pace of her disintegration. What poured finally into Calcutta was chaos and decay.

As you might imagine, I was anxious for fellowship as I moved through these seeming miles and lifetimes of unrelieved sadness, this miserable homeless limbo of a hunger and want so vast and unrelenting that it drained any impulse towards action, the purgatory beyond prayer of this way-station Howrah, so confused, crowded and desperate that it left no room for even the most dessicated and flimsy hope. My eyes searched the gray and phantom crowds for a familiar form imbued with life, a friend and companion.

I anticipated seeing Robin. He and I had arranged to meet if possible and share the same coach down. Scottish John was something of a modest patron to John O'Shea, having sheltered him in his hotel room these past weeks, and was treating him to a ticket on this journey. Dan had some money so he had chosen

sle of a booking office that afternoon and was
o Johns in a berth, second class cum sleeper. Robin
:ither rupee nor paise, had no choice but to brave
; of ticketless third class travel. Company would
deal somewhat, so my eyes darted everywhere,
: lookout for Robin.

bf western vitality and jauntiness flashed about a
ls ahead of me, and I raced to catch up with it. It
in, however, but Sal Friscia, turning beneath the
ain for Raxaul.

buted and pushed towards him. He was at the end of
ss carriage hopping about and straining amidst the
in an effort to read the clumsily typed sheet of
:r that announced the reservations within that

b you know, the yogi from Philadelphia!'' He em-

can see,'' he went on, ''I exit in style – second class,
all in all better than it might have been for this poor
hat's left for me to do is find that grand Sicilian name
ongst these hosts of Biswas and Mukherjees and I'm
my last time amidst this bedlam, old buddy.''
Kathmandu then?''

"Yes, it's the only place I ever really enjoyed here. A short
stay and it's New York and the bright lights once again for me.''

"Returning to hearth and home as well?'' I asked. "Your wife
and daughter?''

"I'm going to give it a try.''

"My time here is almost up, and I'll probably be doing the
same in a couple of weeks. For now I'm going to take a look at
the temple at Konarak. Going to catch that Puri train over there
with John and Robin – remember Robin Brown from Kashmir? I
ran into him just after I saw you the other day.''

A moment's pause.

"Well,'' Sal said, "I guess this is it for you and me. Don't take
any wooden nayapaisa.'' He turned back to his search of the
passenger lists, and I started back towards my platform and

train.

"Hey, yogi!" Sal shouted after me. "Don't give up too eas You stand as good a chance as anyone I ever met, and when y do find It or Him, put in a good word for me, all right?"

I did meet with Robin as well, and together we found a thi class carriage a little less forbidding than the others, and v boarded it. How I endured so many of those rides in third cla quarters is a mystery to me to this day. In the interim betwee these journeys, I would mercifully forget the extreme discor fort and burden. Surely, if I had remembered, I could never ha mustered the nerve to venture it again. Every third class ca had ever been in was packed beyond belief; I had to fight my wa aboard. Arms and legs were shoved out windows in the chokin pressure of the crowd. To find a place to sleep therein was next t impossible. I did manage it upon a few occasions, beneath a sea or curled up in the luggage rack above. Amazingly enough, onc a space was found to accommodate one's cramped and collapse form, it all became not only bearable but slightly pleasant. Th motion of the train itself lulled one into a trance of tolerance even approximating comfort at times. Also, the experience and prepared traveller was never without a stash of hashish opium, or a ball of bhang to see him through it. The entir experience was so intense and out of the ordinary that one ha no choice but to become philosophical about it. Like everything else in India, I wound up loving it in my heart, though my reason told me it was loathsome.

My friend Marc termed travel in this manner, with the added circumstantial embellishment of having no ticket, the "sadhu express." To begin with, the entire railway system in India, from the dreary yellow cantonment and booking offices piled high with ledgers and useless scraps of paper, peopled by sad civil servants who spend their lives laboriously scribbling trans- actions and records that will never be read, who, closing their books at the end of the day, sleep upon that very desk at night, chained and slave to a meaningless ritual, homeless and lifeless save for their office and petty duties – to the first class waiting rooms, which often provide the only hot water or decent meal around for miles . . . one must realize that this entire system is a world unto itself in India and that you become adept within it, both in taking advantage of its facilities and in dodging its dangers.

The process of procuring a ticket is such a hassle in its own right that it at first contributes to, and finally nearly forces, the expedience and delinquency of travelling ticketless. The only way to do this without being caught is at the third class level. The first and second class coaches are well patrolled and regulated. The third class is always so crowded that it discourages a conductor or ticketman from any regularity in attending his duties there. More often than not, a third class passenger is never asked for his ticket. This was never certain, however, and the unwritten karmic rule of the road which governed it seemed to be that if you were driven to the expediency by a sincere and genuine poverty, you would be spared disturbance, but if you had money and chose to travel ticketless, you were almost certain to be hassled by an overly officious ticket collector.

Roused from your sleep or reverie by such a one, you could always offer an authentic poverty in way of an excuse, and you would be regarded with respect by this ticket-taker as a sadhu, yogi, or pilgrim, and he would namaskar and leave you in peace, sometimes even returning with a bit of food. If you had money, however, no matter how much you protested to the contrary, this officer would somehow see through the sham and become more adamant in his hassling, but seldom would even this circumstance result in anything more serious than being put off at the next stop.

The danger of this latter consequence became more frequent during my year in India. Indira Ghandi apprised the literate part of the nation that the influx of penniless westerners was less than a blessing. They were "hippies," a decadent and unwelcome phenomenon, and as such posed the third most serious threat to India's security. We were less dangerous than Pakistan and the Chinese but more of a problem than the language difficulties, which as number four on her list caused riots and antipathy between Hindusthan and Tamilnad. Signs were posted in English in many railway stations declaring that "Ticketless travel is a social evil." Rich and I, travelling to Bangalore, fell victim to a particularly persistent and irritated careerman, who would have none of our avowals that we were sadhus and yogin and therefore entitled to free travel, and he not only insisted on putting us off at the next stop but was also pressing for our being jailed. He marched us towards it at that station but stood powerless and incapable of pursuit as we simply marched through the gate and out onto the road. This occurred, I'm sure, because we did have the means of procuring a ticket and hadn't done so out of a false penny-pinching notion of economy rather than actual need.

Rich and I were actually arrested in a train station once. We had left Benares en route for Agra and were changing trains at Kanpur. As we crossed an overpass to another set of tracks, we were apprehended by some policemen. We had tickets and could not tell why these men bothered us. They spoke no English and insisted on unpacking our things, which at that time were numerous. They discovered our stash of hashish and opium bought in Benares. One of them muttered something, and I heard the word "Pakistanee." I assumed he referred to the hashish. The moment for a bribe passed, and a crowd gathered. The officers marched us to the station jail and, showing off, prodded us now and then with their *lathis*.[6] We waited all day in that police office and watched several brigades of chained convicts march by. The prospect of seeing ourselves similarly manacled was far from appealing and, alas, appeared more real as each hour passed without any English-speaking person of authority coming to our rescue. Finally a portly, mustachioed superior officer did arrive. He spoke English and apologized and laughed about the incident. He returned not only our passports but the hashish and opium as well. In my passport under occupation I had written "teacher." The officer asked me if many teachers in the U.S. smoked charas. Yes, we all smoked it there, I lied. "There is much in this world strange and deserving," he said. "Here it is a filthy and lower class custom this smoking, but I tell

[6]sticks, longer than clubs, shorter than canes, used as weapons.

you myself, I am fond much of it and indulging often." I asked him why then we had been arrested. "Terrible mistake, Mr. Teacher," he laughed, "but much trouble here with Pakistan spies, and my men perhaps are stupid. Pakistanees are no good. It is best that my men are watchful."

During my first visit to Bombay, Rich and I lived for the better part of a month in the first class waiting room of the Victoria Terminal Station. We woke up in the morning and showered there, checked our things in at the baggage claim, and went out to explore the city. Returning at night, we would retrieve our bedrolls from the attendant of the baggage and sleep in the waiting room on the floor or couch. It was in all about the most comfortable lodgings I ever had in India. We were not the only ones to discover this ruse, and during that month there were as many as sixty westerners sleeping there at a time. I first met Marc there. In general, the road scene grew too fast for its own good in India. Certainly the V.T. Station waiting room could not accommodate it, and when it became so large and notice-able, it drew the police, and that dispersed it for awhile.

I recall it in such detail because these aspects of the railroad were so important to the fabric of life for the road westerners during this period of the Great Quest. My journal contained many incomplete attempts to celebrate it.

> "I'm in love with the Indian train
> Śri Mahabiriji, Madman, Ujjain..."

> "mascara running like big black tears
> in the poste-speed dawn of the Punjab Mail..."

As I rode then, with Robin nodding beside me, it was with something like gratitude that I looked upon our present circum-stance, cramped and inconvenient though it might be. We were, after all, being carried by this train on another grand adventure. There was something reassuring in its rhythm, something com-forting in the clack of the wheels upon the track.

It was again my brother Rich, my first teacher in India, who first pointed out to me the psychic amenities and spiritual des-

serts of the train. Journeying to Raxaul, leaving Calcutta behind, Rich remarked once upon the rejuvenation of energy and
enthusiasm that each scene change brought with it, and how,
associating that with your means of change, the train, you
could always lift your spirits by just listening to the song of the
track, hearing the night station cries of the chai and fruit wallahs, observing the regional changes in dress and habit of the
passengers. "Whatever scene you've just passed through, good
or bad" – he referred to my long and fascinating initiation in
Calcutta and the resultant loss of my camera – "it is all blessedly past the moment you board the train, lost in the lure and
mystery of what lies ahead." True enough, dear brother, a scene
once passed is past and equally so. Calcutta, Kathmandu,
Benares, Delhi . . . they are all strung out in my mind like beads
upon a mala, and the connecting thread is the train.

I think the initial and most profound change India had
wrought in me was that it somehow altered my perception and
experience of time. In my first month, week, or even day, I felt
and thought more than I had in the duration of years passed in
the increasing mundanity of a life that had driven me to so
radical a change as India. Time simply became more full, immediately. It was more than ample compensation for the many
egos robbed from me. I thought over these things as the train
whined and hummed and sang her song to me; another experience and change was coming, so I ruminated upon experience
and time itself as I was carried through the tunnel of night.

As I had come to experience more in less time, the more time
there seemed to be in which to experience time itself. I began to
glimpse the wonderful power of an infinite spiral. In itself, that
notion expanded and intensified my life. India had taken much
and given me more. An experience passed was equally past, and
that understanding gave me great power to recall it. In the west,
I had been bound and limited by my linear understanding and
perception of time. The more recent past had more power over
my present than its preceding moments. As those moments
receded towards what I conventionally considered the distant
past, their power to influence my present, and my power to
recollect them, seemed to diminish in a proportionate ratio. My

present, compromised by understanding the past as a linear causal chain, projected an equally diminishing vision of a future. That limitation contributed, no doubt, to the depression that had catapulted me to India.

All of that changed with the shock of experience, loss of ego, whatever, with which India hit me. I still experienced time chronologically, of course, but I began to understand chronology itself as part of a cycle. I felt experientially that I had lived in India before or that I was living several lives there simultaneously – at least one of them, though dimly perceived, much grander and more glorious by far than anything I could consistently imagine. My experiences became spiritual of their own accord without my seeking it, and then to understand them I began to seek spiritual experience. So I had become lost to my life in the west but not quite found here.

A tremendous liberation came, however, with the realization that the successive moments which formed my past did not bind my present. This I learned by experiencing time differently. What happened was that as I began to accumulate more and more past moments in India, I could equally recall those pasts, Calcutta, Benares, the desert cities of Rajasthan, the hill stations I had seen, Mysore to the south – all hung in the same limbo of time. The more recent pasts had no more power over my present than the pasts before them. And the moment I stepped aboard a train to my future, my present was alive in itself, unencumbered by recent or distant past. I had done a poor job trying to convey that thought to my wife in a letter from Kashmir. The liberation I had tried to express with this simple insight was joyous and instantaneous, but I must have known that it would seem a disavowal of commitment and sound even taunting when read so many thousands of miles to the west in a world still riddled with responsibilities and not only bound but burdened by the past. Yet for me, I could not deny that each experience was becoming, in effect, a station through which the train of my perception was passing. As the stations piled up along the track of my memory, I understood that what India had effected in me was a mutation of my perception, from the limitation of linear cognition to the greater freedom and fulfillment of cyclical realization. Perhaps, the thought struck me, the stations of my future, equally in limbo, are equally accessible to my present.

No conductor bothered me for a ticket nor did any other passenger disturb me that night. I remained absorbed in my meditation on Time until the train, careening around a curve, presented me with a splendid amber and coral sunrise.

We left the train at Bhubaneshwar station, and the five of us assembled for morning chai and chillum. It was not hard to find our way to the broken depot and oily yard of the bus transport company. There were two busses that day for Konarak, one at noon and another towards evening. Dan and the two Johns decided to go on directly and procure a room at the tourist bungalow. They gave Robin and me enough rupees for two tickets on the evening bus. We wished to climb and explore the abandoned stupas, temples and shrines, so numerous in those parts that their full number has never been catalogued.

Bhubaneshwar is overall a dry and dusty place with stunted shrub and sparse vegetation around crumbling temple walls. The temple sites dot that Orissan capital and weave in and out of the present life of that city like a mysteriously alluring but useless vein of moss in agate. These temples are, for the most part, small in scale and not very intricate in design, noteworthy mostly for their tremendous number and concentration in so small an area. This suggests an unusually energetic but short-lived burst of reverence and activity upon this predominantly barren plain, sometime in the past, which authorities have speculated upon and dated to the satisfaction of scholarly interest. These shrines are of no curiosity whatever to the local inhabitants, and there is no life around or within them other than the lizards that, startled by your approach, scamper in terror over the walls.

Just as Robin and I had about exhausted our energy and sense of exploration poking amongst these ruins, we encountered a curious sight. There was a long low house nearby which, though not ornamented or distinguished, boasted a freshly plastered wall and gate which declared the occupants wealthy. To this gate marched a line of about twenty-five to thirty lepers. From the house there emerged three servants carrying a few buckets of rice and dahl and some banana leaves. One of the servants carried a lathi and held the lepers back in abeyance while the other two piled the food on the banana leaves in two or three generous heaps. The lepers, the moment the threat of the lathi was removed, pounced upon and fought over the food without nearly the discipline and patience of even the most scraggly, carrion-devouring, winged scavengers.

It seemed to me a frequent ploy of India's to thrust at one in the midst of a quiet, drowsy, and boring moment a furious vision of greed and horror. Once as I was walking outside of Hrishikesh, nearing the Lakshman mandir bridge, a shrill and intense shrieking jarred me out of the dreamy pleasure I found in listening to the blending sounds of the droning flies and the light lapping water. A small colony of lepers squatted in little shaded begging stalls just by the bridge, and they leapt into the routine and litany of their whines and pleas all at once at the approach of this surprised sahib. Upon another occasion, during a night stroll along the ghats during my last stay in Benares, I heard a tremendous clamour of noise from the top of the Dasashwamedh stairs. Going up to investigate, I saw that the beggars sleeping there had been awakened and aroused by a visit from a fat Rajasthanee woman and two of her servants. This good lady, no doubt in an effort to acquire merit and to doubly assure herself that her pilgrimage to the sacred waters had not been wasted, was engaged in an act of charity. Instead of food or paise, however, she was distributing some cloth, cheap beads and bangles, and glass and plastic jewelry. The beggars fighting over the offerings scarce out of her hands frightened her, and her servants were beating them back with lathis. Many of these beggars had fingers and hands so eaten with leprosy that they could barely grasp or hold on to the booty over which they quarrelled. Beads and bracelets scattered and rolled and bounced down the pilgrim-worn steps to the Ganga.

It was quite dark when our bus brought us to Konarak. Despite a moon waxing fairly full, we could not make out any houses or buildings there. In fact, if the driver himself had not left the bus, we would not have known that we had reached our destination. There were no signs proclaiming Konarak nor any visible landmark except the outline of a huge mound or hill which rose of a sudden from the flat horizon. It was a beautiful night, and hordes of luminous stars danced in the domed firmament above. Below, the earth felt soft, somewhat sandy, and very inviting, so we dropped our blankets there and fell into a sound sleep.

Daylight revealed Konarak to be a sandy, impoverished fishing village, seemingly lifeless and deserted. The small inhabited portion consisted of a single lane of bamboo shacks, chai stalls, and broken hovels which posed as eating establishments and boasted grandiose mythological names like the Anna Purna or the Pushpak. This lane was lined on both sides by rows of palm trees which fell not too distantly into a thicket of greenery, appearing a little further on as a veritable jungle of vegetation, unbroken along the horizon. A faint roar announced the proximity of the ocean, the Bay of Bengal, but it was not visible anywhere in that almost undistinguished landscape. Commanding without rival all visual attention was the huge monolith of hand-hewn stone whose silhouette we had descried the night before: rising as if from another plane of reality stood the great temple, the black pagoda, the chariot of the sun god Surya.

The temple, reputed to have once been twice its present size, in ruins for centuries, stands apart in a walled compound wrapped in ancient silence. At the time of which I am writing, cleaning and restoration of the temple had not yet been undertaken, and although known throughout India and to much of the western world by the reputation of its "erotic" carvings, it was almost totally undeveloped as a tourist resource. The state of Orissa did maintain a small guest bungalow there, almost hidden where it nestled in a lip-like crevice in the sandy stretch between the temple and the sea. Of its three rooms only one was occupied, by our friends the two Johns and Dan.

"Some burg, eh?" O'Shea joked, "not so much as a coca cola

*tundi*[7] to slake the thirst."

"Strictly chai and tiffin, mon," Scottish John echoed.

"Real deprivation," Dan agreed.

As it turned out, we spent there a total of five days and nights. Of the few tourists and visitors who came during that time, most came to gaze at the temple but for a few moments, an hour at best, as part of a half-day excursion from nearby Puri. There was one troop of school children, and one afternoon three westerners came through, German, I believe, middle aged, dressed in slacks and short sleeved shirts, carrying binoculars. These latter hardly deigned to notice us, ragged as we were, half-native, probably beneath their contempt. How then were five whole days and nights consumed; devoid of diversion and spare of entertainment, how did we absorb those dreamy hours? There was at least one afternoon spent running on the beach and bathing in the rough surf, a lot of quibbling and complaint over the paucity of refreshment at the eating stalls, where we had always to settle for stale and dried *budgie*[8] hyperbolized as "snacks," and where a small amount of dried fish turned out to be our most bountiful feast of those days. There was, as always, a lot of smoking, and, of course, the temple itself – a riddle to puzzle over and contemplate.

For me the primary paradox was what the temple was doing there anyway; for what purpose had these stones survived the erosion of the culture and vision that carved them? These present day Oriyans who now inhabit this village, are they descendents of the race of heroes that conceived and built this monument? They seem to have no link with that past, these thin-limbed, sullen people whose lives pass in a kind of brute harmony of hand-to-mouth survival. I wondered if they even saw or were aware in any way of the man-made mountain miracle that dwarfed their present reality and made seem so puny the efforts of their stark and mundane lives. The scope and scale of their present existence was so meagre in comparison, how could they accept or survive the recognition of so sweeping and encompass-

[7]cold.

[8]small eatables, fried tid bits, crunchies.

ing an urge for transcendence without condemning themselves for resignation to so pale an alternative? Every inch of stone in that temple was intricately carved with scenes presenting a vision of life so sophisticated, complex and lavish, so bounteously imaginative, that the poverty of present lives could hardly be thought of as imbued with vision at all.

*There* was a culture! Its grandeur maintained by a generous nature, varied and fruitful, peopled by warriors and kings who maneuvered elephants and vast armies into the field, entertained in sumptuous palaces, and considered niggardly any hospitality that offered less than all; a faith that paid homage to *asuras*[9] as well as *devas*,[10] a society that revered both the austerities of powerful aspiring yogis and the sensual delights of celestial *apsaras*;[11] and *here*, a life doggedly unvaried in its pursuit of food, so consumed with eking out the barest necessities of existence, that it could not possibly elaborate, much less celebrate, the themes and relationships of that existence to any higher order. So why had this time capsule from so rich a past thrust itself into the midst of so impoverished a present? Was its moral the transience of glory? Or was it there, perhaps, to inspire, to remind a lethargic and defeated modernity of an ancient, indefatigable, and all-conquering will to express, exceed and create beyond the accepted bounds of mortality?

I had days to muse, to study the disparity between an opulent, noble past and a dull and belittling present; days to space out upon the vision and ideas the temple remnants presented, and nights to wonder where, in the vast desert of present reality, to grasp the source of inspiration. Both ends of the contrast set off deep resonances within me. I gave free reign to the thoughts and feelings that came into play in hopes that the synthesis of these conceptual opposites would result in the exceeding of my current understanding.

The sad, nagging, incapacitating dullness of present day life in Konarak, that exhausted, worn-out acceptance and hope-

[9]devils; demons.

[10]gods.

[11]maidens, musical and lovely, adorning the halls of heaven.

lessness that mesmerized so much of India, was all too familiar an emblem for a depression more personal and immediate. I had known and lived long with feelings of waste and nothingness, had experienced a kind of continuous muted despair. It was a melancholy milk with which my artistic ego was nourished. My Indian journey had simply moved it from the personal to a universal; contemplation of my own lack of fulfillment had been subsumed into reflection on the human condition in general and in particular that suffering portion of humanity that pulls so heavily upon one's sense of justice and rectitude. Preoccupation with personal discontent vanished in the flood of human sorrow India loosed upon me and the world; personal despair was nothing, too small and precious for consideration even in so overwhelming a cry of distress.

Opposite and yet companion to this depression was my developing dedication to art and its capacity to move me into a transcending and idealistically fulfilling aspect of the human journey. Legacy of an artistic heritage, accomplishment in that sphere seemed to me justification, the very meaning in fact of the life process in so sensitive and ill-adjusted a creature as Man. To my agnostic cast of mind, art was God. Then God, don't ask me how, drew into Himself these artistic aspirations of mine, and my worship, also developed during my Indian journey, became more direct though far less formal. Somehow, I came to know that God was at the center of everything and was both the object and subject of the kowledge I sought. And so for me, the meaning of the temple at Konarak was just that – it was God, God, God, always God proclaiming His own existence, fairly screaming it there in the wastes; upon that dull plain of depression and poverty, the temple in its isolated and undeniable grandeur said nothing else but that "It is all Me – Catch Me, if you can."

One morning, on the wall around the temple, we encountered an aged if not venerable vedantin, a priest, orthodox and conventional, tired and worn in service, a man whose complaint was this very absence of God to modern day Orissa, India, the world as he conceived it. He was clean shaven, wore thick glasses and that sort of comical headgear, a saffron cap with ear flaps. Carrying a huge open black umbrella for shade, he moved slowly beneath it, tortoise-like, deliberate and ambling at the same time. He invited us to his home for chai.

The small bamboo shack in which he lived was surrounded that day with puddles from either a mysterious rain or a misguided attempt at local irrigation. The whole of his world during our encounter seemed soggy and dripping, about to be reclaimed by the sea.

"Nobody cares," he started, "for these things nowadays." He motioned towards his books and *papier-maché* altar pieces. "Yes, you are god-seekers, I am sure, but where are your robes? I know you. You are young and impatient, and the discipline, I fear, is very much in the lacking with you."

We were amused by the sudden directness of this man and did all we could to encourage the communication in him.

"You wish only to find God through smoking. I know. But it is filthy and destroys too this body, sacred temple of him *Jaganath*[12] who is everything."

He showed us a book by Evans-Wentz. "Now this man was true seeker. I have letter from him. He interviewed my guru, *darshan*[13] you know." He showed us a photograph of Śri Yukteshwar.

"Nobody cares these days for devotion or duty," he continued. "That is the thing! In my time, you understand, a *chela*[14] was truly a chela. But you, you wish to be Masters all at once. No patience. That is the pity. Yes, in my time, you would serve a guru for many years satisfied with a glance only. A small beam – bliss – but what do they know? And I carried water too. To this very temple, but that is in a former life. Did I show you this letter from Doctor Evans-Wentz commending me for some assistance I rendered him in translation and matters like that...?"

He drifted off in this manner into an obscure tedium and,

[12]name for the black form of Vishnu popular in the state of Orissa.
[13]audience with a holy eminence.
[14]disciple and servant of a guru.

pardon the judgment, a very petty contentment. This swami passed by me completely as one of many in a long parade of pompous pedants. He satisfied some note of yearning in Dan, however.

"I liked his vibes," he said. "Quiet, unassuming-like."

It became obvious that Richard Horne and his party would not make it with the acid for the full moon. Tired of waiting, Dan and Scottish John departed late that afternoon for Puri with some addresses the swami had given them. Robin, John O'Shea, and I stood firm in our resolve to pass the full moon at Konarak. Vision, thank providence, is not dependent upon circumstance or chemical catalyst, and we, at least John and I, were not disappointed that night.

We started out together, the three of us, there upon that wall, smoking a chillum. The temple and all its carved details appeared evenly illumined in the early moonlight, beckoning us towards some prearranged rendezvous. Descending from the wall, each of us, almost ritualistically in measured step, moved towards our as yet partially perceived assignations.

I lost track of Robin first fairly soon. His eyes and interest were drawn almost immediately to the third level of carvings above, where all the figures were in postures and attitudes of sensual and erotic release, unconstrained but also formal. At each corner and turning of that row, larger coupling forms stood out.

"Ah, the *yab-yum*," Robin muttered, "oft-described, difficult to picture from description only. There, the impossibly contorted *mithuna*[15] . . ." He wandered off, apparently engrossed in his own musings, depicting and classifying, exploring and codifying, pursuing and fulfilling as much as myself or anyone else, I have no doubt, the particular force that had drawn him here, the deity whom unacknowledged he nonetheless served.

John and I remained together for awhile longer. We followed at eye-level the scenes of battle-strife and pastoral-calm that seemed to spring into life before us. It was as though those very rocks existed only for our understanding, had compelled those ancient artists to draw them out in precise imagery, so that we,

[15]particularly imaginative and athletic positions of sexual intercourse.

latter-day spiritual archeologists, might peruse at leisure their meanings. Redeemed then from dumb silence, emancipated now from their stone stasis through our reception, the images began to flow together. In liquid liberation did they unveil to us their secret paradigms and enigmas, unshrouding the sinew and muscle of their testament to Time. War in its pageantry we see as nothing more than an inevitable extension of contradiction and conflict in personal honor, and peace, as the synthesis of the same. There, upon the plain of strife where armies clash, sage counsel is delivered and received beneath the sheltering canopy where sit the kings and priests, and here, upon the well-tilled fields of peace, appear again tents beneath which *maharajas*[16] and *brahmanas*[17] meet in advice and celebration appropriate to its time and place – no endeavour repulsive nor attractive, all equal to all. Each moment and scene, rendered with the same care, followed an unbroken and even line into one of the great wheels of the temple.

It all seemed so simple. Everything resolved in the turning of the wheel. The heights and depths of any linear tableau were all levelled by the cyclical vision. All of our comings and goings, war and peace, the evolutions and involutions of culture itself, the ancient, glorious and modern, mundane Konarak are all turnings of the wheel. All forms of sensate and compulsive life rush towards the hub of the wheel and spin out again centrifugally towards the circumference in the dance of this great chain of being. And the great wheel itself to which our ephermeral and fleeting destinies are hinged is but one of many supports to yet another more complex artifice, a chariot of the gods.

Almost in a trance we climbed upon the wheel and ascended to a second level of pictorial representation. Here the gods themselves appeared. We moved among them and their powerful association. Vishnu's vehicle and mount, his great *vahana*[18] Garuda stared out at us, arresting our attention for the moment with his sharp-beaked austerity, commanding, with the tenac-

[16]kings.
[17]priests.
[18]vehicle, mount; that which transports, carries, or relays Deity.

ity of his taloned purpose, our homage to that he served.

"I beheld the Garuda once," John said to me in a disarmingly normal and matter-of-fact tone of voice. "I was smoking at night with some sadhus; it was in Hardwar. I saw a beetle crawling along the log fall into the fire, and then, I swear, as his shell was consumed in the flames, I saw his astral body, soul if you like, drawn along a thread, ascend into the atmosphere. I know that cremation is the best way to dispose of body. Burn away all that pain and suffering associated with it. Just then I felt a presence behind me, and turning I saw Garuda. Somehow, I felt he had just landed, just held there for a moment, genuflected towards me as if to say 'everything you have seen till now is nothing,' and then I felt more than saw the ruffling of his wings and he vanished. I tell you this for what it is worth. I shall never forget it, and I can hardly ever communicate it. But I saw it just as sure as we are here."

Perhaps it was at the suggestion of a pointing figure of Surya that John moved southward along the ridge. The stones were warm to our touch, vibrant with the heat absorbed by day. We could be drawn, it seemed, into any number of nocturnal corridors. All sensate passages were open to exploration. The feel of the rock, a scent in the air, a shape at any turning; the great chariot extended itself in almost every direction with infinite invitation. Only an occasional chill sea breeze would arrest us, calling us back into the passing moment and into our hesitant bodies yet inadequate to measure the mysteries. I saw John climb down towards the cemented-in entrance to what we had assumed to be a main prayer hall, and I lost contact with him about then.

I began to climb towards the uppermost part of the chariot. By day I could not get very far in that direction though I had attempted it on numerous occasions and through varied approaches. Each ascent was terminated either in a sharp break and drop or by a government-erected baricade, solicitous of tourist safety, impossible to circumvent. Somehow, on this night, I found myself beyond my former limits and above previously accessible heights. Below me was the conventionally regarded erotic sculpture, and just before me, beneath the great dome and chariot crest, was a cavern-like hallway supported by pillars carved in the forms of apsaras.

I could trespass there and walk beside these celestial maidens. They stood just as tall as I, these divine musicians, but they were much broader, larger-limbed, and fuller in torso. They were held in a stoned physicality much grander, more voluptuous, luxurious and ample of body than I. The chiselled tresses of their hair seemed to lap lightly with the wind, and they themselves glided and sauntered in the half-heard heavenly harmony of their instruments. The moonlight fell full upon their almond eyes, the sly and sullen lips of their mute beauty. Wonderfully generous breasts swayed pendulous, rhythmically, and their fluid hips shifted and flowed with the line and beat of the *mrindingam*, the long two-headed drum of south India.

A kind of natural celibacy had come upon me in my Indian wanderings, not a principled abstinence, mind you, but an almost imperceptible withdrawal of sensation and desire. India was not a nice place in which to experience body, and I assumed that most of us seekers there had drifted into a lack of want and lust, a loss of those libidinal drives that were in India just too inconvenient to be dealt with. A quick lascivious round in the "cages" of Bombay early on had seemed to release the residual urges of my western virility, and since then I had done without sexual act or want, and almost without any thought of it, at least these ten months. I viewed it humorously as yet another ego stripped by that great thief India; compensation was a growing pride in my spiritual achievements. When I had puzzled over this transformation in my more serious reflective fits, I felt that as much as anything else it was due to an unwillingness in myself to take responsibility for any thought or emotional image beyond that of a twelve-year old boy. I felt my devotion and aspiration most comfortably housed in a pre-pubescent age and feeling; *brahmacarya*, [19] don't you know.

But now my unexpressed manhood would brook no denial. It

[19] (literally "teacher of Brahma"); first of the four ashrama or stages of life, that of a student and celibate.

rushed upon me, overripe and demanding. I was seized with a passion long-pent, full-blooded and warm. Shaken with yearning, I was ravaged in an instant with desire and want and a mercilessly pervasive sense of my own incompleteness. An urge to kiss those enticing thighs was all but compulsive. I wished to run my hands over and clasp such bounteous bosoms, and I dreamed of racing with these women through the ages in pursuit of the elusive consummate promise. These were the strongest sexual promptings I had felt in my Indian life, and they rushed over me with undeniable fervor.

But just as instantly they withdrew themselves from me, these lustrous apsaras, retreated back into their stoned and frozen indifference. Neither mockingly nor sweetly, but with the clarity of dispassionate fact, I heard them declare, "You have left no place for us to enter."

*It was so that night as I thought and paced and sat amidst these now distant sculptured goddesses, watching my thoughts dance and pass with the moon.*

Something like this I had heard before, quite clearly on the Amarnath yatra, only then it had seemed teasing and taunting. As the Spirit we sought became more certain, the conditions and terms for finding and receiving it became less clear; Marc and I, in our attempts to articulate it – and sometimes we came close – always put it in terms of our efforts to exceed ourselves, to transcend, supercede and soar above these frail vehicles to touch the gods. But the more accurate though slippery truth, which one knew however briefly in these moments with the Spirit so full upon you that the hairs of your body stood to meet it and your flesh tingled with the thrill of it and each pore opened to receive the message, what one knew in these moments was that the gods were seeking to touch us. It was not personal, private, or individual. They were seeking, aided or not by our efforts, to touch our time and place, to penetrate through us the phenomenal reality in which we were both born and bound. We were being used for that. Poor mind-blown vagabonds, we were nonetheless the best our time could afford for the experiment.

I don't know how many customary feelings and identities break in a moment like that, how many well-worn patterns, thought-forms, samskaras,[20] dissolve in those moments of sudden liberation. I do know that I try to track and trace primary mind and being through as many channels as my courage can endure and my will persevere, try to stalk them to the antinomies of time and space, hound them down to their elemental dualities, and resolve those too, God willing. It was so that night as I thought and paced and sat amidst these now distant sculptured goddesses, watching my thoughts dance and pass with the moon. This then was the justification, this was the power that held, commanded and ordered one's journey. Yes, the gods needed some reality to enter through, and your only merit was your capacity to surrender.

From this height, I could see the ocean as the sun rose. Resplendent counterpart to my own illumination, the dawn stretched before me in roseate fire. I swirled back and rested

[20]thought tendencies, inherited traits, inevitable grooves or predictable ruts in an individual's process of perception.

upon a niche carved in that stone parapet. Feeling the entire temple shake for a moment, I thought it began to rise ever so subtly. Somehow, I knew I was seated upon the very charioteer's mount of that great structure. I was carried for a moment with the sun in its diurnal course, and I saw that the whole of ancient beloved *Bharat*[21] lay before me and that it comprised all that had ever or would ever come into being and that there was no end to it as it curved along the horizons becoming the rondure of the great world itself.

Robin was sleeping when I returned to the tourist bungalow, and John was trying to do so. We would depart about noon, and by far the best thing we could do would be to get a few hours of sleep. John was as restless as I, however, and I could sense that he too had passed an extraordinary night at the temple.

"Did you get it?" he asked as we lay there.

"At least part of it," I answered, turning onto my side, and then added drowsily to myself "as usual."

An old, grey-bearded, toothless sadhu was crouched outside the Bhubaneshwar train station. We sat down with him to pass the hours until the arrival of our train to Calcutta. He leapt to his feet at the sight of the gooly of hash Robin brought out of his pack. John motioned him down with his hand raised, palm outward, shoulder-high. "Beyto, beyto," be seated. The sadhu fell back to his squat and Robin passed the hash to John who had already whipped the chillum out of his pouch.

On the matter of dhuni etiquette, my friend John O'Shea would take second-place to no other sadhu. He showed that matted-haired mongrel the way a chillum should properly be prepared, the amount of respect, love and devotion that should be poured into Śiva's offering if knowledge were to result.

Travelling with and learning from various itinerant sadhus, John had come easily to exceed them at their own game. Something in him was sensitive to the feeling, in tune with the real spirit of these ancient rituals. Ceremony was a part of his na-

[21]ancient name for India when it was thought to be the entire existence.

ture, and he tried to express as much of it as any occasion could bear. The manner in which these once reverent formalities were practiced along the degraded contemporary sadhu circuit offended some native purist instinct in him, and he regarded it almost as a duty to set a good example at every dhuni.

A young businessman-type, also awaiting the train, joined our dhuni. His curiosity was aroused by the sight of three sahibs squatting there, and the resident sadhu swelled with pride at the sudden popularity of his otherwise lonesome and unobserved vigil.

"How is it," the businessman asked, "that you have left the riches of your own land and come to such a poor place as this India? You don't mind, please."

This question was part of what had become a rote and annoying catechism to the traveller. No matter whether your guise were that of a tourist or a hardened sadhu, the string of inquiries from the English-speaking locals was always predictably the same. The "Why have you come?" was but one form of the more common "What is your mission?" and this along with the unvarying "You are coming from?" and the sing-song "What is your name?" were certain to invoke anger and elicit abuse from the interrogated pilgrim. John, to my surprise, treated the question seriously and the questioner with respect.

"You must not speak always," John answered in pidgin English "of India as poor place. Don't you see that we sahibs have come, given up riches, as you say, to live like this to worship India. You should be proud and happy. We love India. You should too. If you speak 'poor, poor, poor' all the time, then you will stay poor. How can you change if you look only to that which is weak and helpless?"

The sadhu, picking up on John's tone, began to berate the businessman with a string of incomprehensible utterances, seeking confirmation from us with a proud look that implied "You see what I must put up with." The businessman was affected neither by reflection on John's advice or reaction to the sadhu's curses. He went on with a "You are smoking? This is a bad custom, only good for *chandalas*[22] and rickshaw wallahs."

[22]outcasts; pariahs.

"*Ek naranjan*," John went on in Hindi.

"*Ah, acha,*[23]*teek,*[24]" the sadhu agreed, rolling his head. "*Ek naranjan.*"

"*Ek naranjan*," John went on, directing it mostly towards the businessman but also proud to show off a bit before Robin and me. "One is God. *Do sukhi:* two are friends. *Teen markatpat:* three are quarrelling. *Char dukhi.*"

"*Acha, char dukhi,*" the sadhu babbled.

"Four are in trouble," translated the young businessman.

"Do not always repeat what others say," John offered the young businessman in parting earnestness. "Feel for yourself first. Then maybe, someday you understand why we have come to live like this. Namaskar."

John pressed his thumb into some of the fire's ash and then marked each of our foreheads with a vertical streak. The sadhu proffered his brow, giggling with delight, and the businessman too was pleased to be so distinguished. He took leave of us with his hands clasped and his head tilted in a sincere namaskar.

Cramped as we were, travelling "sadhu express" again, Robin was nonetheless able to sleep. We rolled through many night stations where waiting passengers leapt up from their sleep and squeezed with all their luggage into our compartment, already filled beyond capacity. The whine of "*chai garam,*[25] *garam-chai*" pierced the air.

"You know," John said to me, "that we must someday return to Konarak to finish our *puja.*"[26]

What I did know, whether or not I was finished with Konarak and no matter what the content of the mail which either I would await or already awaited me in Calcutta, was that India was not yet finished with me. I felt that in my next round with India I could do far worse than to absorb from John what he had learned. He seemed to have emotionally stabilized his life as a sadhu and wanderer to a much greater degree than I and to have

[23]"yes" or "I see"; signifies agreement or at least that the listener is following.

[24]'teek' or teekay – O.K.

[25]hot or warm-hot tea.

[26]devotional prayer and service.

unquestioningly accepted the open-ended nature of this stage of
his life with a kind of security that I could only admire. Our
fancies carried us on future journeys. Together we would explore the south all the way to Cape Cormorin, and perhaps we
would push on to Ceylon from there. Certainly, we would stand
in mutual awe and perhaps share visions before the great
southern temples of Trichinopoly and Trivanderum.

"It's the *mudra*[27] that inspires me, turns me on, and even
holds me together," John volunteered. "I saw the potential
almost immediately when I arrived. After Japan I was excited
about ritual and how the high points of culture are held and
remembered. As shabby and sad and ridiculous as India is, it's so
easy to see that this place was once the highest man ever had it
together. You know what I mean. Mudra reveals that.

"Look," opening his palms he formed a delicate lotus with his
fingers.

"But this is not the place or time, all crowded like this. I'll
show you sometime. You need to really get into it with your
whole body. I know that you can control the atmosphere of any
place and occasion through mudra. The dhuni is an elemental
energy flow, you see, and it can easily be controlled by mudra to
release more mudra and energy. That's what real chillum smoking is all about. The thing about any mudra is that it is perfect in
and of itself. If you know perfection in at least one thing, then
you can recognize it in any other thing that has attained it. In
Hrishikesh I saw this cat. He knew what mudras were about.
They said he was mad, walked with the gods, you know. Some
said that Krishna had entered his form and taken possession of
it. He was a divine flute player, Radhakrishna he was called,
and he just walked around all day playing the flute. And you
know, he controlled everything that happened in that town by
the finger mudras on that flute. It was beautiful, never a gesture
out of place."

Howrah Station greeted us with the mad clamour of screaming porters and coolies fairly attacking the arriving train. We

[27]perfect symbols of aspects and postures related and signified by finger and
hand positions. Essential element in dance.

squirmed through easily enough. A tram carried us across the bridge and through Dalhousie Square where passing the American Express, we half-in-jest performed a quick puja to Lakshmi in hopes that the next lap of our adventure be blessed with prosperity and fortune. As we passed the Esplanade and on up the Chowringhee, I spotted a tall, bearded, and bespectacled westerner, who, despite the early hour, was out for a stroll and was besieged by curious Indians. Robin continued on the tram towards Ballygunge, but John and I disembarked at Sudder Street with the intention of stopping by the Astoria and finding out what had detained Richard Horne and the others.

A French hippie who was now inhabiting that room told us that they had checked out two days before and were off to Khajarao in the company of an Indian who by description could only have been Dr. Śivamurti Praṣad. John and I laughed. They missed us; we had missed nothing.

We strolled the streets aimlessly, killing time until the American Express would be open. There awaiting John, in an unsolicited letter from his mother, was a ten dollar bill. So Lakshmi had heard and smiled on us. This was worth between one hundred and one hundred and thirty rupees on the black market, and we hastened over to the New Market area to compare the prevalent rates with several of the numerous "change money" boys.

When we emerged from the labyrinth of stalls and alleys that makes up the New Market, it was as rich men. We decided to celebrate and splurge a little with a fancy breakfast at the Grand Hotel. We strutted past the fancily turbaned and beplumed Punjabi doorman. Armed with wealth and our recently reaffirmed spiritual camaraderie, we were ready for anything that Calcutta and, in particular, the Grand Hotel might offer. Do sukhi.

An elementary truism gleaned early by those on the road is that "nothing that is meant to come your way can fail to do so." The acid had escaped us at Konarak, but we enjoyed the vision nonetheless, and now in the unlikely locale of the Grand Hotel we were about to stumble upon a considerable quantity of the chemical itself. I found this agreeable with a growing feeling of mine that experience and dope alike generated higher and purer revelations when, rather than sought, they came to one, as it were, of their own accord.

We ran into Harry Glaum at the front desk, and it was he who tipped us off to the presence there of LSD and the American spiritual tourists who possessed it.

"I'm peaking now," he said, and thrust a telegram towards us as though it would explain everything. It was an urgent message that his father was ill and his immediate return home was demanded. A ticket was awaiting him at the Pan Am office. I think the telegram had originated in Chicago and had reached him through the American Express. We aided him with his checking-out maneuvers as he seemed to be having difficulty with his traveller's checks and the bill. He seemed as loquacious now as he had taciturn before, when our paths had crossed briefly at the Ballygunge flat.

"Yeah, it's sure going to be one hell of an airplane trip," he laughed. "I told you I was tripping, didn't I? It's probably the only way I could get there from here."

"Where'd you get the acid?" John asked.

"Upstairs. There's a whole bunch of whackos up there. You'll love it. You know who's there?"

"Who?" I asked.

"Lou Gottlieb."

The name meant nothing to me.

"Man, didn't you follow the Limelighters? They were really big, like the Kingston Trio and the Weavers. Gottlieb was the funny one, you know. He's up there with a whole bunch of people."

The Punjabi doorman helped him with his baggage towards an awaiting cab. We turned back inside. For a moment I felt kind of sorry for Harry. What a dream it would seem to awaken on the other end of this trip back in Chicago. How much could the mind take, I wondered, with a tinge of worry about the means that would ultimately carry me from this labyrinth back home, wherever that was, when my time would come.

"See you later, fellas." Harry said lamely. "Oh, yeah, if you ever run into Jim Shaw again, don't trust him with nothing. Our trip in Kathmandu was a complete disaster."

He was gone in a moment, and we hastened onto the elevator and ascended to the next floor. A girl with wirey wild hair was wandering the corridor. We later found out that she was named Rena Morningstar. She was wrapped only in a lungi and prayer shawl, and you could see her breasts beneath as you often could with village girls. She namaskared towards us as she passed and called out "God bless you, brothers." We knew we were at the right place.

Except for its name, there is hardly a vestige of elegance left about the Grand Hotel. All pretense of luxury and distinction vanishes beyond the lobby and balcony, and the hotel becomes one long series of sordid doors set in the dingy green corridors.

Still it is one of the only places in Calcutta that offers hot water and western toilets, and the few businessmen and legitimate tourists from outside of India who found themselves passing through that city during those years of its degeneration were most certain to be booked into the Oberoi Grand. Such was the case with the incongruous group we were about to encounter.

How this particular crew was assembled, for their quick dalliance with the subcontinental mysteries and the resultant assault their psyches received for the effort, struck me at first as something of a puzzle; easily enough explained, however, in the ensuing time I hung around them. Though most of them appeared in their twenties and seemed representative of hippie America, the range in age and status was undeniably vast. Gottlieb, whom I didn't meet at first but whose name was constantly being spoken, was, I was told, well into his forties. More advanced even into middle-age was one Donovan Bess who was laid out on the bed as we entered, a victim perhaps of a preceding night's experiment with opium or of dysentery, or any of the numerous incapacitating possible initiations to India. His name was familiar to me as I remembered it from by-lines in the San Francisco Chronicle during my years spent in the Bay Area prior to my departure for India. At the uppermost edge of the age spectrum was an unfortunate white-haired woman, at least in her seventies, whom I felt must have been realizing too late a long neglected or denied desire to see "romantic" India. She spent most of her time there huddled on a couch in the lobby, almost babbling to herself and appearing catatonic when approached. I don't know which she feared more, the riot and chaos of Calcutta or the frenzy of her travelling companions. What they all shared in common was California whence they came, perhaps some unarticulated spiritual expectations, and the certain breakdown of their preconceptions about India, whatever they might have been.

There were Paul and Judy, a pleasant couple about my age; Lorelei, a pretty but silent, sad-seeming siren who carried an air of incipient doom about her; Robert Garcia, a Mexican-American from the Mission district, jovial, out-going, perhaps an unabashed sensualist (he it was who would run in periodically with news of some narcotic or flesh fancy to be had in the neighborhood for what to him was a ridiculously low price); and an artist and poet from the Haight-Ashbury named Michael Bowen. These along with the aforementioned Miss Morningstar – Gottlieb's muse, professional free-spirit and love-child – occupied several adjoining rooms, and the doors always stood open to accommodate the heavy traffic. It seemed a continuous party there, overflowing into the corridor, beyond the control of their own tour structure or the hotel management, an atmosphere abandoned enough to attract John and me without hesitation.

In the little more than a week which followed we became involved with this company readily enough, visiting the Grand daily, partaking of a few lavish banquets with them, spending a night or two in their rooms, showering, and in other ways taking advantage of the social and material amenities possible. Mostly we enjoyed, I confess, the praise and admiration that various of them lavished upon us at moments for our capacity to endure the mystic morass and muddle that was overwhelming them. Great changes had swept them along in the last few years in America, just as we had experienced something of the extremes of those psychic ripples, tides, and waves in India. We needed to see each other for this time to comprehend a bit more the scope and complexity of our kindred journey, and, perhaps too, we were drawn to each other out of an intuitive understanding of a destiny we were to share, some glimmer of recognition that we were together fording yet another stream towards the river of the Great Awakening.

That first morning their energy was not only frantic but scattered as well. Rena was wandering the corridors stoned; Bob Garcia was attempting without much success to administer to the needs of a nervous, ill, and more than slightly apprehensive Donovan Bess; Michael Bowen, even though he dashed between this room and his to continue a painting, seemed to pick up on us the most, anxious to draw us out into conversation, welcoming us as relief from his other companions; Lorelei, walking about, could hardly manage the lower register on the bamboo flute that held her attention; Lou Gottlieb was not there, had been gone since early that morning on an adventurous lungi-buying expedition into the inner recesses and bowels of Calcutta; Paul and Judy seemed stable enough; they were simply enthusiastic about everything. There appeared at the door, identically clad in saffron robes and wearing, I swear, malas of plastic prayer beads, two bearded western devotees or aspirants. They appeared to me a kind of vedantin Tweedle-dee and Tweedle-dum. Vince and James by name, they were the only ones at all concerned with the purpose of that particular tour. In vain they tried to instill some sense of obligation, if not interest, into the disintegrating party, pointing out that the leader, Ashok Fakir, had gone to great trouble to arrange a special bus which would take them across Howrah to the historic Dakshineshwar, Ramakrishna's own ashram.

"Ashok hopes that there will be a little better showing for this than there was for last night's film on Vivekenanda," intoned Vince.

"Let's not disappoint Swamaji," echoed James.

Ashok himself made an appearance a little later. The look he cast about the room was a combination of disgust and condescension with an omniscient implication of "I thought as much." His appearance at the door was brief but sufficient for me to form a very definite negative impression. He appeared to me a kind of comic book version of the cliché guru, portly, turbaned, clean shaven, smug in appearance, the very stereotype of the western layman's concept of the Hindoo (double O) Swami. Alas, Ashok seemed all that was conventional and uninspired in the teachers and ashrams to which I had said "no," all that I had come to avoid in the advertised and Congress Party sanctioned spirituality of this maddening country. Later I found out that he had been "discovered" and sponsored some years back by an American poet who passed through Calcutta. He had had some success in San Francisco, where apparently any huckster of "consciousness" could gain a following and had now returned to Calcutta, really to visit his ailing mother, using the spiritual tour to gain his own free passage. Air India had rescinded on the usually-demanded dozen when there had been a last-minute cancellation and had granted Ashok a free ticket even though he could only manage eleven paying customers. He'd have been hard put upon to manage even that if his two devotees, or rather their parents, had not been willing to pay their own fares, and I shudder to think what salesmanship might have been used upon that poor white-haired lady.

At the time, however, Ashok seemed to me successful. I thought these Americans took him as the bona fide article, the best India has to offer the cause of Enlightenment. The whole thing filled me momentarily with a renewed depression. So this is the America I would be returning to, I thought snobbishly, the same old commercial, crass, and mediocre reduction of all experience into product. The intensity and sincerity of my own quest, one that I felt had exacted so demanding and sometimes debilitating a toll, seemed betrayed and undermined. Perhaps that is why I refused that morning the first offer Paul made of some LSD. No such reservations bothered John O'Shea, however. In one quick swallow, he "dropped" the acid without question.

I went across and down the hall a bit with Michael Bowen to his room. He said he wanted to show me some of his paintings. Water colors were spread out upon the bureau. The work in progress was a *mandala*[1] resembling a color wheel. A male winged angel stood to its upper left and a serpent flanked its lower right. He leafed through a large pad of absorbent paper showing me paintings and sketches he had done in Pondicherry and some from Madras, places they had stopped briefly before coming to Calcutta just the day before. They were all in a psychedelic mode that had blossomed and then glutted in the Haight-Ashbury art renaissance the year before I left. Unlike Sal's, Michael's style or content had not been affected by India.

"Quite an outpouring," I said. "Are you always so productive?"

"Yeah, this is nothing. It just sort of pours out of me, you

[1]graphic symbol of the universe or cosmic forces, usually complex, concentric and symmetrical.

know. It's been my thing for a couple of years now. Keeps my head together. Otherwise I'd probably be running around like a half-ass with the rest of these gumballs. Man, they hit India like sweet freaks in a pastry shop."

He allowed that Gottlieb was different, interesting enough, a more mature sort of character. Lou ran an open commune in Sonoma County called Morningstar Ranch. Michael had visited it once or twice and found it an interesting experiment in the "alternative life styles that were emerging all over the States."

"My old lady's a dancer. She took off to take part in a workshop for a couple of weeks. I had my shit together so I thought I'd link up with this group going to India. We got that kind of relationship. She does her thing, I do mine. Anyhow, I thought I'd check out India, find out what was going on first-hand. I'm going to split from this rinky dink outfit pretty soon though. Thought I'd trip on up to Kathmandu. They say that's a real groovy place. It is, isn't it? I think a whole bunch of these birds are going to break off, except for the poor slave bastards in the saffron monkey suits. Can't trust Ashok. I think all these Indian hottentots – big maha bullshit, you know – want to turn everybody into zombies. I don't want to wind up back in the States running around with my head shaved and my prick cut off."

"Is there a lot of it going on back there now?" I asked.

"Shit, yeah! There's Krishna freaks on every street corner. It's worse than the Salvation Army at Christmas."

Michael showed a wide grin through his beard. It revealed a gap in his upper front teeth. I remember thinking that he stood the best chance of any westerner I had yet met of getting out of India essentially unchanged.

When we returned to the first room, John was sitting quietly cross-legged with his eyes closed. He began to extend his right arm upwards, his thumb and two forefingers pointed out and the two last fingers were folded in. Gracefully his elbow hinged and straightened over and over again, and he seemed literally to draw the energy from the atmosphere above and around him into his form at the chest. Stimulating the *anahata*, I thought, and received a contact high as I imagined him flowing with the swirling and undulating *kundalini* as it traversed the *sushumna*, releasing appropriate color plays and light shows at each *chakra*.[2] John's fingers began to form elaborate and delicate patterns. Like a divine cat's cradle with an invisible connecting string of pure *prana*,[3] a whole sequence and series of inter-linked movements and motions were unlocked and exhibited. Some of the finger gestures seemed similar to those in sculpture and painted representations of the Buddha, some seemed to come from dance, and others seemed wholly new, spontaneous, created in the moment or recalled from some long dormant or forgotten programming. All were beautiful.

His body swayed, and slowly he rose to his feet. There began a dance; some of it seemed furious as he spun about with his fist of his right hand, thumb pointed down, sweeping fast small circles about the crown of his head, and some of the motions were slow and studied, almost painfully deliberated upon, and he seemed compelled by some sort of inspiration to sway smoothly and without effort from one motion to another. For a finale, he grabbed my staff which I had left in a corner and leapt about in semi-martial movements. When he came out of this trance, his face was flushed and beaming, and a vein up the center of his forehead jutted out prominently. His reddish hair and sparse but long sandy beard stood out and floated, encircling his face like a highly kinetic aura.

"Mudras, remember?" he said and winked towards me.

"Looks like Tai-Chi, only fancier," Michael said. "I'll bet that really serves to keep your head on straight out here, keeps you balanced and centered, huh? Where'd you learn that?"

"It's a form of perfection," John answered. "I never learnt it

[2]refers to classic vedic and yogic description of the raising of consciousness in which the latent power, kundalini, coiled like a serpent at the base of the spine on the subtle and causal body, begins to rise and pass through the seven chakras, energy nuclei, stimulating them and releasing their respective powers and perception – The anahata is fourth up, usually pictured near the heart and is the chakra that releases the Will. The sushumna is the ethereal tube or passage through which the kundalini is imagined to flow in its rising.

[3]breath, self-perpetuating energy of the cosmic atmosphere.

anywhere. It's just in me. And it doesn't help me do anything. I serve it.

"During my first acid trip in '66," he continued, "I knew I was one of the lucky ones. It was in the Haight, and I dropped into a new world, an enchanted one. All the colors in Golden Gate Park were never the same again. I could see a high-intensity shimmer on everything. The world was no longer grey or dull. That vision became my master, and my job was to put that gleam and shimmer on everything. As I came out of that first acid trip, I put magic properties into a piece of light wood that was in the apartment where I dropped. In the Marines I had a kind of swagger stick, now I had a magic wand. That was the beginning, a tool, when I came down to help me remember and serve the vision. I'd walk around and command things to look up, reveal their sparkling essence. I'd shake the wand at anything, and 'ping' it would be blessed. Everything began to look the way it should look. Things came down in time, of course, and I had to leave the Haight and move on to serve the vision. The magic wand was child's play. It was replaced by love and passion for mudras as I began to understand the more permanent and eternal aspect of things."

During the week that followed I visited the Grand by day, and my nights were spent at Ken's flat in Ballygunge. There my company was Robin Brown, still awaiting his means of exit, and David Bray, who seemed to retreat further and further into his silent and distant cave of isolation. Even though I saw a lot of the touring spiritualists downtown, I didn't really get much closer with any of them. Paul and Judy seemed quite friendly, and they were interested in John's and my Indian saga, in the changes that had occurred with us, but still I kept my distance by intention. I just sensed something superficial and temporary in their presence there, and though I was quick enough to share the luxuries and diversions they offered, still I remained loathe to offer them any of the understanding I felt my journey and experiences in India had produced. I wished to maintain a sense of superiority as it was important to me to feel that my alliance and bond with India partook of depth and commitment whereas

I saw them flirting with a merely dilettante exposure to the motherland. I watched with wry and somewhat cynical amusement the collisions of attitudes and personalities that took place in this group as they tried to hold together in the startling, novel, and unique circumstances India presented.

A large meal was ordered from room service one night, and Lorelei, who felt in a celebratory mood – perhaps she had mastered some of the troublesome fingering on the flute – requested a bottle of red wine to accompany the dinner. Vince drew the line there.

"You can't do that!" he fairly screamed. "Don't you know that for what you pay for that damned wine you could keep a good-sized family from starving here?"

Rena too was often given to promoting compassionate responsibility for all mankind. If there were ever any food left over, rather than let the bearer remove it, she would gather it up and dash out with it proclaiming that she was off to feed some beggars. I actually witnessed her in a scene like that one night. Returning from my own meal at Nizzam's, crossing the grey and dusty, blank-walled, and hopeless square that stood behind the Grand Hotel between Banerjee Road and the New Market, I beheld Rena passing amongst the huddled and loitering misfortunate street dwellers there, actually tossing *chapatis*[4] and *roti*[5] their way. *"Prashad, prashad,"*[6] she called. With her was Robin Brown, amused no doubt to see the way "that particular little beggar scampered." What a contrast the haughty Scotsman's form presented next to Rena's whose movements suggested that her highest aspiration was to melt and merge with the mute, downtrodden, homeless, and slightly astonished recipients of her charity. "Eat well, my brothers and sisters," she cried. "It is His will that none go hungry. Mother's breasts are full and generous. All may partake, with the new age there is plenty."

That was, by the way, the last I was to see of Robin Brown in India. His passage to Bangkok and maybe all the way to Bali

[4]flat flour bread, like a pancake or tortilla.
[5]bread.
[6]holy food; an offering.

must have come through for suddenly he was gone without so much as a word or even a note of his departure. I did see him years later in San Francisco, however. I ran into him wandering the shell and skeleton of the then wiped-out Haight-Ashbury. Still driven by the changing winds of terrestrial perambulation, he was en route to Mexico, thence to South America. He still denied the existence of any purpose, goal, or haven to the journey, was not the least bit curious to investigate what I had claimed to have found. Farewell for now, Robin Brown! May you find respite from the ancestral furies that drive you, and peace as well in some hitherto uncharted and inexhaustible paradise!

Somehow I never personally encountered Lou Gottlieb during any of these sorties to the Grand Hotel. He had always "just left" or "stepped out for a moment." I even suspected briefly that he was a collective hallucination that the group had constructed to provide sanction if not sanity to the indulgent and delirious experiences in which they were participating. It was clear that, in general, Ashok had no authority whatsoever and very little esteem in their eyes, and in so far as they made reference to any intelligence more comprehensive or higher than their own, it was always "Lou said this" or "Lou thinks such and such."

Though rooming and eating together and spending much of their time as a group, they were, nonetheless, each exploring their own avenues of sensate and spiritual knowledge quite independently. Donovan Bess would in an accustomed reportorial fashion question John and me about yogis we had encountered or systems of meditation we practised. Once he asked us in thin-lipped seriousness if we had ever seen any feats of *tantric*[7] levitation. I hadn't but told him of the time in the ashram in Ujjain when a sadhu using his penis lifted me up about half a foot as I lay supine upon a wooden board. There were ropes tied at each end of the board, and they in turn were tied together in the center making a construction like a swing or cradle. Standing on top of a bench the sadhu wrapped his insensate penis

[7]the *tantra* in its simplest terms is worship of Divine Śakti, the power in Nature (prakṛti).

around the central knot, forming with it a kind of strap or handle. He then lifted it with me lying there and rocked it back and forth a couple of times. Donovan was more impressed by the report of it than I had been at the actual performance.

Bob Garcia came into the hotel one night with an Indian girl who was obviously one of the denizens of Free School Street. He had probably picked her up at Isaiah's or some other flesh parlor. He took her up to the room and had her smoke a chillum with all of us. I could tell from the tattoos on the backs of her hands that she was Muslim. She had probably come as far in cultural liberation as he had. On the whole my visits to those rooms always produced something surprising and unusual.

I felt more familiar and comfortable with Michael Bowen than I did with the others. One afternoon we went together to see the famous Jain temple in north Calcutta. I had missed it the year before when I was myself more of a tourist, and I pointed it out amongst the trips listed on Ashok's itinerary for the day as the one most likely to be of interest. As we stepped into the cab, Michael pointed to a billboard. It displayed a crudely painted picture of a razor blade, and written above it was the brand name "Ashok."

"You see what I mean?" Michael asked. "Is that trying to tell me something or not? I tell you the guy wants to cut them off. Ashok Fakir! Faker, more likely!"

At the highly ornamented and bejewelled temple, Michael told me that he really was fed up. The time was drawing near for his escape to Kathmandu. He offered to take John and me with him and said he was willing to pay our way. Even though the mail I was supposedly awaiting in Calcutta had not yet come, I was game for this change. John and I went as far as to have visa photos taken, and we laid plans to go to the Nepalese embassy and show the minimum currency requirement, advanced by Michael, to complete the visa process, but that particular plan would not come to fruition, as it turned out, and that was one possible detour to our destiny that we were safely and happily spared.

During this time Jim Shaw returned to Calcutta. He had scored hash. It was sitting in a safe place now at the airport, and

Jim wanted our help in repackaging it and getting it together for the next stage of the deal. He offered a share in the profits. From the sample we smoked it was of negligible quality, in fact, what we called "bootblack hash," worthless to even a casual consumer, let alone a connoisseur. Jim had been "had," ripped off. I could even picture the culprit, a Nepalese madman who stalked the Hanuman Dhoka in a fez-like cap and preyed upon the naive and newly arrived. Anyone who had been there any length of time learned to avoid him and his offers of ersatz and inferior hash. Had the quality been up to John's standards, he probably would have participated, at least enough to bless its safe arrival in the States with a "ping" from his magic wand, but as it was, he was not only disinterested but even insulted by the offer. As for me, regardless of quality, and even if I had not been warned by Harry Glaum not to get involved in business with Jim, I would not have been interested.

I had learned my lesson in the one abortive hash fiasco to which I had reluctantly consented. Drawn into the life on the road, the main problem, along with extending your visa of tenure there, was finding the financial means to prolong it. Inevitably an export scam was hit upon. The most valuable product was, of course, hashish. During my stay in Kashmir, just prior to the decimating onslaught of hepatitis upon my form, I was drawn into a short-lived scheme with some friends to send charas to California. I purchased my share, one-third of a kilo of the best we could find (not nearly as fine as that available in Nepal, I might point out) with my friends Eva and Loren, a couple who had a small houseboat on Dal Lake. It was in that boat that the plan was hatched and executed. Loren, whose electric energy bespoke the unmistakeable signs of genius, would have none of your commonplace cans of chutney or stuffed elephant schemes of concealment. He hit upon the original idea of our disguising the contraband as works of *papier maché*, a famous Kashmiri handicraft. We were stoned, of course, at the time of execution, and the rough and uneven balls which we hoped would pass as native necklaces were ludicrous. As sense came upon me, I demanded my share of the initial booty. I wound up smoking that very stuff for the rest of the summer, and each time I had to crack open a hardened and encrusted ball, it was a bitter reprimand to me and a graphic reminder that an innocent and amateur consumer such as myself had no business meddling in such sophisticated and professional matters.

Even before that I had become wary of doing anything extraordinary or going out of my way solely on the motive of financial gain. When my brother Rich and I had arrived in Bombay for our first visit there together, we found an acquaintance lying ill and unattended in a Sikh gurdwara where we sought a couple of nights' refuge. We had seen Tom Zwicker before in Kathmandu. He liked to hold forth at the Blue Tibetan on the merits of macro-biotic diet and warn other westerners there that they would rue their casual and unguarded dietary desires. But it was he who fell victim to some incapacitating stomach disease, and he lay moaning and perhaps dying when we came upon him. Rich and I saw him to a hospital and helped him find a sympathetic person at the consulate who would aid him in getting home. He had feared contact with any authorities because his journey in Asia had begun with his criminal action of jumping ship from some merchant marine vessel. We became his intermediaries. Things worked out favorably for Tom, and he was fed well, nursed, and, his former misbehaviour overlooked, given passage on a ship bound for California.

Tom was grateful to us. He offered to do us a favor. Pointing out that sitars which were inexpensive here could command a high price in California, with the recent popularity of Indian music to be considered, he suggested that we invest in one which we could send with him and that he would cable us the money upon sale in the States. It required a bit of persistence and bother on our part, but we did it. When Tom sailed, he carried with him the best sitar that time and our finances could then provide, but we never received any money nor heard any word of what became of Tom or the sitar. Later I surrendered entirely to Providence, of course, and I swore that I would not do anything to extend my journey or make it more comfortable, nor would I henceforth initiate any action that had as its motive the material well-being of this poor vehicle of consciousness.

Jim Shaw resumed residence with me at the Ballygunge flat, and he accompanied me some to the Grand Hotel. He claimed to know Gottlieb from the States, had visited Morningstar, of course. For me, Jim's company wasn't as fascinating as it had been before. His mind was on the hash still sitting, possibly leaking tell-tale odor, at the airport, on his expectant wife in the Phillipines, on just plain getting out. When we awoke one morning, there was a clean-shaven, tall, handsome young man pacing about the rooms. I almost made the mistake of telling him he was welcome to stay in that luxurious "crash pad" before I realized that he was one of the original and legitimate western occupants of that flat. His name was Peter Van Gelder, and he was the first of the group of music students to return from their trip to Kashmir. He was busy packing. His plane for the States would leave that evening, and he had much to do. The others would return any day now, he said, and he believed they would be departing stateside pretty soon as well. As for him, his wife Marsha and baby daughter Rupa had already returned to California more than a month before, and he was anxious to rejoin them.

Before packing his serbahar, he treated us to a recital. Peter was perhaps the most gifted of all the westerners I had witnessed attempt to absorb and master the nervous complexity and the sorrowful resonant timbre of Indian music. His muscles flexed, and every sinew in his forearm pulsed with taut reverberations as his fingers furiously plucked the strings. As he played, I remembered again the peculiar pitch or tone I had heard or rather sensed in that room when I had first entered it that morning of my return to Calcutta, which now seemed so long ago. Peter seemed to possess the musician's proverbial mistrust of language as I could elicit nought but terse monosyllabic replies and no conversation whatsoever in response to my attempts to learn the story of his travels and study in India. In way of an answer to my inquiries about his musical background,he showed me a record jacket of a group called "The Great Society," one of the earliest to emerge and then disband in the San Francisco scene that gave birth to the great era of rock. Peter had been lead guitarist in the group. He also showed me a record album which told me something of Ken and Josh's background. It was a recording of a college group from Toronto called "Boys from the Big Town." Four young lads were pictured, all with short hair, clean shaven, of course, and wearing matching suits. A paraphrase of Dylan's notorious line came into mind, "you would not think to look at us, we were famous long ago."

Peter did volunteer one story I found of interest. When he had first come to India, almost a year before, he and Marsha had visited the Taj Mahal. Rupa was then an infant, and she was asleep upon Peter's shoulder. For no apparent reason, she suddenly awakened, straightened her back, looked all around and cooed in the most satisfied manner. Peter and Marsha thought that she had sensed a higher, more exquisite than normal energy and perhaps was even having a "former life flash." It interested me because Rich and I found our hearts beating extraordinarily fast when we first beheld the Taj. The excitement had grown as the bicycle rickshaw drove us along the wall, and we were beginning to thrill as we entered the arched gateway. When we saw it shining there across the garden – a pure and radiant hymn of fantasy amidst the humdrum – we literally whooped and danced for joy. "By God, its' still there, something of beauty – the old Arabian Nights' grandeur a reality! Adulthood couldn't fool us, brother, this world is still a place of magic! The all-seeing eye, the temple of gold, the legendary elephants' burial ground – I'll bet it's all still here, brother! We've made it, by God, we've made it!"

The visit to the Grand that day produced the information that Michael Bowen was at last putting into execution his plan to break off from the group and depart that night by plane for Kathmandu. Lorelei was going with him, possibly Paul and Judy as well. There was no mention made of John and I accompanying them, and it seemed to me that Michael must have changed his mind about taking us with for he tried to avoid us as he busied himself with "last minute" details. That day also brought my long-postponed rendezvous with LSD. It was towards evening when Paul offered me the acid. I suppose I did not wish to deal with the downtown nighttime vibrations of the

Grand in such a vulnerable state for we chose to change the setting to the relatively more peaceful atmosphere of the Bally-gunge flat.

Only Paul and I partook of the sacrament, but Judy looked on supportively and Jim Shaw was there too. We passed in silence the seemingly interminable length of time that one waits and watches closely for the at first almost imperceptible and then somewhat alarmingly overwhelming signs of an altered and expanded state of consciousness. The darkening room began to dissolve in waves which rushed towards the single point of light, a burning candle in the center of the room which became the focus of meditation. I could see the molecules dancing around the flame feed and transform themselves into the element, radiating out in light waves more intense and pure – particles of past cognition offering themselves to the fire of transmutation, emerging renewed from the forge of present perception as shimmering sight and vision to be. A sudden superflux of energetic thought in resplendent matter born anew to twirl and gyrate within without the ceaseless flow of circumstance – mind and will in motion whirl vast futures passed in each and every atom's sun the seed complete and the whole contained, consumed and consigned again to myriad moments circling moth-like about the wick of time, the candle heart, the pinpoint of illumination. Two eyes across the reach of world, myself in Paul peering at Him in me wishes in melting merger surcease of enmity, but unremembered alien will breaks the trance as Big Jim's black and beefy hand upon Paul's shoulder pulls and turns us twain.

"Come on, man, you'll miss that plane to Kathmandu."

With the help of Jim Shaw, Judy swept a startled and bewildered Paul off into the night of another world. The three of them vanished in ephemeral phantom flight leaving alone again inevitably I to ruminate upon the secret source and fathom full the mystery, to be shown again the elusive wonder of it all, to try once more to grasp and hold the immanent why and emanant how of things.

I first took lysergic acid dithelemine-25 in early March of 1965.

In the less than four years between that experience and the one of which I am now writing, LSD was instrumental in affecting the consciousness of half a generation in the west. I suppose anyone taking it for the first time was as little prepared for what they heard, saw, felt, tasted, smelt, and, above all, thought under its influence as was I. The difference between information and experience was particularly vast on this subject and there was nothing you could read or hear about it that could come even close in conveying the change of perception involved or the resultant bliss or terror of the psychic shock of witnessing at least some ego-level of your identity dissolve and die. The world appeared changed and changing ever afterward; never again would it be as it had seemed – indifferent to, unimpressed and uninfluenced by individual perception and cognition. A new dichotomy was created around and due to LSD: quite simply, there were those who "knew" and those who did not.

I was in graduate school at the time, my 25th birthday was rapidly approaching, the difficulties in my married life seemed particularly acute just then, and an increasing involvement of my idealism in the popular radical political outlets of the day heightened my sense of alienation from my studies, my nation, and my life in general. Though I had been cautious and prudent during the preceding years in my dalliance and experiments with marijuana, I somehow leapt without hesitation upon the opportunity to try LSD.

There was a deceptively off-hand tone and manner in the way it had all come about. The discussions and actions which led to my taking LSD that pre-spring San Francisco Saturday all seemed, before going into the experience, completely arbitrary, casual and unrehearsed, even random and impulsive. How singularly purposeful, intentional, and ultimately inevitable seemed those same circumstances upon emerging at the other end of it! Throughout, whether I laughed or cried at the dissolution of various dominating ego formations, there was an overwhelming and compelling certainty to the vision, an air of inescapable predestination, poetic and cosmic determinability, which made the means of induction, a tasteless, odorless, invisible substance ingested with a sugar cube, seem ludicrously inappropriate and negligible. I could accept the chemistry involved as a loose metaphoric example of the changes, but not as an explanation and never as the cause, surely, of such cataclysmic implosions and explosions of my conscious understanding of being. It was obvious the LSD was only a clever vehicle employed by some rationale or force well beyond my puny comprehension to sabotage technocratic logic and material defenses and to rescue some intelligent, inquiring process of self too long stifled and imprisoned. I was deeply and profoundly humbled.

Yes, awe, reverence, and almost worship were restored in an instant, but true understanding and, above all, surrender were still a long way off, for although my appreciation of the riddle and puzzle of life was renewed and my dedication to exploration and knowledge stimulated and expanded, still the general cast and tenor of my mind and heart remained atheistic. I now know that my encounter with LSD and the dosage of altered consciousness I endured was just a touch premature. I was at least a year and a half too early to completely and unequivocally be able to feel God working within a human persona, and I resisted with fury any suggestions or hints of it.

I would have none of the *allap* or falling *ghat*[8] strain of sitar when my friends placed it upon the record player. Too strong and terrible were its suggestions of going deeper and further within, and too fearful was I of what might lie on the other side of that seduction. I preferred the exuberant familiar ascending staircases of Vivaldi. Could I not tarry longer in enjoyment of the ennobled thrust and surge of western dialectic? Must I submit to debilitating and annihilating eastern passivity? The implication and urge for synthesis was already there in that very first acid trip, but I took it as a threat for I would not, could not, really, let go yet of the education and responsibility that I felt had been so painfully invested in me.

Whatever it was that LSD did to one, or rather allowed to

[8]allap is the invocation, ghat is a descending series of notes; terms employed in Indian music.

happen, as unsettling and astonishing as it could be, it was nonetheless, and this made it even more powerful in its impact, not entirely unfamiliar. The awareness being experienced was not really new but rather a resurgence-with-a-vengeance of a perception long forgotten, ignored, even suppressed. "Ah, yes," came the thought, "I remember this." Childhood easily recalled, traumas, disappointments relived, doors opened that had been slammed shut in anger by wounded pride – a lightheaded giddiness, drugged disassociation, giggles, mockery perhaps, as laughter from somewhere cascades at the seriousness with which you had taken it all. I could remember brief, silly, liberating moments spent in dental chairs where, with avoidance of pain as an excuse, I was permitted time "out of myself," the dreamy merry-go-round anaesthetic of some early surgery before that, and, at last, not quite felt fully, a flash of the first "going under" when through sudden startled stupor I was yanked from womb to dream again. With the experience induced through LSD, as with those others, I was alert to a certain whispering which I could not quite locate – off in another room perhaps – a whispering (had I heard it more clearly when I was younger?) concerning my progress. Did I know yet, they wondered, who I was. It became a clear companion metaphor after that LSD trip, a promised reality, a room inhabited by fellow cogniscenti, illuminati, a room I would enter and take my place, once I had "figured it out."

"It's all perfect, you know." It was the voice of David Bray. He had not spoken even as much as that previously. Apparently he had picked up on and entered my present acid-induced trance, and he was strikingly articulate, if enigmatic, as we met briefly in the same wave-length of communication.

"So perfect, in fact, that there is nothing to do about it but see it. At least for me, that was it. I've checked out, you might have noticed – came, saw, expired. It should work, you know."

"What had happened?" I didn't verbally ask (I was in a state where I understood too much, it seemed, to form words) but directed the question at him by thought.

"The whole show went for me in Benares, that was all. I saw it

you know – there – the whole crazy, wild, delicious expanse of
it. Just saw it so there was no need to see again. There went the
whole show, right there. You're seeing it too – but there is
something for you to do with it, I can tell that. I haven't got
that, don't need it maybe. The whole show went for me in
Benares, don't you know? It should work for you though. It's
quite perfect!''

Dawn approached and David Bray, frozen in intense contemplation of the perfection which he tried to hold – geometric,
crystalline, pure and invisible – cupped in his palms, drifted
away in the sliding lens of my changing vision until he was lost
in the wide angle of infinity.

LSD had done its part in the conscious arousal and stirrings
that had accelerated and made possible the perusal of one's
karmic file. It had wrenched, threatened even to destroy, the
function of time and the process of assimilation, and, therefore,
it could serve only as a temporary cathartic and never as a
permanent panacea. Saints and sinners were born overnight,
destinies divine and derelict sped to their conclusions and there
beckoned opportunity to settle swiftly large accounts in the
cosmic ledgers.

With sunrise came the specific locating of time and place, the
relative, topical, terrestrial data regarded with due consideration – date: November 14, my internal calendar reminded me
that it was also my son Nathaniel's seventh birthday; occasion:
my sixth acid trip, third in India. I recalled the anticipation and
expectations of the one that had come to me in Bombay on April
2nd. My 28th birthday had just passed, and I was still looking
forward to my first acid trip in India. The coincidence and
collaboration of the drug that had "blown my mind" with the
place where I had come to learn that the "blowing" and mind
itself were all God – this coincidence could not help but be, I
thought, a significant landmark in my conscious evolution. The
colony of us that had settled in Goa (and it was still quite a small
one at the time) had literally prayed for the arrival of some acid
to consecrate and clarify the ethnic and moral ground and
landscape we had heroically traversed and dis-covered. It was,

we thought, the finest thing the west could offer the merit of our pioneering efforts and spiritual stamina.

The acid, when it finally did arrive, came through the wrong form, a dealer with profit as his motive. The price placed upon, and games played with, the commodity had the effect of dividing rather than further integrating our group. The fact that consciousness is one and indivisible was forgotten in the hassles over who should "drop," when and how much dosage, and the assumption of shared knowledge was abandoned for the insecurity of "are you on?", "did you get off?", and "what's it like?". Egos we had thought long dead resurfaced immediately. Not only had it not provided the cohesive, bonding, and reinforcing properties we had hoped, but for Marc and me it didn't come at all in the bucolic, peaceful, paradisial setting we had intended. The acid came for us instead during our desperate-paced and frantic city escapades.

Marc, always one to push beyond any accepted boundaries, spent his birthday, April 1st, in the Colaba section jail of Bombay. He had stripped naked and run the streets howling, beseeching in acid madness that everyone come out of hiding, reveal themselves, love one another, and, above all, come together in mutual recognition and sharing of the cosmic purpose that had drawn us isolated exiles to cluster in these intemperate outposts. I heard of Marc's incarceration when I awakened the next day at the V. T. Station waiting room, and I went down to sign for his release. That night I took acid with the vague notion of somehow fulfilling and redeeming his excess. The night sparkled for me, and the sunrise over the Gateway was a splendid one. Seven Sikhs jogging, their top-knots neatly tied in handkerchiefs, bouncing and swaying, seemed Surya's steeds transformed, couriers of a brighter dawn. And so too this dawn was bright with promise, Ballygunge all aglow to salute with me in reverence renewed the majestic pageant of phenomena.

Morning brought the return of Ken and Mary, Josh and Gayle. I remembered Ken easily from our brief meeting in the Rex Hotel, Bombay. He carried about him the same unmistakable boyish enthusiasm. The others I hadn't met before. Mary had been Ken's girlfriend for the year, but they were going through a

change in relationship. She had been bored with India for some
time, had taken dancing lessons to allay the feeling and find
some common ground with the fanatic musicians with whom
she lived, but it hadn't really worked, and she was impatient to
get back to America. Gayle and Josh seemed to have a deeper,
longer-lasting relationship. They had all enjoyed their vacation
in Shrinagar.

I was verbal at this point and asked them if they had gotten to
the countryside around and told them that I had spent the
summer at Nishat Bagh across Dal Lake.

"We heard something about that scene," Ken said. "You guys
must have blown a few minds, huh?"

Was it that we had been the first fairly large band of westerners there that caused the stir; had we been particularly callous
to local feelings, I wondered, or was there something inevitable
and purposeful in the Shivite-like destruction we had seemed to
inadvertently leave in our wake? Sometimes it seemed to me
that in our desperation and intensity of seeking we were like
locusts upon the extant culture. These musicians, coupled and
stable, by and large, seemed to absorb what they needed from
India in so much more measured and civilized a manner.

Jim Shaw had returned sometime in the night though I did not
notice him until now. Ken recognized him from Hong Kong. The
mystery of how Jim and Ken had met was cleared up. Simply,
Ken had returned to the west for a brief visit to his folks and then
back to India via Hong Kong. He seemed to have inexhaustible
funds at his disposal, and it opened a hitherto unimagined vista
of quick – even chic – bi-cultural exploration and maneuver-
ing. From the nature of my own journey in India, I hadn't
considered the possibility of one being able to move easily and
swiftly between the East and the West. The two worlds had
seemed so inexpressibly distant, separated by unbridgeable gulfs
wider than miles and deeper than oceans.

"What a flash!" Ken exclaimed, "to be back there suddenly
after you've been here for awhile. Everybody ought to do it
just to keep from getting too settled in the head – you know,
compulsory shake up. It would be good for you every six months
or so.

"When I was back," Ken continued, "I passed through San Francisco, so naturally I checked out the rock scene. Went to both the Avalon and Fillmore ballrooms. Man, you know, they're too zonked out to dance anymore. No one's dancing, I swear. They're just sort of sitting on the floor and moaning and undulating to the music."

This talk of the West brought us to the subject of the tourists at the Grand and impulsively we decided to hightail it down there. Mary stayed behind but Josh, Gayle, Ken, Jim Shaw, and I speedily swept down Lake Road to Rash Behari where beside a triangular park always stood a line of waiting taxis.

"The Grand Hotel," Jim Shaw directed the driver, "and step on it!"

Another wave of the trance came over me as the taxi rumbled downtown. I was semi-hallucinating as we entered the Grand. My companions seemed to race ahead of me, receding down the corridors of time, leaving me alone once again to grapple with some yet unresolved and still disturbing levels of self-communication. I was aware again that an essential part of the recent me was dissolving and transmutating and knew that I would never quite be the same again as I emerged from the other end of this. For me there is always a transitory moment of sadness when all of the messages uncommunicated, feelings unexpressed, rush upon one with a wistful nostalgic finality. It is a kind of leave-taking without proper adieu. My brother Rich came to mind: so long it had been since I had last seen him, so many changes had occurred since our last conversation in that death-smelling Kashmiri hospital. I wished very much to communicate with him – was it possible that I would awaken in some plane of vibrational existence that could not support both Rich and I, who were in fact really one and only pretended our differences for the sheer company of it? – to send some note in a metaphysical bottle towards whatever island he presently inhabited. Since we all breathe and are maintained by the same prana, could I not find a frequency therein to direct and channel a message towards him? It seemed I could, simplest thing imaginable, and as I pondered it, I tripped over the foot of someone who was turning the corridor in my direction.

"Tom Zwicker!" I shouted coming into the present in an instant.

"Oh my God, hey man, you look real good!"

Tom took me down the hall and into his room. There were several brand new neatly-arranged backpacks and sleeping bags in one corner. He introduced me to his girlfriend who was an attractive Japanese-American. They were in the process of checking out and flying up to Kathmandu. Tom apparently was doing the circuit again, only this time on his terms.

"You look good," he repeated to me, impressed by my outfit and thinness, no doubt, as though I were wearing a neon sign which proclaimed "yogi" or "realized." I didn't tell him I was tripping at the time, nor did I bring up anything about the missing sitar. What followed was what Tom volunteered.

"It's so good to be back, man, if you know what I mean. You wouldn't believe how hard it is to feel high, to just get off in the States. It's all gotten a hundred times more totalitarian and uptight, you know what I mean. I had to do *anything* I could to survive, you know. Now I'm back home, baby, and I'm not going to waste any of my chances. You guys who have hung on here, my hat's off to you, you've done the right thing. You look so good, man, so righteous, holy, you know what I mean."

"In the end it's all been good for me, Tom. Everything that has happened to me," I told him," has been perfect. I'm grateful to all of it, really. It all helped to get me to the place where I inevitably must be, right? And it's not over yet. I love you, Tom, wish you well." I staggered out of the room and did not see him again.

When I found the room that my companions had settled in, I proceeded directly to the bathroom and started running some water in the tub. The water rushing over me lapped the porcelain edges of the tub as though it were some distant shore. The sounds of the dripping faucet and the fan in the next room and whatever other sundry hums and drones that made up the atmosphere seemed both ominous and comforting. Whatever I could not quite lay to rest in the unplaced reaches of my mind,

I was calm in the reflection that I was a stranger to the company and land in which I would wash ashore – no preconceptions or expectations to fulfill or disappoint. Under the influence of acid it became obvious and palpably demonstrable that circumstances were engendered by thought formations. The more one pursued a particular line of thought the greater the labyrinth of mental circumstances he created from which to emerge. So, LSD made second degree yogis of many who could foresee the endless tangle and infinite complications possible to the unchecked mind. If the means of tuition had been artificial, as the meditation purists opposed to drugs argued, the experience and lesson was nonetheless real. Hundreds of intrepid voyagers understood directly and instantaneously what could not be communicated through thousands of years and endless translations of Patanjali.

As with every birth, it was naked and defenseless that I entered the world – in this case, the main room of that suite. Still wet, I lay down on the large bed. The highly resonated and perfectly modulated voice of a professional speaker filled the room. He sat in the middle holding forth to Ken, Josh, Gayle, and Jim. Rena was there as well and Bob Garcia. The speaker's head was large, with a prominent semitic nose, and his black and greying beard and hair seemed leonine. He wore glasses with black heavy frames which, though obvious and outrageously contemporary, did not distract from his over-all biblical appearance, like an elder of the tribe as Blake might have etched one. As he bobbed and bowed his head in emphatic speech, his vibrational field changed dramatically, and he himself seemed to move in and out of various primal patriarchal archetypes – Moses, Father Abraham, I recognize you, born-teacher, rabbi, guru grown upon American soil. It was, of course, the now almost legendary Lou Gottlieb. I recognized him; I had seen him before, seen him from the streetcar, seen him besieged by hungry and curious Indians the morning of our return from Konarak.

"The whole problem in the proverbial nutshell, don't you see, is in letting go. It kills modern man but that's what he's got to do nonetheless, let go. The old tenacious instinct, the primordial

*It was, of course, the now almost legendary Lou Gottlieb.*

impulse to clutch and grasp and hold on, with the dying breath to hold on – that's what he's got to overcome. It all starts with the land. The land becomes the property of an individual or an institution or some special interest group, then all that grows and feeds upon the land becomes his or their property, and then that which lives there – women, children, all become the property of an individual ego and its insecure compulsion to acquire and accumulate. It's mine, *mine*, don't you see? – then possession becomes nine-tenths of the flaw.

"Morningstar began to teach me – painlessly, on the whole – how to let go. 'Let go, Lou, let go,' it said at every corner and turning. The trees breathed that – let go, let go. I tell you it is the veritable mantra of that blessed piece of earth. So, it declared itself, through me and through Ramon and others, declared itself, 'land access to which is denied absolutely no one.' If I don't control what goes on and takes place on that land, then what directs what happens? The land itself. It has its own destiny to fulfill. It calls to itself those it needs to perform its own will and cosmic intention.

"Don't you understand that the land is mother? Mother earth, Mother Nature!! It gave birth to all of us. How then can we possess our mother? In the global history of nations, with the migrations of people, it is Mother India that as a separate, geographical, cultural, or political entity understood that first and still stands for it. India itself was the first – and maybe only, as far as I know – place, country, conglomerate of people, call it what you will, that in spirit and action became essentially land access to which was denied no one. No one was resisted, no one was told 'no,' neither the Aryans, the Muslims, nor the British were repelled at her borders. They were all given free access to come in and deal with the land in their own way. Ultimately, they all succumbed to the land and had to do her will, don't you see?"

He paused a moment and raised his eyebrows in punctuation of the incontrovertible logic of his theories.

"Maybe it's easier for me to disassociate and disattach myself from possessiveness with respect to the land. It is the redeeming quality of the Jew – perhaps his only redeeming quality – that he is not by instinct a landowner. Maybe it is his history that he has to thank, that in hundreds upon hundreds of years, he was denied ownership of land, had to develop other interests, less cumbersome, more mobile, like banking, finance, and the traits and talents that made him for a time master of Europe but always so upon a land that he temporarily inhabited only by the grace and permission of others. So his investment was more in his seed and not in the land. They did not identify with the land principle, the old territorial imperative. Not until recent time, that is, with Zionism bringing about the limited chauvinism of identity with a specific locale. Really the Jews need no specific homeland to give them identity. They are not really a people or race and certainly not merely a religion. What they are is a caste – they're the brahmins of the world. I only came to understand that here. The moment I came here I felt and knew I was home. These people know it. They see it in me immediately. I am as at one with Bengal as I am at home on Morningstar!"

Lou looked up and gazed directly into my eyes. Something in

him hesitated a moment, sought permission somewhere inside of me to go on.

"Aha," he said, "do I detect one of the brotherhood of the All-knowing, the omniscient? Ahaa, LSD in our midst!" He licked his lips.

"Why," he went on, "is it an irresistible impulse when feeling high, illuminated, free, to divest one's self of the constricting garments, habadashery of custom, raiments of convention? To be free of it, free of possession!! To stand naked before your maker, undisguised and unabashed!! I love it! At Morningstar we have had considerable encounters with the Custodians of the Law, shall we say, the local constabulary, the gentlemen in blue who from time to time come to check out the dancing maidens and nymphettes, the reefer tokers and bung-hole pokers – you know Mencken's old definition of the puritan, someone who is constantly afraid that somebody somewhere might be having a good time – well, they came to Morningstar all the time using zoning ordinances and imagined infractions of some law or other as an excuse. You know the best way to confront them? Bare-assed naked!! That's right, just drop your drawers and they have no defense. It is an infallible, evolutionary tactic!! They retreat immediately, abashed and ashamed, for they need all their accoutrements to maintain their sense of themselves. I tell you, one man, or better yet a woman, standing naked can turn back an army. If Ghandi had known that, Britain would have been out of here in two minutes.

"It is a popular misconception that hippies are a peaceful people, flower children, make love and not war and all that. Hippies are at war, I tell you, with everything. They do not use force, but they are nonetheless at war. They are the modern kshatriyas of the world. The warrior caste, no question about it! They fight with nakedness and their refusal to do anything but that which they wish and that which pleases them. That's the teaching, that is what is pointed out to Arjuna – svadharma!! Don't you understand, what in God's name is svadharma? It is, as the hippies so eloquently put it, doing your own thing. What an old fashioned and off-the-mark translation is 'duty'; thing, baby, it is doing your own thing! If everyone would insist, regardless of argument, cajolery, persuasion to the contrary, insist upon doing his own thing, the world would change in a moment, overnight. I have seen it. I can't resist it. Everytime I myself find myself getting uptight, I turn around and there is another naked hippie dancing his svadharma in front of me, and a voice inside says 'Lou, Lou, let go, let go, baby, let go. It is the only way to your salvation!' "

Ken, Josh, and Gayle had gone back long before, and the day went through many changes of mood as I remained in the Grand watching various scenes, all seeming allegorical and significant, unfold before me. I was the witness and enjoyer. John O'Shea had appeared late in the day, and when he saw me at last stirring my supine and now clothed form and making my exit, he called me to attention with an earnest namaskar and slipped me five rupees with the advice "don't spend it all in one place." For awhile as I wandered, I felt it to be a cosmic assignment to spend or place the five rupees judiciously. I imagined various far-fetched effects of my giving it to this beggar or that bidi wallah with a "keep the change," but I could make no decision and in the end wound up the next morning with the five rupees still in my kurta pocket. I knew I would not spend it on a taxi or other means of conveyance back to Ballygunge as my intent was to walk myself into exhaustion, thus working out the last adrenalin of acid and being able to crash in blissful slumber.

I found myself that night walking the entire length of the main artery of Calcutta. The street went through four changes of name, and I puzzled over the red street signs wondering if they conveyed secret messages – Chowringhee, Jahwaharlal Nehru Road, Asutosh Mukherjee, Shyam Prashad Mukherjee. At last I came to Rash Behari and turned left, remembering that I was heading towards Ken's Ballygunge flat, the inevitable return to the point of departure, another circle described.

It was a very delicate balance that I walked that night. I hovered between the vulnerability of total suggestiveness, a surrender that could carry me into any number of alleys or random byways, and the application of enough will to keep me in a steady direction, moving towards my goal. I both enjoyed and suffered the imagination that if I stared long enough at any of the numerous other pedestrians, I could command their gazing into my eyes and that if they did so, then I would penetrate their disguise and see that they were each of them someone I knew, perhaps myself. I did not wish to go that far nor did I wish to ignore anyone's existence, dismiss it as insignificant, unnoticeable, of no importance to myself. And so in this delicate balance I recalled a yogic trick I had learned during that Bombay acid trip. At first I had had a flash of a high mortal attrition rate of those aspirants that had launched themselves within this lifetime upon The Path – and with it came that old familiar, loving feeling that I was destined for the supreme goal, no matter how difficult, or how many others should apparently fail. As the acid had begun to wear off, I was given a specific piece of knowledge as a means to prolong and sustain the high I was experiencing for awhile longer. I realized that what exhausted one, brought one down, made it necessary to crash was the expenditure of will in one's own desires. I had realized that if I willed nothing for myself but put my form in motion and service according to the will of others, then rather than become drained I would be replenished with energy. Thus for three days I had sat in a room at the Rex Hotel and did not stir unless it was at the bidding of others. I did not consider my own stomach and did not eat unless others reminded me or wished my company during their meal. I was neither hungry nor tired, but in the end I could not carry this out indefinitely. Bit by bit, my self and subtle longings began to come back to my cognition, and soon enough I was back upon the wheel of desire, satiation, respite. This night, too, walking the length of Calcutta, as the acid allowed me to see easily my last complicated thought projections, I became overwhelmingly drained and tired with myself, totally spent by the persona of my cognition. "I" this, "I" that, always the interminably troublesome "I." I saw it as clearly then as I do now, in writing so repeatedly that single vowel, as years later I now sit recreating that "I" used up so long ago.

Entering the flat I saw my staff standing against the wall in the corner of the main room; beneath it lay my now worn

Tibetan bag. How well I knew the meagre contents of that bag: my passport, random letters, my sporadically-kept journal, and a slightly soiled pair of white pyjamas. Suddenly I became posessed by the idea that I must divest myself even of these last things. I shall lay claim to them no longer, I thought. The idea began to amuse me that anyone coming in from anywhere could pick up these few items and continue to play out the hand or game where I had left it. As for me, I was anxious for the next step. I could sense that room of the fellow illuminati, brothers and sisters in consciousness, opening before me. It seemed that I had been in that room often recently. Clearly I could see green curtains stirring lightly and quietly and then parting of their own accord. I could almost see the occupants of that room as they stood up to greet me. I moved in to embrace them but fell asleep in the same instant.

don't know exactly when or precisely how it was that the certainty came upon me that Father was about to reenter our lives. It just began to seem that he was the conclusion to which these recent circumstances were pointing and that the intense and potentially combustible energy we were experiencing was somehow or other summoning him. I began to reinterpret all the episodes of my last weeks, including the voices at Konarak, with him as the central force or guiding factor, thread or hand behind the scene.

Lou Gottlieb had something to do with it. He was a man anxious, even desperate, to meet God. He saw Him at work in everything. Random glances on streetcars, words overheard in chai shops, contacts made through New Market runners, all seemed to indicate to Lou that the breathtaking ecstatic culmination was at hand. "One brief hour to madness and joy," he was fond of quoting, and he would with great vigour and conviction tell us of a recent encounter of his that was surely a precursor to the "Last Judgment."

"I was on the tram this morning coming from the American

Express, and I felt a pair of piercing eyes. Right through my back I felt them. I turned and saw this compassionate-looking young man staring at me. This afternoon I saw him again in a juice stall where I stopped. And this evening at Chico's when I was changing money I saw him again. His name it turns out is Kalyan Bhattacarya. Well, don't you see? Kalyan means 'blessed.'"

Another time he asked me if I had ever received a mantra. When I told him "no," he rejoined: "Then you must go see Ballak Brahmacarya without delay. Have him whisper a mantra to you. I tell you it will accelerate your evolution." If my hesitation or lack of enthusiasm betokened skepticism, he would counter with, "Well, it certainly can't hurt."

One evening as I left the Grand Hotel, I saw Don McCoy standing head and shoulders above everyone else on the Chowringhee. There was no way to miss him, and I had been waiting for him. I knew Father could not be too far off.

At Ken's place Don told me that he had flown up from Pondicherry and that Shotsy, Sheila, Buz, and a young man they'd picked up at that world ashram were following in a day by train. I wondered why he had flown and left the others to the rails.

"Because I was sick as a dog, that's why. Sick the whole time I'd been in Pondicherry, and I know why."

"Why?" I asked.

"Because I'd judged Father, that's why. If I hadn't judged him for something he said, then we'd have never gone, and we shouldn't have. He was right. There was nothing there but the same old uptight lip service."

"What do you mean?" I asked.

"Look, I hadn't meant to come here at all. Sheila'd been going on for awhile in raptures about India and how it was her cosmic mission to come here. Well, I just wanted to stay clear of the place. I happen to like my own place, things in their proper order, and besides I wanted to stay at Olompali and keep it together with the kids and all. Buz it turned out wanted to go to India and that pleased Samuel Lewis, their teacher, and I thought it was fine because Sheila would have an escort and everything, but suddenly I do find myself here, I really don't know why, and when I joined them at the Spiritual Summit Conference, they had already been to Pondicherry. Well, before I knew it, we had all these plans . . . go back to Pondicherry, turn them on to some acid . . . oh, we were going to do a million things. Then we met Father, and it all stopped. Well, that was fine. I mean that was the way it really should have been, us surrendering to him and getting off our trip and all that. But then I judged what he said. It didn't seem he really could be who or what he said. It just seemed he was taking over our trip, that we had no more say in what was going on. Well, I balked. Whatever happened to our plans to go to Pondicherry, I wondered. I went there sort of to show him he wasn't everything because, to tell you the truth, I didn't have any more interest or business in Pondicherry than an ice man in Alaska. I'll show him, I thought, but he showed me, of course."

"What do you mean?" I asked once more. "Who do you think Father is?"

"I want to tell you a story," he said, fixing me with a long earnest stare. Don McCoy was a man who spoke little if at all unless he had your full and undivided attention. He reminded me of the Ancient Mariner as he carefully and precisely chose his words as though there were nothing in the world more important than that which he was about to tell, and he wished to scrupulously avoid coloring it in any way which would detract from the facts of his tale.

"Before I met Father I had several visions that after I met him I realized . . . You know when you have a vision, you don't always know it's a vision until later, after some time passes. I suppose it was some sort of vision that established us at Rancho Olompali to begin with. That's where I lived with my children and where Sheila and Bob lived with their kids when it all began to happen. About twenty-six of us were living there and trying to establish our own life style, based primarily on doing just exactly what we wanted. Acid had a lot to do with it. I mean we took a lot of acid. The main part of the ranch was pretty close to the road and back up in the valley, sort of nestled in the breasts of these two beautiful mountains, was the deer camp where hunters used to stop. A friend of mine had fixed up a place there to be a Buddhist

monastery, tatami mats on the floor, everything nice and ordered. There was a stream nearby, and it was just a beautiful
place to go and meditate.

"I had moved up there in August, and on this one particular
day, I hadn't done much, had dropped some acid, and in late
afternoon as the sun was pretty far down in the sky, I saw this
huge thunderhead of a cloud which immediately attracted my
eye. I had taken acid, but this cloud was definitely there. I
watched it for I'd say about ten or fifteen minutes, and during
the period of time that I watched it, I noticed that it started to
change, that the visual images that I was seeing in the cloud
actually started to change. And it started out being like comic
strip characters. First it was like – I don't know what came first,
but definitely there was Mickey Mouse and Porky Pig and Bugs
Bunny and . . . it would change from one face to another, and I
was just . . . ah . . . really spellbound. It was almost like a cartoon
I was watching in the sky. Pretty soon the face changed to what
looked like the north wind, my picture of what the north
wind . . . ahh . . . deep set eyes, a long white flowing beard, his
mouth in a blowing-like . . . you could just almost hear the wind
go 'whooooo' from its mouth. And then from that it changed
into something that I'd never seen, a face that I'd never seen
before but I instantly recognized it as the face of God. And . . .
uhhh . . . it stayed there for maybe ten or fifteen seconds and
then it started to dissolve and go into . . . well, more back into a
cloud again, not taking on any more discernable images. I just
thought 'That's very far out. God just gave me a little peek into
what He looks like, and if I ever see Him I'll recognize Him.'

"Well, a couple of months later I find myself here at this
Spiritual Summit Conference, and during the second day of it
this man appears. He came looking like a beggar, but he had
such a countenance or such an appearance that it was one that
was . . . uhh, arresting to the eye. This beggar just sort of showed
me his presence for a few seconds in the doorway just as we were
leaving that day's proceedings. He showed himself to me for just
a few seconds but I remember I nudged whoever it was who was
standing next to me and said 'Wow, look at that man. I'd

certainly like to meet him. He looks like he knows what he's doing.' Nobody else there knew what they were doing, it seemed to me, certainly, least of all myself. So then he disappeared from that doorway and reappeared in another doorway. As we were all coming out of the auditorium, we came to stand in a big circle in the lobby, talking about a lot of nonsense, I suppose, and Mr. Finley Dunne, the director of the conference, was standing on my left, and maybe about five or six other people when suddenly this man that I had seen in the doorways came and addressed Mr. Dunne. I couldn't hear what he said, but Mr. Dunne walked off. The man stood there very quietly, just with his eyes cast down and his hands folded, didn't make any attempt to communicate with anyone else. Finally, Mr. Dunne came back and said 'I'm sorry I couldn't arrange the ten minutes for you to speak, the schedule was just too filled up.' This man said 'That's all right. You needn't be sorry. You tried. I understand.' And then he looked right at me – The man looked right into my eyes and said 'I have other means of communication.'

"Well, it was like a bomb exploded there. I grabbed this man by the shoulder, and I said 'You tell 'em, brother,' and he jumped into my arms and I jumped into his arms and we danced around and jumped up and down and laughed and cried and he lifted me off the ground and I lifted him off the ground and it was just an ecstatic experience."

He fell silent. I waited a moment in vain for him to continue, but it was as though he had said all that he had intended, more indeed than was necessary, and, falling back into his more normal tight-lipped state, he made it clear that he would volunteer no more.

"What are you trying to tell me, Don," I asked "that Father, the beggar, and the face in the cloud are all one and the same?"

"That, yes . . . and more. Father, I'm sure now, is everything; I can show you reference to Him in the Book of Revelations. I understand now the feet of bronze and the face no one can turn from. But it is more than the face. There is one more thing I should tell you.

"I had another vision late last summer. Perhaps it would more properly be called an audition since I didn't see as much as hear something. There's a holy mountain in Marin County called Mt. Tamalpais, and I went there one afternoon to clear my head. I lay out on the ground and stretched my arms toward heaven, and finally I sort of floated out of my body. I was not on acid this time. I described it at the time as a 'samadhi experience,' but I see now that all visions and experiences out of body and so forth point to the same thing, and there is no need to give them different names. This was a voice I heard, and it spoke perfectly clearly and said exactly, 'Stop trying to change the world, Don, and change yourself. This world is my perfect creation which I have created for your enjoyment, and it is only your faulty vision which keeps you from seeing that.' Now, doesn't that sound familiar to you? You know if I were never to see Father again and had to remember him from just what I've already heard ... you know when we were at the Astoria ... In all those hours he must have said millions of things, and they all pointed to the same thing really: 'There is no world to change, only yourself.'"

The next day Don took some large rooms at the Grand in preparation for the return of the others. The day after that, I remember it as a Sunday, they did return. There was a great deal of commotion and excitement. It seemed they all already knew Lou Gottlieb; some knew him from California where Don and Lou were considered brothers and leaders in the vanguard of commune experiments. All of their paths had crossed as recently as a week before at Pondicherry where the arrival of one group over-lapped for a day the departure of Ashok's spiritual touring party. They were flashing on the implications and effects that this present trip in India would have on their American life. As for Don and Sheila, they planned to take Father to Olompali, and Sheila had a very definite "and we'll live happily ever after" way of talking about it. Lou, conversely, was going to establish a Morningstar East somewhere in Bengal, purchase some land and then declare it "land access to which is denied no one."

Lou showed me a post card he had had printed up. It pictured the Morningstar symbol, a star of David with a heart and torch in the center. Beneath it was printed: "Good News for Modern Man. God has revealed the meaning of original sin. It is private property, and the cutting up and dividing of Mother Earth. Put a Morningstar in your window. It declares your home as 'land access to which is denied no one.' See who your land will draw to it. Your first guest will be the prophet Elijah. Your life will become happier and easier, and your sex life will improve. Om shanti."

Sheila produced some newspaper clippings from the Pacific Sun. They spoke of Rancho Olompali, of the progressive attitudes there, how the running of the ranch and the education there was determined by the children. There were pictures of Don and his children and Sheila and hers and above the photos the headline "Chosen Family believes God wishes them to establish new order."

I got a chance that morning to speak to Buz. He told me a little more about their recent visit at Pondicherry.

"When Sheila and I had been there before – we stopped there on our way up to Calcutta – it was like we had the 'open sesame' or something, carte blanche to the whole place. Of course, we did have a letter from Murshid, that's Sam Lewis, and we know Pir Vilayat Khan, and in the ashram library they had the books of his father Hazrat Inayat there, so all in all it was working like magic. If we could come back we would definitely be granted darshan with the Mother, fine rooms made available to us gratis – you know, there's kind of a spiritual kiwanis club at work in these places. Well, the night we went out to Father's hut, it all seemed to be fitting together, particularly when I noticed that the one picture of any guru Father had on his wall – I mean everywhere you go here there are pictures of at least six or seven gurus, just to be on the safe side, I guess – well, the one picture Father had was of Aurobindo, and the only book evident there was a copy of 'Life Divine'! So I figured Father'd be delighted with the chance to go to Pondicherry, but when we offered to take him, he acted hurt and said, 'You're leaving me for that which is already over and dead.' He told us that they wouldn't receive us at Pondicherry, and I thought that was ridiculous and 'sour grapes' and all because I'd just been there, and I knew they were going to receive us with open arms. Man, you couldn't believe the change in the place! They didn't want to receive us at all, by no means would grant us darshan with the Mother. They tried to forcibly eject us and we'd done nothing. You know a lot of those guys posing as yogis there are really jocks at heart, sophisticated bouncers. They probably would have gotten rid of us but Don started shouting 'lip service' and 'infidels' so loud and furiously that he really intimidated them. I have to laugh about it now because there was Lou being all serious and muckitymuck with them and Ashok and trying to pretend he didn't know us, and there we were blowing it for him completely. But really I don't know what made the difference between our two visits except that we'd met Father in the meantime."

As if on cue, Father suddenly appeared in our midst that morning. He was exactly as he had been before, same brown shawl, same white lungi, same benevolent smile. They all tried to tell him different things at once: Shotsy was appalled by the thirty some hours she'd spent on the train; Don of how sick he'd been; Sheila something about the Mother. It all pointed generally to how uncomfortable they'd been since they had last seen him and how glad they were to be with him again. Just as suddenly they all seemed to remember other things they had to do. Don went off to look for Lou who had left before Father arrived. I found myself alone for the first time with Father, and my heart was pounding and my hands trembling.

We weren't alone long enough to break the silence when Vince stuck his head in at the door and said, "No, Lou doesn't seem to be here either."

Ashok's head followed immediately with, "You'll excuse please but we are looking for Mr. Gottlieb."

When he saw that Father was present in the room, he dismissed Vince and tarried a moment. What transpired seemed most peculiar to me because Father said nothing, not a single word that might have caused it or any comment in response to it.

"Ah yes," said Ashok, "I see that you think I have forgotten India since I left. It is not true really. My heart is constantly crying for India and at same time glad to be back here...at home, you know...there is no place really like Bengal...but also sad feeling because it is necessary for me to be leaving this place again...and too soon, I must say.

"Yes I have gained weight," he said, touching the girth about his middle which in contrast to the beggar seemed excessive indeed, "but that is due to the kindness and hospitality of my American hosts and friends. Really they are too kind in means and ways in which your comfort and well-being too they are seeing about. Of course, they are in seriously lack with spiritual desserts, fulfillments and all these matters which here we are so fortunate and lavish in abundance with. Much is to be done there, I tell you, in the uplifting of their spirit, and it is full-time and arduous work, I assure you."

His tone became increasingly whiney and apologetic. It appeared to me that he was acting the part of a subordinate appealing extenuating circumstances to his superior in accounting for his mission being only partially or inadequately accomplished. This whole scene astounded me because I couldn't understand what it was that compelled the unction and self-confession from Ashok. Father remained absolutely silent throughout. Ashok, almost bowing and scraping, finally made his exit.

This departure was followed immediately by Don poking his head in at the door.

"Father, would you like to meet our friend Lou now? He's just across the hall."

I was right behind "the beggar" as he entered the room so I had a full view of Lou during his initial meeting with the man it was becoming increasingly natural to call "Father." Lou stood on the other side of the bed and lowered his head in a sincere but more or less routine and formal namaskar. Suddenly he was smitten, I suppose as I had been by one of those bolt-of-lightning glances, for Lou began to call out, "It's Him, It's Him, by God, it's Him!" His body shook in a paroxysm of laughter. "Hoo-hooo, haa-haaa," he dissolved with a delirious hilarity of ecstasy, in a divine hysteria of happiness. "Bhagawan," he sobbed and wiped a few tears that had started down his cheeks. I don't know what in fact happened next, but what I saw and have continued to see every time I have remembered that meeting was that Lou and Father leapt towards each other from opposite sides of the bed and met in the air in a merging embrace, and, I swear, they were held there for a timeless moment, suspended gravity-less as one, and then, pulling apart, lightly landed again each at the side of the bed from which they had started, Father upon the door side and Lou at the interior. They finished then their namaskar of obeisance, each to the other.

In the moments that followed that room developed into a place of congregation for a fairly sizable group. Almost by appointment the seekers and gnostics, the most earnest or desperate of the pilgrims, the thinly or highly disguised devotees began to gather. This, then, was the authentic "spiritual summit conference," assembled neither by public promulgation nor through media advertisement but brought into being by the accumulated moments of what we would come to understand more and more as supra-physical communication.

A roll call of those in attendance I feel is appropriate for historical record as well as the narrative demands of this particular account. There was, of course, Father, the centrifugal force of it all; balancing him, the two Śakti powers that had first been drawn towards him to stabilize and transmit the revelations through their respectively consortive and maternal personalities, Shotsy Wallace and Sheila McKendrick. There was Buz Rowell, Don McCoy, and Lou Gottlieb as already mentioned.

Reclining upon the bed throughout the following scene was Govinda, a young man disaffected with ashram life whom they had picked up in Pondicherry. His name had been Lenny Steinhoff, and he had been a pharmaceutical salesman in his former life in New York. About a year previous, after suffering a premature heart attack (he was only thirty), he began to explore the possibilities of a spiritual life and became a devotee of the guru Satchitananda. He had recently come with that saffron-clad holy man and others of his similarly apparelled followers on a quick spiritual tour of India. They had passed through Hrishikesh just days prior to my stopping there, and they had been welcomed and honored by the also saffron-robed attendants at the Śivananda Divine Light mission where I was refused a single night's lodging. They had gone on to visit the south and then Ceylon where Lenny had had a falling out with Satchitananda. The tour went home without him, and he moved on to Pondicherry hoping to find a new and more compatible master. It had been Satchitananda that had blessed him with the name Govinda, and Sheila, spotting the little lost Jewish boy in him, who had given him his first acid trip there along the beach of that province.

And now, like myself and the others in that room, he was no doubt a bit bewildered but happy to find himself a part of this network of communication which seemed to be forming of its own predetermined volition. It included, also drawn from the by now nearly defunct Ashok Fakir tour, Donovan Bess and Bob Garcia. Rena was there, quiet throughout and for the most part hanging childlike by Lou's side. Jim Shaw too was called into our midst though he made frequent exits during the proceeding illuminations. Also present, a sort of sadhu delegation representative of the road veteran constituency of Shivites, were John O'Shea and myself.

In all we numbered the same as Jesus and his disciples as they gathered at the seder which has come to be known as "the Last Supper." Such correspondences in numbers, positions, personalities, and activities in the spirals and patterns of spiritual pageantry occur more and more frequently to each individual form of mentation as it comes more and more to witness and participate in the flow of cosmic occurrence. This accounts for the popularity of numerology, astrology, and other occult sciences with the spiritual seeker. I do not put overmuch stock in these sciences myself. Since the terms and forms of the great game are constantly shifting, certain significant formations must inevitably repeat, but to ignore these patterns would be to exclude a good bit of the poetry through which the Divine lets you know that something very special is happening. With this flash of correspondence I mused upon the juxtaposed meanings of the last terrestrial moment that Jesus was together with his disciples and the play that would begin with this corporeal reunion with our Father, and I wondered if we weren't, perhaps, picking up where they left off. It came to me that all Scripture, no matter what the terms of the individual culture and language, must be the same since it unlocks and releases the same power; so all chants and prayers are mantra, and the sermon on the mount is a perfect upaniṣad. The Last Supper then was nothing other than one of the most historically significant and best recorded dhunis of conscious time.

I had become fascinated by the concept of the dhuni from the hours I had spent with hardened sadhus. They meant by it merely the smoking circle to which they were delightfully addicted, particularly those that took place at night about the fire. I came to see this dhuni or circle as the concentration of mental energy necessary to invoke the Divine, and the fire at the center, agni, as the combustion of knowledge which results from a successful communication. Both as a metaphor and a reality, the dhuni is omnipresent and ongoing, and the *sadhak* or aspirant comes into various recognitions of and participations in it.

Lou Gottlieb much later confided to me of this same scene, "I looked about and Father had drawn a perfect circle about him. I mean in number and persons we represented a perfect cross-section of American culture and its urge to change, moving foetus-like through transition in the re-birth canal. A former Berkeley intellectual like you, ex-radical turned yogi and all that – a debutante in Shotsy, a housewife in Sheila, a Mexican-American, and of course, a black – a middle aged straight like Donovan, and a middle aged kook like me. McCoy is an American evangelist, and Buz a boy scout – even a dropped out marine, O'Shea, imagine – it's too pat and perfect. And, as in any gathering of highly determined spiritual folk, there was, you'd notice, a high incidence of the 'chosen people,' the yehudi nicely represented. I considered myself something of an expert on American forms of spiritual awakening, and he had them all. 'He can't fail,' I thought; by all that's holy, he had us eating out of the palm of his hand." This last was uttered at the time with a slight note of bitterness and a fair share of lamentation.

Lou was saddened by the reflection that some who had been present at that momentous Grand Hotel encounter were no longer with us. Having suffered doubt or other reasons for change of heart – indeed Lou's own course had not been that steady – they had chosen to disassociate themselves. No matter, I now think; that was only a beginning, and it was bound to go through then unforeseeable changes. For me it wouldn't continue to feel right if it didn't. The important thing is not so much the changes but that it go on. In a fall from grace I would hope to find great solace in remembering that it nonetheless goes on, that in some forms somewhere it goes on. The participants vary in *namarupa*, name and form, but the dhuni is eternal.

Jim Shaw had a lot on his mind, indeed too much to sit quietly very long.

"Look, man, I'm thinking of Kaiko," he said to me. "She probably left the Phillipines for Hong Kong by now. I got to get out of here. But I just came from the airline office and you know I don't have enough bread for a plane to Hong Kong. Also you need some damned exit visa or permit and that's gonna cost me bucks, I know. You know what I best do? I think I gotta go out to that airport and break into that hash and start selling the shit right here so I can get some money to get out, but it probably wouldn't bring enough here to make the difference, huh?"

"I can't help you, Jim," was all I could reply.

Jim bounded out the door.

Buz picked up his guitar and started to play. He was striking notes and chords with open tuning, and the resonances he received were uncanny. They filled the room and seemed to usher out any of the commercial or plebian vibrations left about those quarters from any of the doubtlessly many sordid and mundane scenes that had transpired there. Buz's music was transforming the Grand Hotel into a temple, and we listened transfixed and amazed to find ourselves, when the music stopped, gathered about Father in a perfect dhuni formation, attentive to learn why we had been summoned and thus called together from our ancient slumber.

"Now do you see why I have worshipped America?" he began. "I knew you would be the first to come and save me. I appealed to you for that because America gave me my birth. Remember when I met you, Mother?" he asked turning towards Sheila, " . . . and you" to Shotsy. "And I told Anne Parkinson the same

thing. I called you all 'Mother,' and Don I called 'Father' because I looked to America as my parents, and I sought your
protection as such because I am only two and a half years old,
don't you see?

"For forty-five years in this form I worshipped and studied
America...read all your journals, even 'Popular Mechanics,'
saw all your movies. I know you and love you, why? Because
America was able to put any idea into application...and the
world was jealous of them for that. But don't you see that it is
precisely the ability to materialize an imagination that shows
real power? It just must be possessed by a positive imagination...for the sake of the whole creation, isn't it?

"Then too, even before I was awakened, sometime in the
early sixties, maybe sixty-two, I saw...I said 'Mishtu, hey the
American children are all growing long hairs and beards and
they are leaving their families.' I came to see that you were
rejecting everything...why? Children of the atomic apprehension, you were the first to freak out. You hippies, you divine
infants...that's what is 'hippy,' divine infantilism...I love
you! The first to freak out...freaked out by them, now you are
really freaking them out...because you have rejected all that
had come to be the basis for them.

"What a freak-out!" He roared with laughter and slapped his
two hands together. His whole body rose from its half-lotus
asana grounding, rolled around in a convulsion of humor, and
resumed the same postion with Father holding his head in his
hands and still laughing. "Hey Buz," he said, "remember that
picture you drew of me at the Astoria? Do you still have it?"

Buz went amongst his things and easily produced it. On Indian notebook paper and using one of those unreliable
Bharatipur pens, employing many criss-crosses to create a very
dark image, Buz seemed to have captured a figure that combined
all the aspects and modes of wrathful devourings. In position it
seemed a rendering of Kali but its sex was indistinguishable in
the dusk-dim activities of anger.

"Yes, I could look like that," Father said, "but, hey, Buz, no
need. I'm not really going to freak anybody out. Actually, the
world is going to come into this with such a big laugh that we'll

enjoy that laugh for years to come. The laughs we are having now the world will enjoy for years, even many centuries to come.

"Now if I am only two and a half years old, how old can you be? So you were right to call me 'Father' because I was the first to freak out and see, and I have seen what is inevitably to happen and what we must do, and I am Father in that I accept to look after my children, each and every one. Divine infantilism is very good because it is so unattached to everything, but the world truly needs our service and for that it is necessary that we grow up a bit. There are things we must do in our adult forms and for that we must assume an adult intelligence. Remember when you came to our mud hut that first night after we met at the Spritutal Summit Conference, remember that I turned to you and said 'You have come to the hut of the future king of India – India of happiness and love achieved through its own heritage of yoga,' and you Americans, bless you, came out with 'We have come to the king of the planet.' When I accepted, remember that I said 'Since I am a slave of your will, I accept... please remember that SELF RESPECT IS THE WAY TO THE LIFE OF TRUTH, KNOWLEDGE, POWER AND LOVE.' I am a slave of your will. Others seek liberation. I seek enslavement. By truly serving your will to create a world of peace, prosperity and happiness I come into the existence as His will because it is that. The will of Time is to create an evolution of harmony, Śiva Kalpa, and we find true fulfillment and freedom through serving that. So there is much you must know – you must know how this form came to be as it is.

"You must know the story of this body as an individual body because what it underwent is so illuminating. You must know the story of the Zero Hour, the midnight of June 14th-15th, when the form Ciranjiva, when in this form, I died... completely, all the deaths.

"Don't you understand, Lou?" he said turning to Gottlieb who had been nodding his head in heavy assent ever since Father had begun speaking of freak-outs and had carried on this visible agreement into the subject of death. "Understand that this process of immortality which we are undertaking in earnestness... which, believe me, immortality is no longer an abstract aspiration of science nor a vague ancient promise of scripture, but it is a reality. It has already been achieved − in this form. And if your forms are to become immortal, then it is necessary that you witness your own death, many many times.

"Why, now that we understand, do we undertake this process of immortality? Is it not enough to understand? Because to be possessed by such an understanding is to have nothing else to do but to put that understanding into application, and the redemption of a suffering and dying humanity demands that we do it. You all share that aspiration, to redeem a dying world − that you all have in common. In one way or another that led you all to come. So there is a job that we have to do together, and it is such a nice job and we will enjoy it so much that we'll want to stretch out and stretch out the time of our enjoying it... thus, immortality follows as a course. We have really but to listen... and understand that what is happening has already happened. And it is Time's will! But to understand the time is to enjoy the activities that Time produces through you, and to be unconscious or oblivious of it is to suffer the activities that result through Time in you.

"To redeem the world we must preside over this moment in creation. We must see that there is as little as possible suffering... in any of the forms. Mortals must attain happiness, not to mention the gods. I promise you not a single tear in a pair of eyes."

This found a deep response in another part of me to surrender. The "man of sorrows" persona that had guided a good portion of my Indian journey wanted to hear this, needed the promise that the expanded vista of suffering and misery that he had come to witness had reached its limit and that Time's will was toward the reduction and not further multiplication of grief.

"And so we must to make a contact point, must throw ourselves into the activity to show how to enjoy activity − not by attachment to the type of activity or the result of an acitvity but by enjoying the flow of activities that Time chooses to produce in us. What activities we do not enjoy will not stay in the existence, believe me!"

"I see it!" Lou fairly shouted. "Why, it is the old-fashioned but inevitable transference of properties, the material and spiritual dialectic, a question of the haves and have-nots. Suppose we set up a trade between America and India. America gets what it needs, a new way of looking at things, maybe even knowledge, and India gets the matter it so sorely wants. America is over-flowing with goods, so much that it wastes everything. India recycles and uses everything so much that its matter's basically exhausted and useless. Now to do maximum good, the good old U.S. of A. should give away its goods. It's beneficial for its soul to give for once instead of always selling, for we are speaking here of nothing less than the antidote for gluttony. The Americáns can give away their garbage. The hippies need employment, real honest, purposeful, ecologically healthy employment. We'll have them comb the countryside and pick up the aluminum beer cans that are just clutter there and have them recycled, and they wind up over here where the villagers convert them to solar energy machines. Ramon showed me a book where by using a solar energy machine, a simple parabola made of aluminum, say, you can generate enough energy for any household needs. It's a clean and efficient alternative to electricity, oil, and a lot of messy things, but the Americans can't experiment with it because they can't afford not to waste, of course."

"No, Lou, that is not quite right," Father said gently, "though it is true that America's junk can physically save this place, and it will, properly applied. Don't you see, Lou, that it is not America's fault? Rather they have been generous. America has already given India many billions of aid and can you imagine a man like me still starved? So where did it go? Into the cunt of a kankibacha prime minister who is riding a mule of a president . . . but that is nobody's fault. That too is the will of Time. Also, it is not quite right, Lou, because the polarization of matter and spirit has already taken place and has been going on for a long time now so what is needed is not merely an exchange. That alone will not answer or serve. What is needed on all fronts and from all sides is *synthesis*. You have seen one Śiva Kalpa? Well, what is printed there? 'Beginning with the subtlest forms of spiritual and supra-physical existence It is moving through all forms of knowledge including the grossest forms of material pragmatism embracing both *avidya* and *vidya*, ignorance and knowledge in the universal and unanimous synthesis of Matter and Spirit...'" he paused a moment and continued, "'...in the vast comprehensiveness of Its higher order of existence.'

"So you see, it is all expressed already in Śiva Kalpa. You must read Śiva Kalpa...over and over again. It is a distillation of volumes, even libraries of past attempts to express knowledge and truth, and it exceeds them because it is successful. It took a tremendous concentration of Time and Space in this person, a re-union of Communication between the Cosmic I, the Human I, the Collective I of the Period and an individual i to achieve such perfect expression in the I that now speaks to you. For months after the zero hour I wandered through various planes of thought and wrestled with numerous forms and forces of demonic confusion, *rakśasas*, they are powers too, and I was not able to communicate this to the earth plane. I was not able, and the I speaking now is a knowledge, not able to make contact with the human sphere, not until September 19th, 1966, from which we now date the commencement of Śiva Kalpa."

"September '66," Lou mused. "That would be the same period of time when a vision of the Mother descended upon Morningstar. That began our era of revelation there."

"Hey, I just remembered," John whispered to me. "Remember that acid trip I told you about, the one where I picked up the magic wand? Well, now that I think of it, that was early summer '66, maybe June 14th. I'll bet I was tripping on September 19th too."

"That's when my brother Rich arrived in India, June '66. I'll just bet it was the 14th," I said, trying for the life of me to recall what I might have been doing mid-September two years before.

Jim Shaw reentered just in the wake of these personal associations and correspondences, bubbles of private verifications in the voyage and process of our absorption of His-story. He was huffing and winded, a definite messenger from another energy system, tired and a bit battered from errands in a world less than mental. While we were coursing easily about the cosmos, Jim had had great difficulty going a few blocks in Calcutta – trying to get out. It seemed impossible, and he was momentarily irritable.

The rest of us had shifted a bit, stretched, some were pacing about. Sheila probably, and Shotsy, never one to sit still too long, certainly were in motion, taking a physical "breather" from the static intensity of our last round in the dhuni. Something in the way Shotsy carried herself touched off a spark of latent hostility in Jim. Perhaps it was that no matter how wired or wrought Shotsy might become in dealing with the energy and circumstances of our common present, a deep-rooted air of superiority, some successful sense of breeding would never permit that she become distressed, would never succumb to that apprehensive impotence that had gotten hold of Jim. Maybe her self-absorption registered upon Jim as indifference to his plight, which had become his point of sensitive focus. Whatever it might have been, the result was an unexpressed, but nonetheless, observed and operational psychic assault upon her from Jim. To John O'Shea, what he witnessed was definitely a moment of unresolved tension from some past life association between them.

"Did you see that?" he asked me and then interpreted: "The heavy disagreement that caused that little action probably has its roots back on the plantation. Did you see how it came over them and kind of took them both by surprise?"

That struck me as a bit too cliché to be the literal explanation, but definitely the exchange displayed something of that unoriginal resentment of the dusky and the insecure for the light and assured. Jim himself could not be sure what it was – he just had no power to initiate or check it. Some power there was, however, to protect Shotsy or Miss Charlotte from it. It was quelled with a glance from her eyes, a quick glance that hardly deigned to recognize the disturbance yet was sufficient to overpower it. The hostility receded, hopefully expired and transcended itself through some adequate glorification, but it was all too subtle and immaterial to be certain. I suppose it retains itself in my witnessing memory by its significance as an early example of the divine powers of gods and goddesses, appealed to and invoked by Father, powers actually beginning to reside, play, and protect themselves in our forms.

"What is it you want?" Father asked Jim as the energy began to concentrate itself again in dhuni fashion. "No, I mean it simply," he went on after an uncomfortable silence. "You can tell me. What is troubling you?"

"Well," Jim started, swallowing hard, "Father...it's my wife. I left her in the Philippines. I should meet her in Hong Kong. I got involved in this...well, anyway, I can't get there, and she's pregnant. I haven't the money to get there..." He almost said "Sir," it seemed to me, but turned it into a trailing off "Fath...ah."

Father's eyes were closed a moment in brief, but one felt complete, consideration and absorption of Jim's situation. "Well, just sit down for a moment," Father went on. "Running around in every direction will not get you anywhere.

"The thing is this...Nobody really knows what he wants, or rather he wants different things at different times. He wills one thing to begin with and then before that will, which is actually an action loosed from the mental and vital worlds upon his physical circumstances, has a chance to enact itself, he contradicts it by willing something quite different in another desire moment, and so it goes on accumulating until a man is so caught up in the network and web of the contradictory desires that he has willed that none of them can possibly materialize to any degree of satisfaction, and the man becomes convinced that he is impotent to effectuate anything. Isn't that the lot of the modern world?

"You have to will one thing only and hold that will against the arguments and objections of a weakening skepticism. If you can do that, you will see that the world is moving in a way to enact your will. But you by then understand that the true will, the rit chit, the Truth Consciousness, the Real Idea of existence, has already been willed and is in operation creating the circumstances and has just been awaiting your awakening to realize that, so, of course, you do not will anything which contradicts that because by the perfection of your own nature you are becoming one with that will...and it is His Will, the will of time, My Will!...and remember again, I am not only this form that is addressing you.

"We do not want to plunge the world into a further broil of contradictory ineffectual wills, not to multiply and further divide into contradiction and limitation but to bring to a happy conclusion and resolution the unfulfilled moments, the undelivered promises, the unanswered prayers. So it is best we will one thing: the peace, prosperity, and happiness of everyone. And it has already been willed, in a way so unique and resourceful, so pleasant and delightful that it will surprise and captivate all of you in the eloquent simplicity of its natural unfolding . . . and we have nothing to do really but understand and enjoy it. If you can, I promise you that every day will be better than the one before . . . 'breaking joyously,'" he began to rock, "'into the rhythm of greater and higher waves of illumination, intensifying towards the growing light of a self-existent Knowledge spontaneously awakening to Itself as the Sun of Truth, receiving the world from the murky depth of an obscure physical bondage into the enlightened height of spiritual freedom by the transforming radiation 'of ITS *jyoti*,' glorious Arc-Light. Bom Shankar Bholenath!! All Śiva Kalpa again, you see. The will and imagination joined, the Self-Conscious Will of *purusha*,[1] the man of Omnipotent Imagination . . . Such a will and such an imagination and such a power and *lila*[2] that the understanding and aprreciation of it and thus the self-conscious participation in it can only be developed and stabilized in forms of love – true lovers of humanity and life. And for each share and portion of power your capacity to love is tested in truth and expanded by grace. Since you are already creatures of love, you can do as you like. I don't and never will say 'Do this' or 'Do that.' Do as you like, but don't oppress anyone . . . that would only result in your own circumstances becoming oppressive, almost immediately. The world does not need to be oppressed any more. It is not for that but rather for service to the world, a service of love, that gods and goddesses, kings and queens, and all forms of greatness are being

[1]The Self, The Consciousness, The Cognizer, The Soul – its counterpart in the essential duality is prakṛiti, Nature.

[2]the game; the play of It all.

awakened.

"Remember when you are tempted into rancour and resentment in encounters with the still recalcitrant forms of ignorance, remember that they too are Me and that they too enact My will, and love them for the role they play and the glorious role they afford you. When I tell you these things like 'do not judge,' 'don't oppress anyone,' I am not giving you a new set of commandments. Hey, you Moses!!!!" Father laughed and slapped Lou's knee. "You got into such contradiction over ten 'do this' and 'do not's' that to resolve them they multiplied into billions of 'do's and don'ts,' so many that no one of them stood any chance of not being contradicted by some thousands of the others. What a scramble! I am not here to give laws or teach anybody. My friends can observe and learn through the practice and fulfillment of their own nature the easiest way to evolution.

"There is no need for rules and laws, no special diets to become points of contention later, no tiresome asanas to maintain your consciousness. Consciousness will maintain itself and expand itself in forms of love. Our understanding and love of the creation together will assure our agreement. That is only self-respect, respecting the Self in each other. That is inevitable and natural at this level of communication because 'Mental Being is Self Consciousness, Self Consciousness is Self Respect and SELF RESPECT IS THE WAY TO THE LIFE OF TRUTH, KNOWLEDGE, POWER, AND LOVE.'"

Father paused a moment, a moment which expressed itself in me as a chance to come back into a more transient and immediate person, and I noticed that at some time during the recent revelation Jim Shaw had again exited. This time he had done it with uncustomary invisibility.

"How fortunate we are," Father continued, "to be alert and witness to this particular change and play in consciousness. Śiva Kalpa, I tell you, will become the fullest expression yet imaginable within His omnipotent dreaming. All the ages hitherto coiled and released within the infinite spiral of His imagination in time were but a preparation for the great moment which begins and is Now. Prior to this, consciousness struggling to awaken experienced itself but in a solitary moment, incommunicable in the frustration of so enormous a gap between knowledge and ignorance. But now there are many emerging from Maya's delusive sleep, and we will enjoy the expression together. Within this first wave of awakening there will be 108 gods and goddesses appreciating and thereby creating the play. We are the *prathama brahmaṇa*, the first knowers of Śiva's Becoming. Awakened by His Nature," (here Father gave a loving and grateful look to the three goddesses present, in particular Shotsy) "He can now enjoy the activities of His willing prakṛiti, Nature, to further divide in joyous play this moment of understanding and the illumination of his essentially indivisible *virya* or spirit. You see, I but paraphrase and reexplain Śiva Kalpa. It says it in the Śiva Kalpa document under 'Perfection.'

"That is ... Time will awaken the Self in all of us to the same realization that it is My play, and with that we will begin to enjoy the existence. But we cannot awaken all at once, overnight, because then there would be just one big flash that would consume all of time and Time would cease to exist. So the play and game is controlled by Time extending Itself through different forms in different moments of realization and recognition, and we wake up in successive moments in time and enjoy our awakening and the awakening of others together. For this Time must prepare Itself in each form for the awakening of knowledge, and it has prepared itself in your forms mostly through a seeking to overcome the contradictions that plunged you into such a misery – from which you saw no escape – the apprehension of 'the world running headlong towards its inevitable cataclysm,' the atomic-intellectual world of death-dealing ego. All of your leaders and teachers further freaked you out with their compromises with this downward trend in the course of things. So that idealistic spark of greatness within each of you would not succumb, and rather than compromise with their vision of the world, you left to seek a new and greater world or die in the process. I understand! What is death? To a man of honor death would be welcome if he could not live in this world without denying Truth. I felt the same way in this darkening India. 'My God,' I thought, 'if a man cannot live in Truth, I'd rather embrace death. Mother, make me a leper,' I prayed, 'but give me truthful fulfillment.' And so this sense of Being, the *satyam* and *śivam*, what your English Bible refers to as the 'I am,' was prepared to be awakened in you, and through this supra-mental preparation you became capable of receiving the form of supra-mental knowledge which now addresses you . . . and will continue to address you into the *sundaram*[3] of a greater, more comprehensible, and ultimately omnipotent future.

"Not everyone, however, has been prepared to the same degree, and you must be merciful upon them for that. You cannot force your consciousness upon anyone who is unprepared. You must always start within the limits of what is already known by those with whom you are dealing – so I am doing that with you – and gradually, gently, lovingly, you bring them beyond the bounds of their present limitations. And then," he laughed, "you can cut out from beneath them the ground they formerly stood upon and which anchored and held them to a limited form of comprehension . . . that is only if they are forms to be awakened. Not all forms can be awakened within this moment of time. Some will live out a mortal existence, but even that existence will be infinitely happier than they presently dare to dream or hope. That is God's promise to all men for all time . . . because it is the human plane in the mortal moment of cognition which is capable of recognizing Itself as supra-human and immortal. The 'I am' of which we spoke belongs uniquely to the human sphere and comes out of the increasing contradictions inherent in the human condition.

"Do not feel superior to other forms of Being. They are already conscious. They have always been conscious and awaiting man to recognize his role. The cow, the tiger, the worm, the maggot, all, all are infinitely and totally conscious. There is no contradiction in their lives, but there is not much chance for the expansion of existence in them either. That is why through infinite-seeming lifetimes consciousness moves through forms

[3]Satyam, Śivam, Sundaram (सत्यम् शिवम् सुन्दरम् ) – the triune perception that underlies the explanation of time and the creation as set forward in Śiva Kalpa. Satyam – Truth; Śivam – Consciousness; Sundaram – Beauty of the harmonious existence.

aspiring to birth in the human plane of existence... so it can experience those contradictions which will become the occasion of awakening.

"So you must appreciate the struggle and be thankful to all of those things which placed you in the series of contradictions that triggered your own awakening. Worship your parents, honor your teachers and former leaders – no rancour against any of them – but at the same time do not be limited by any of them. You are the means of their salvation. You are the future they projected, even though they themselves denied it. Be limited by no one nor no thing, be bound by no consequence; at the same time, revere all distinctions and fulfill all relationships. That will require hardly anything from the infinite capacity that you shall be developing.

"So you see, it is not a scientific rationalsim, nor the dead intellectual existentialism of someone like Jean-Paul Sartre," he said imitating a heavy French accent. "Though Jean-Paul Sartre said one thing that is very good. He said 'Words are actions provided they are arranged with a definite plan for change.' That is true. That's how my words are arranged, and that plan for change is already in action in this world. You have only to understand the words that express it. Nor are we merely the emasculated spiritualism that has paraded itself as religion in the past. Do you know what really is 'religion'? Re-lig-ion, to tie again – it should maintain the thread which connects us with the Creator and shouldn't be a ligature to society or business. Do not constrict yourself by thinking either I or you fall within the purview of what we have already seen... either in the recent or distant past. We must be malleable and sensitive to serve a future which is ever new and expanding, increasing in spontaneity. We cannot limit that future by reacting with the repetitions and inertias of what is already known and therefore exceeded.

"You'll understand this more easily when you come to know and understand Vishnu, my grandson. He is one year old now. I have been listening to him since before his birth. To prepare the world for the future he is dreaming, I have come to destroy the ignorance and thereby create the basis for knowledge – creative destruction, that is *pralaya*."

This Sanskrit touched off the antique but comfortable role in Lou of the precocious student, anxious to play himself off against the teacher. "Father," Lou interjected, "isn't it true that within this present age of awakening there have been many forms of knowledge suddenly appearing to prepare the recipient audience, mankind, for the advent of the Divine? Aurobindo's 'descent of the supra-mental power,' what we in show business so lightly and perhaps unappreciatively call 'warm-up acts' –by which I mean that there are many masters and meanings that have begun to express themselves to our consciousness, at least, let us know they are there, as it were. What do you think, for instance, of the Maharishi and his methods?"

Lou, to begin with . . ." – there was a touch of piquant irascibility in his voice. Witnessing this, I lapsed into the judgment that Father was displaying anger, and I wondered if he had not exaggerated how much he was above such petty emotions. ". . . to begin with, one of the most important differences between ignorance and knowledge is that knowledge reveals, ignorance seeks. And knowledge does not always reveal itself to the seeking nature of ignorance. Ignorance in order to transform itself must be able to hear the self-revelation and self-communication of knowledge. Why do you begin by limiting me to what you already know? Haven't I said that what we are to see will so far exceed what has already come that it will stagger imagination? Why do you start with comparisons to such puny forms as the Maharishi or talk about those who are not present here, those whom you only know via media? Media is only one degree above the merely informational level that has driven you all crazy.

"If I thunder upon Nixon, or Golda Meier, or Indira Ghandi, or Chairman Mao, or any of the so-called leaders of this modern world, you will applaud. But if I say anything negative about the equally pernicious and limiting spiritual leaders, who, dressed in robes of ridiculous pomp, are bound as much by their chair of office as any politician, equally incapacious of learning anything new or true . . . if I thunder on these saffron-clothed monkeys, then you will think I am 'jealous' or 'envious.' Don't you see that these fools need their heads cut off before we should even touch the politicians? Didn't you see at the so-called Spiritual Summit Conference that they could not reach agreement, that none of those great men of the world's religions could reach agreement? The best they could do was pray for time – that prayer was heard, I can assure you. Other than that they could only speculate how to spend money – six million dollars for an inter-faith monument in Washington! As if the world needed more monuments or temples. There are so many already and what good has it done? Six years ago world scientists similarly gathered at the U.N., and the only thing they could agree upon was that at the present rate of consumption, reproduction, and pollution, the planet earth could not maintain a human population for more than five to twenty years maximum. They said they would reconvene in a year to suggest solutions. They have never met since . . . and your press is silent about this. So is the Church, to begin with. It is those who are in lip service to God who hold the world in its contemporary form of thralldom, much more than the politicians. First it is the gurus, and the priests, and Popes who must change themselves, then the academicians and scientists who pervert knowledge, and finally, the politicians who corrupt the physical existence only."

Lou apparently wasn't satisfied with this. "Ah-ha," he said "just as I'd imagined! It was the same with the musicologists in my university days, as they say, and it was the same with the stars and prima donnas when I hit show business. No one likes to acknowledge a competitor. All the holy men of today, I notice, are high and tranquil upon all subjects except one – other holy men."

To tell you the truth I have always been grateful to Lou for raising this objection because if I am honest with myself I must confess that something of the same reservation resided in me, only I hadn't the nerve or power to verbalize it within Father's presence. I am glad, therefore, that Lou so early brought it to a head because this very confusion has become a troublesome stumbling block to many. The difference between the relative and the absolute must constantly be considered and absorbed, the relative in one's self exceeded through surrender to the absolute.

"Please, Lou," Father began again, more consolingly, "I'll make you a promise, but in order for me to fulfill the promise, I must be given absolute freedom . . . to serve you. Don't limit me, please, by what you already know or think. Do not think that I am merely this form that addresses you, nor the personality through which it takes expression. I am not a person still envious or in competition with anything else in this world. There is nothing any longer for me to attain or realize, no benefit for myself can come from any activity or interplay with this world. As a person, I died. I maintain this form only as a service to Knowledge, and through it Knowledge expresses Itself to you. Now I know what I am doing in every single form alive to the existence at this time. I know what I am doing in a form like the Maharishi as well as I know what I am doing in the form that now addresses you. I know the limitations that still bind other forms, and I know the manner in which I have liberated this form from such limitations. Therefore, if you listen with the true inner ear of consciousness, you will understand, and that understanding will bring about the same power in you. But if you immediately limit and judge, if you are thinking while I am revealing why it is that I reveal what I do, if you weigh it in terms of motive or consider it due to any condition or circumstance, petty or grand, on my part, then you are limiting the whole vision its power to express in you . . . it will go on anyhow, but your own understanding of it will be limited.

"Do you begin to comprehend? I know it will take time, and it will be natural in you when it finally comes – not all at once does each petal of the lotus of understanding open. We are going to enjoy each other's company for a long time to come. Let's not start it off by fighting and judging. All right?"

In writing now of our early encounters with Father, I am trying to preserve the integrity of the growing awareness of his power as it developed in us. Yet, I do not pretend that I am uninfluenced by the years of listening and association I have enjoyed since then. Indeed, I could not hope to recreate Father's speech patterns, mush less the content, if it were not for the accumulated experiences of the following years. I took no notes at the time of which I am writing. In fact, my efforts at keeping a journal of my Indian travels broke down just at the time I first met Father. Things started happening too fast to keep up with and seemed to take place in a mental sphere of change to which literary musings and reflections were just inappropriate.

There is one thing which I did not know then but have subsequently learned through observation and wish to point out now lest a reader sense something artificial in the construction of these verbal sessions which I am here referring to as "revelations." When this mood or trance was upon Father, which was and is virtually a constant, particularly during such a period of stimulation when Father was suddenly blessed with so many ready and willing ears to receive his knowledge, he did much more than just talk. He seemed to control the very atmosphere and our responses as well. Thus, it seemed that he orchestrated the entire session. Seldom was a revelation broken by an untimely interruption, and upon those few occasions when it was, retrospect would later illuminate that he engineered those seeming intrusions to further elucidate by irony or example the very things he was revealing. Father would build in his speech, and he could hold us motionless for hours (I remember one session of uninterrupted and non-stop revelation that went on for seventy-two consecutive hours during which we would listen to him in shifts), and when he would come to appropriate moments of pause, often punctuatd by a rhetorical question or with an "isn't it?" or an "all right?" as above, it often heralded a change of energy that would break the static intensity of revealed knowledge with a flurry of physical activity.

The pause we are now considering brought about the reappearance of Jim Shaw. He was wildly excited and anxious to communicate something to us. At the same time Lou Gottlieb dove somewhat frantically amongst his things and started pulling stuff out of a valise in search of something.

"You won't believe what just happened to me, boys and girls, brothers and sisters," Jim began. "The gist of it is I'm on my way to Hong Kong and that's for sure. Yes sir, I went back to that same airline office, got the same dude who gave me such a hard time before, only this time he seems to be winking at me behind those dark glasses. I mean either he was confused, bug-a-booed somehow, or he was just plain set on helping me out. He issues me the damned ticket, and I swear to you I am at least five hundred rupees short in cash to pay for it. Brother, he hands me some change! Next, he waives the exit visa requirement seeing as how I'd only been here less than a month. But he never mentioned that before. And he asks me if I need any vaccinations fixed up upon my health card. Can you dig it?"

We all smiled, most of all Father as he rose to his feet.

"Bhagawan," Lou said, "I'd like you to accept this." He offered something woolen that looked like a red and black serape.

"Please don't call me 'Bhagawan' if you are only going to judge and limit me. I don't need your accolades, Lou, only your understanding."

"Take it as a peace offering then and a genuine act of my contrition," Lou, never at a loss for words, countered. Father turned the object in his hands, trying to figure out just what sort

*His demeanor changed entirely, and his right arm shot directly into the air. "La cucaracha," he shouted.*

of garment or blanket it might be. Unfolding it revealed a vertical split in the center, and it became obvious that it was not a serape but a poncho. Father slipped it over his head. He stood still a moment, absorbing the feeling of it, and then he suddenly burst into action. His demeanor changed entirely, and his right arm shot directly into the air. "La cucaracha," he shouted.

We all laughed hysterically at Father's ability to instantly change himself. In mannerism and look he became the cliché stereotypic image of the Mexican. I realized that he could assimilate himself into any culture easily. Perhaps it was that I was howling at this more than the others that caused Father to turn towards me, or, more likely, knowing everything else, he knew without being told that I was the film fanatic amongst us.

"Have you seen," he asked me, "Wallace Beery as Pancho Villa? I loved him a lot. 'Give me all your money,'" he said in a first-rate imitation of Beery, "'or I'll blow this train sky-high.' How I loved that! The daring, you know. That's greatness, when one man is not afraid to face an army. My own family was like that, but that was some time back – before they lost everything, including their valour. Pancho Villa, I loved him! My nickname is Panchu, you know. Still my old friends, the ones that are not afraid to talk to me, call me 'Panchu-da.'

"Isn't it fascinating," Father began again in a tone of voice which, though casual, commanded full attention, and so the dhuni formed again to receive another revelation of Knowledge. "Isn't it fascinating how easy it is to see that even in the ignorance and throughout the mortal measure of our lives there are so many hints and clues to our divine destiny and immortal becomings? 'Guided in darkness, now in light...' Our name, given in the mundane world, can reveal the seed of our inspired flowering. My name, for instance, 'Ciranjiva' reveals my ma's intuitive hope or prayer for her son. It means 'eternal portion' – 'ciran,' that which is eternal, and 'jiva,' that portion of the Atman or world soul which incarnates as the soul or living entity in the individual. It is also one of the many names for Śiva, Ciranjiva, a very powerful form of the name and far less common in application than Śankara or Rudra. So also my nick-name has reference to Śiva. Panchu, panchu-da, from panch meaning 'five,' of course – panchagaota, panchagushaha, so many adjectives applied to Śiva employ the number five: Śiva as yogi is He who has overcome the five senses; Śiva as dispenser of boons to mankind is He who has provided the five elemental conditions of perception. Of course, the five elements and what you term the five senses are directly linked, intertwined causally and interdependent. *Akasha*, ether or space, provides the condition for hearing. Air, Vayu's element, permits the sense of touch. From Agni, the divine inner fire, sight is born. Liquid lends the taste or *rasa* to life, and smell emanates from the earth element or *bhur* plane of perceptual existence.

"This is pure veda, pure gita, and pure truth I am telling you now. Those are the forms of my lower existence, the *apara prakriti*, and above them are the three cognitive faculties and so it is said that there are eight natures to God and His play with the creation, and how He cognizes Himself in His creation.

There is *manas*, mind, and *buddhi*, the intelligence which is more properly intuition than intellect, and finally, *ahamkara*, the self-sense or that which perpetuates a sense of individual identity, what western psychology inadequately deals with as ego. Ego is a small part of it, that which allows activity or work, *karma*, to come through it and is also that part which involves into the delusion of thinking it is the cause of activity, the doer of the action. But God is that too. The creation is not complete without all of its parts. You see, all of our thought and speech is divided first into the essential duality which makes perception possible: the witnessing subjectivity, that is, the cognitive faculties of mind, intelligence and ego, and the acting objectivity, nature or the apara prakriti, what in elementary grammar is called a predicate. Nature acts and is the object of action, and consciousness, the purusha, witnesses and is the subject. It is so simple how I project Myself into every form and activity in the existence! Substance and process are both Me! There are four degrees to this self-cognition in nature. The first, and that most occult to knowledge itself, is when there is no division between the subject and object and the subject and object are one by identity. And the second..."

We sat rapt in breathless awe, and our minds merged in an ease of comprehension as Father took us through the ages and levels of self-identity. The object and subject divided but had direct contact and knowledge of each other, then dividing into further distance a medium became employed through which the one learned of the other, and then through mass multiplication a condition and world came about where there was no direct knowledge and so much media that mere information alone was possible. And Father went on revealing in a manner that was not solely cerebral but moved with such vital intensity into a concrete and tangible-seeming physicality that we all felt the knowledge to be our very own, in truth simple and self-evident. Several times Lou Gottlieb spontaneously broke out with ecstatic acclaim and what for him was an expression of ultimate surrender. "At last," he shouted, "I have found someone smarter than I! I'm so tired of hearing myself speak. Smarter than I, tell me something!"

We were still just in the beginning of our relationship with Father, and not all of the implications were clear. One thing had certainly advanced over my two other moments of priviledged recipiency to the Knowledge. I now very definitely felt a spiritual camaraderie and divine kinship with all the others who were in that room. It seemed to me that we were all the most fortunate and also deserving of souls, mahatmas, not merely survivors but those who prevailed through the struggles of seeking and now were receiving our just deserts. More and more as the revelations went on, it felt that we were not only the blessed ears of reception but also creators in our own rights; subtly, without knowing when or how it began, it seemed that we were in the midst of a great scheme that had been brewing since time immemorial, and in moments we moved from total unawareness of it to the illusion that we had always been conscious of this divine plan and so each of us felt the drama to be our own. Fulfillment, individual and collective, hovered over this congregation like a resplendent rainbow.

Sometime during the rest of that afternoon, Jim Shaw made a more or less graceful and definitely happy exit. I did not see him again for four months. And now, taking on a life of its own, regardless of individual comings and goings, the revelation rolled on as the evening gathered slowly without, but time within that room stood still.

We are indebted to Donovan Bess for the first actual recording of Father in revelation. Sometime during the later part of the day he surreptitiously filled a half-hour cassette. I did not know it at the time and only discovered the tape much later. There is ample evidence on the tape that it belongs to that day's proceedings. I choose to incorporate a transcript of it here so that the reader may have a more direct experience of Father revealing, and, free for a moment from dependence upon my powers of recall and re-creative abilities, may soar above the third-level, medium-relayed knowledge of Father, a mere reflection, no matter how inspired.

"...Nature which has spiritual contradictions – these spiritual contradictions are a necessity for spiritual existence of creation. Without contradiction there is no creation. Material contradiction in its last stage gets into infinite contradictions, contradictions becoming harder and harder every day to put up with so that through these contradictions you divide the time into mere fragments of existence. Look here, the past moment is the father to the present moment of contradiction. Now we are in a moment of synthesis. Now we are seeking synthesis, and we are making synthesis on all sides, in everything...something is coming up as resistances. When we touch the resistance it transforms itself into an active support. But if everything becomes active support and unified just like one, it becomes a picture, static, just as the cosmos is static. It is retaining its form according to the terrestrial time of creation as imagined by the material scientists and astronomers as only 12,000 crores of years – one crore means 10 millions and it is only 12,000 crores of years – and the birth of the solar system is only 4,000 crores of years, and it is only 3,500 crores of years the birth of earth. But it has suddenly taken its birth from a great explosion of matter, that is the big bang theory of existence.

"Now, this is the scientific idea of the world today. The world today is a world of science...only science has given us so many

bad things, but it has given only one good thing. It's the austerity of thought, a certain process of logic – we might call it
'ratiocination,' isn't it? A certain process of logic – it's an austerity of thought. It doesn't submit itself to the desire of an
individual. It doesn't submit itself to the preference of an individual. It compels every individual who goes through the
process of a scientific thought. 'E is equal to MC square' is the
conclusion of a certain thought process which manifested itself
through Einstein and is retained in calligraph . . . not by the
production of another Einstein.

"Now, what happens . . . so, we begin with that scientific rationalsim. There is no scope for individual preference. It is
compelled on a modern man. You needn't compel the Indians
– if you can compel the topmost ten, the world moves according
to that. Let us not put an already contradictory world into more
contradictions between leaders and their followers. We compel
the leaders to follow our order, order of knowledge. If they refuse
to obey, they only find their own exit. This process is the nicest
process, the most . . . the simplest, easiest, and perfect which
knows no failure. Failure is created by a limitation of knowledge
which moves through contradiction. Here there is no contradiction so far as the physical world is concerned. But when we
overcome the physical contradictions of the physical existence,
we begin with the contradictions of Consciousness, pure conscious stuff. They are all luminous bodies, astral bodies . . . and
we can kill there, kill ourselves a million times without losing
ourselves, our own identity. We have to take it, you know. That
I have suggested. Lou, didn't I tell you so? That we shall have to
accept a death for a few seconds and that is a physical death as
well. You will go into oblivion and feel a sense which is more
akin to the actions of LSD. But it differs from LSD in that you
suddenly get a sort of living without weight for some time, that's
all. But you get a great shock, a shock which in the medical
expression is called a cerebral shock. I had to go through various
cerebral shocks. I lost a few of my arteries in the brain. I was
dead for some time, and I was perspiring like anything . . . in a
bus, and a man who was accompanying me, a relation of mine,
was in good dresses . . . Since I was perspiring . . . well, I was

oozing...I was...so he didn't hold me. So I saw that my body was falling on this side and that side. The pain ceased, and I found that somebody else is suffering from a terrible pain in the heart and the head. And he's losing sense. But I kept the sense in the body, and the natural activity of life revived the body. If you take out my heart, even then I will go on living and talking. If you put a few hundred bullets, even then I'll go on talking. It's very easy. And the wounds will heal themselves very quickly. It's easy. You can put the Himalayas into the Indian Ocean, and send the Indian Ocean washing the whole land to the other side of the Himalayas to the Gobi Desert. But you must permit some time for this to happen through a logical process of...well, ahh...geographical reactions. But if you want it to happen immediately, the time ceases to exist. If you move very fast, the time ceases to exist. Einstein said this in a material way – anything acquiring the velocity of light will turn itself into light. But you see Einstein's contradiction. You just listen:

"I don't say do this or don't do that. Whatever you like, that will be good. Beer cans, very nice! No beer cans, very nice! What will happen you can not precipitate. It will be precipitated by the will of the time. If it is necessary, it will take shape. You have to think about it, that's all. I'll tell you how to make the world move by sitting here. Then you throw yourself into the current. Why? Because to let people know you are doing it. Because you need fame. Why? So you can teach better, so that everybody listens to you. What they have to do? Not to act, but to listen. Without listening nothing will take place. But if they refuse to listen physically, we have a supra-physical method of making them listen to our will. That's what I am going to tell you. That's what is taking place now. You have to understand – it is Me, not you. The moment you understand that, that is surrender.

"Now, I'll tell you what happened on the eventful night of 14th and 15th, June, 1966. Well, I surrendered myself completely to the will of God, without making any judgment for anything. Who kicked me, I said you are doing the right thing. Who loved me, I said you are doing the right thing. So I said everything is being done by His will, which I don't know. If I will something and if it doesn't happen, I get hurt. But if somebody cuts off my ear I say you have done His will. I surrendered myself as such. And what happened? My wife left with the younger children and my eldest daughter was there. She was not married at that time, and my mother was in Calcutta – so we were two. We were sitting, we were sleeping in the two rooms. Well, it was during the night . . . I was meditating. I used to do a lot of meditating. I was always in meditation. I used to be. Now I never get into meditation. Meditation takes hold of me sometimes. And when meditation takes hold of me and gets me into a trance, you have a certain feeling. You must have. Now, I try to come back from that height. There is a height from where it is difficult to communicate. I must make the body go on. I am trying to show you that a full light makes the body cease to exist. So we have to live for another thousands of years in the creation of knowledge, so we are going to . . . If, say, actually 3,500 million people die of starvation, what does it matter? Nobody dies, just as nobody is born. Well, they haven't had any knowledge, so they left their body. Well, anyway, if they haven't any knowledge, but if they want to change the world, then, even then, they'll get old and have to shake this body. And whenever you shed this body, you become one with the existence. But you retain your individuality. Why? Because you have to gain knowledge in body, not in a supra-physical existence. Suppose you die. You become one with the whole existence, but even then since you have assumed an identity, even then you live in the astral body. You maintain your identity, but you are conscious that you are everything. Even then you maintain your identity, just as Ciranjiva is doing that. Ciranjiva doesn't think he is other than Don or Lou or Sheila or Shotsy or an ant or a maggot. They are all equal to Him because it is He who has placed Himself in so many forms and so many natures."

Lou: "Who is this?"

Father: "This is existence. Because existence is one and indivisible. So when you see division, it's existence which looks at itself in so many ways . . . and forgets that he is the Creator. For this oblivion an ignorance is necessary. And existence being Almighty, He can forget Himself in so many forms. You retain your physical form only by a tremendous will of ignorance. So ignorance is not a bad thing. Ignorance is a necessity. So we see the end of ignorance. We have created the bodies. We have multiplied. See, one existence has multiplied itself into so many bodies and forms. Now these bodies and forms will understand we are one existence. So all the bodies are actually effectuating the initial will of creation. You cannot change the will. Neither can Ciranjiva. And that will is manifested in the moments of fleeting time. Look here: We and the universe is a movement in which all the successions of moments . . . the past is progressing and increasing by the inclusion of all the successions of moments into a present which is very much elusive. You cannot look at the present, which is at the same time the beginning of all the moments of the future. So seed and tree are your own imagination and ignorance of your own movement, but the whole cycle makes you think it's a static sort of evolution. Nothing exists.

"Look what Śankaracarya says:

> asta kulacala sapta samudrāh
> brahma purandara dinkara rudrah
> na tvam naham nayam lokah
> stadapi kimartham kryate sokah
>> bhaja govindam
>> bhaja govindam
>> bhaja govindam
>>> mudhamate

It means that neither you exist nor I exist nor anything exists. It is only an imagination which has materialized itself in one body and is thinking that all these are bodies. But he has forgotten that it was a moment, it was a moment of his will or a will of his moment, which is effectuating itself in a process which we call time. So let us not stop time by reaching the end all of a sudden. I have reached that end. It will take millions of years for you to reach that end. So whatever you will, I'll do that. Beer cans, all right. Why not? So anything you do will be good for the world since you love humanity. No other law is a necessity.

"Look here: I'll tell you what happened on the 14th and 15th night. That's the most important part of the thing. You'll immediately begin to understand what happened and how you were informed across the oceans.

"Śri Aurobindo says submit yourself to the will of Mother. Who is Mother? Aurobindo could not explain because it's a self-communication. God was so long ineffable, inexplicable, unseizable by thought and incommunicable by speech. Why? His will. He hid Himself under so many veils of ignorance. As the veils were increased the opacity also increased 'til it became absolutely gross and dark. Because no matter exists – it's the self-cognition of conscious existence which divides its knowledge into so many forms. Now this realization will come a little later. What happened, how I got into this realization?

"Well... A man must become a person without any desire. Any preference, either for murder or for rape or for a kiss or for charity, they are both my desire. Then how this bestial world is going to be turned into a world of love and understanding? Well, let us understand that first it is the primary necessity that it is God's will which makes a Ramakrishna, a yogi like Ciranjiva, and a pickpocket who is standing on the street. No difference, actually, you have to understand that it's His will, and you are nobody to judge it. Unless you are the Creator. But you are the Creator, the self-oblivious creator. Therefore you are apt to judge the Creator Himself... being a created stuff... in your oblivion. Now this self-communication is called yoga, not to become numb in body. I have given you a body to enjoy it, not to suffer its existence. But I made you suffer this existence because I have to multiply Myself. This multiplication was done in ignorance by sheer animal instincts, and everything you have built you have built... Have you gone through Frank Harris, an American writer? Well, he used to write pornography and a great writer too. In pornography there is art. There is understanding, and it is a confession, and he was also jailed perhaps. He was an editor of a big American magazine. He was just thrown out for his ideas. He said now... D. H. Lawrence, he's very pornographic, but he's put a flavor in pornography. Pornography is nothing but your judgment. It differs from man to man.

"I might cover the world in darkness yet retain my spiritualism and show you that you have to bow down to even a lower form of spiritual awakening... Preparing an ignorant world, multiplying myself through ignorance... We don't possess bodies. Nothing exists. Now if we reach that point very quickly, the world ceases to exist because in reality nothing exists. It's a tremendous will which holds all these forms in existence. Only you have to remember that we are that.

"But before we reach... well, all activities are prompted by the status of knowledge. You cannot will anything that is beyond your knowledge, so you begin to will as soon as you get a little knowledge. That's what Mahesh Yogi did, and before he perfected himself, he wished something. It happened to a certain extent but not fully. So the world was still going the wrong way about, the way toward hatred and misunderstanding. We have to bring it back. The easiest way is to listen to the plan I am going to tell you and understand what I am going to tell you, but physically, wherever you want to take me, you take me. But I tell you I don't need any material method... medium. I can present myself throughout the whole world at the same time and speak the same thing from everywhere. And I can get myself photographed... physically, and get the photographs all sent and create a row and that will make the time move so fast that in a few months we can come to the end of existence. We shall have to create again. Why take all these troubles?"

Lou: "Actually, the photographs have already been taken."

Father: "No, I never say that. I can appear in many places at the same time and talk, and I get my photographs taken, that is in the future. You know I have only to will it, but I never will it. Why? Because if I will it, it will happen. And no sooner it happens, the world ceases to exist. Because everyone is not prepared like you, so you are not taking pity on the others. You are becoming rude for the others. Love means it must be an infinite love. If I do anything, anything miraculous as Jesus did – Jesus did so many miracles. Let us not will or desire anything, but let us understand the desire of the time spirit.

"What happened? I was meditating. I surrendered myself to Mahakali. What is Kali? Kala means time and Kali who manifests time. Now this is Kali. What I did I was meditating...Mother, I surrender myself to you. You either give me fulfillment – that's my prayer – you appear before me in your...well, I was seeing Her eyes...I was...She was talking to me...a very nice sweet voice, and do you know who She is? My youngest daughter. I recognized Her for a long time. And if I tell the story...well, I'm a scientist myself, you know. I tried to get rid of my youngest daughter. I hadn't the money for an abortion. I was very much hard up. But I was a worldly man, so what I did? When she was born I put some poison into her face, but you know there was a chance of a post-mortem examination, and if any poison were found, I'd be jailed, you know. But I had more children to look after, an old mother, an old father, and my wife. You know sixteen times I sold my blood to the blood bank...in one year, getting only 160 rupees in nine months! After that they drove me out, sixteen times in nine months! You know, I always used to feel that my eyes were getting in, my ears were getting in, I couldn't listen anything, but my consciousness was perfectly all right. I said it is God's will, it's...I never believed in God. So long there is blood in me, my family shall not starve. I shall sell my bones, but shall never bow down my head. Since then...I couldn't make money, you know. You cannot earn anything in India without bowing down your head. I come from a feudal family, you know. Well, for prestige we would jump into thousands of people, armed men, with a sword – 'Shut up!' but we lost our courage.

"Anyway, I said 'You must appear.' I was saying that almost every moment, every day. But She didn't appear. Only I used to look at her eyes, mouth, ears, sometimes feet, but not the whole form. She appeared, luminous body, and said, 'Well, Son, what do you want?' She was about eleven, twelve years old, Indian age...just, just yet a girl, but won't be a girl tomorrow. That was the form Beautiful! Ornamented! Divine arms! She appeared. She appeared just in front of me. Just a little high. She didn't require any footrest, you know...nah. She said, 'What do you want, my child?' I said, 'Mother, tell me that you won't leave me again.' She said, 'Granted, then what do you want?' Then I said, 'Well, this is not a trick, this is not a maya that

you'll go away again and that you'll give me certain things for
the enjoyment of this worldly life then fly away again so I'll
have to seek you again, I shall forget you again in these worldly
enjoyments and worldly desires?' She said, 'No . . . you asked for
the worldly desires. I have created the world for your enjoyment. You are my son, so I have made this world so that you can
play with the whole world.' I said, 'Humanity?' She said, 'No. I
give you a power over Space and Time and all it contains. I give
you the power to play with the Past, just as you can play with
the Future. All is inherent in this moment.' I said, 'Mother, I
want to go to America . . . and Swami Vivikenanda was given
five minutes time, and when he addressed the Americans as "my
American Brothers and Sisters," who were used to listening
"ladies and gentlemen," and they responded out of the warmth
they received . . . and Vivikenanda talked for hours, and for
years. Hours and for years. So give me . . . he was clapped for five
minutes. I want to be clapped for half an hour.' She said – now
look at the dialogue – then Mother said, 'You'll be clapped all
over.' I became very happy. 'You address them, and they will
become happy, and they'll begin to clap.' I said,
'Mother . . .' I became very happy, and I said, 'Mother . . .' She
was talking to me, just like you talk to me. I said, 'Mother, now
you are very naughty again. You see, now if they always clap
whenever I address them, they become very happy and begin to
clap, I won't be able to tell them what I want to tell them.' So
you resist the knowledge. You see, Mother played with me. She
said, 'No, you address them and they clap, then you begin the
address, and your addresses are their awakenings.' Then I felt
very happy, you know. Then I said, 'Mother,' 'What you want?' I
went on asking, 'I want this, I want that,' and She said, 'all
right, all right,' and after asking a few things, I said, 'Say you
won't leave me again.' She said, 'No. Once you have got me
wholly, when I have integrally manifested myself, I cannot go.
I'm attached to you.' I didn't understand what she meant. Then
what happened, you know . . . well, I said, 'Mother, I want one
thing.' She said, 'What?' I said, 'Well, in Śiva Śastra, that is in
the knowledge of Śiva, it is said that he is the greatest yogi. He is
the only yogi amongst the gods. He is the symbolization, the

symbol of a yogi. So, he desired something and you assumed the form... Can I have it, Mother?' And you know what happened? In a twinkling of an eye, she became a very voluptuous blooming lady, beautifully dressed in divine clothes, came down from the upper level and knelt before me in a typical posture and said, 'My Lord, how long will you stay asleep? Don't you find that your children are going to destroy themselves? Wake up, My Lord. I am just your will, whom you call "Mother."'

"I fainted. I fainted with joy and with a possession of power which nobody is going to feel is true, because two persons feeling the same thing means the end of existence in a second. Because it repeats itself, repeats very quickly... so fast that every human form is awakened in a second, and they merge and become light and exceed even light. It's so logical, but to explain this requires time... say, a few hours. You'll have many questions, but this is the end, this is the hypothesis, and we must begin from a point by a certain construction which is not rigid. We can change the constructions, the principles of the construction will be retained. So you see, I'm not speaking, I'm not listening, I'm just thinking aloud... and so many forms have begun to understand. This is Śiva Kalpa, a period of good imagination or the will of Lord Śiva. So you see, I've appeared at this moment as Lord Śiva. Not Saviasachi. Who is Saviasachi? Who can fire – he is also right – who can fire both sides, on the spiritual side and on the material side. Because on the spiritual side there are spiritual contradictions. Once you are on the way to spiritualism, you want to destroy. That's what India did. And on the material side they want to destroy spiritualism altogether as America did. But the end of materialism is spiritualism, and the end of spiritualism is materialism. So you see, the Himalayas can go to the Indian Ocean, and the Indian Ocean can move right up to the Himalayas..."

Here ends the tape, but the talk and the warmth and love it engendered went on – and, indeed, are still going on even as I write this, and, thanks be to His omnipotent scheme of things, shall go on, world without end, amen.

It became increasingly clear that Father's ability to reveal and our capacity to receive would soon outstrip that environment. The Grand Hotel and its transient circumstances seemed exhausted of its potential to provide an adequate setting. More time would be needed to absorb what Father had to tell us, and a move to his home village was suggested. Here Lou Gottlieb came nobly to the fore. Years of touring in the entertainment world, one night stands, living for months on end out of a suitcase, had made swift maneuverings and facile exits second nature to him. He took charge of everyone's baggage and the checking out procedures, and accomplished it all economically and with as little turmoil or confusion as possible. Within seconds, it seemed, that entire scene proved its ecstatic indifference to time and place and evaporated from within the confines of the Grand Hotel.

There were two reasons why I was not swept along with that change. What few things I had were at that moment at the Ballygunge flat so I would have to break off from that group to get them. More importantly, I did not wish to share, as much as I loved the group, their first days of adjustment to life in an Indian village. Time and circumstance had stripped me of my luggage and needless weight, and I felt that paid my dues so I had no wish nor need to watch or help them get stripped of theirs. Being so recently from the States, they were carrying entirely too much baggage, mental as well as physical, according to my judgment. And so I watched them all exit, Father as well as the others, in a ball of buoyant and felicitous energy.

I was not alone, however. John O'Shea too chose to remain behind, perhaps for reasons akin to mine. What it was that made Shotsy and Sheila remain I don't really know to this day. Sheila much later told me it was because she knew John and I needed them at that time. Whatever the reason, we were delighted to find those girls keeping us company when the rest had parted. It even seemed momentarily like the fulfillment of Konarak's implied promise. Śakti power, both John and I thought in unison and sort of winked at each other: just what we had lacked, needed, and, dare we admit it, craved.

ohn and I stopped by the alleyway before the Elite movie house to catch a smoke with a rickshaw wallah who had hissed and motioned us to join him. It was a good and well prepared ganja chillum, and John took the last pull, drawing it all in, leaving only slight ash clinging to the giti stone. This the squatting wallah blew out of the chillum, replaced the giti and stuffed the filthy rag that served as safi back into the conical end of the chillum. Sadhus passing through Benares would not condescend to saving such an inexpensive and dispensable clay chillum. They would with pomp and ceremony smash it after the first smoke. The chillums they saved were their own personal stone ones about whose use they were finicky, and the history of which they would expound in haughty bragadoccio. But our chillum and dhuni habits were more flexible, and I hope we honored each class and person that offered us the beneficence of smoke. John tikaed his head in approval, and this more than satisfied the grinning wallah. We surveyed the situation before us.

After some friendly conversation and a lot of beautiful feeling between us, Shotsy and Sheila had sent us out to procure tickets for that evening's showing of the film *The Ten Commandments.* Due perhaps to some residue of pride, we had neglected to tell them that we hadn't any money. It had been over a week since John had received his slight bounty, and money, no matter the amount, never lasted long with people who had become used to having none. We had eaten well, treating ourselves to mowglai paratha for breakfast almost every morning, and had again well forgotten about money or any necessity for it until the dilemma of this moment.

That chillum was most welcome indeed for in the after-glow of it, the solution to our problem seemed very simple. It's clear, John reasoned, that the ladies really wished to spend some time with us, and still a bit conventional and stuck in American social games, they had suggested a movie as an excuse. This made sense to me, particularly to the old movie snob I had been who couldn't believe that anyone would genuinely and seriously wish to view Cecil B. DeMille's version of the life of Moses. We would just tell them that the tickets were sold out.

John and I alike had considered ourselves holy men for some time now, and devotion to truth in principle rendered us awkward in the practice of anything less. Even so harmless a lie as the one we were considering was beyond our powers of effective perpetration. The ladies exposed us in an instant, and we were uncomfortably treated as though we were errant juveniles.

"It's best to tell the absolute truth with us," Sheila's reprimand began. "We'll always be truthful with you. Shotsy doesn't request trivial or unimportant favors. You can be certain that there is a good reason, an absolutely divine reason, for everything she says. I have to take care of her and see that her wishes are carried out. They're always simple and pleasant."

The impersonal manner in which this was said took some of the sting out of it. They became strangers to me again in an instant, and I was fascinated anew with just what might actually be going on with them instead of what I thought they were all about.

Shotsy, I'm sure, intended no cruelty with her remark, spoken so off-hand and summarily, but it hit us hard in contrast with

Sheila's more gentle probings.

"It's the money, isn't it?" she declared. "You don't have the money, right? I never let money effectuate anything I say or do."

They supplied the money, and we found ourselves seated in the balcony, watching a larger than life Moses receive the ten "do's and don'ts" from a disembodied voice that was supposed to be adequate representation of the wrathful Jehovah. I enjoyed the film immensely despite my reserve of latent cynicism. The chorus of "ooohs" and "ahhhs" with which the Indians greeted the special effects as the ten plagues swept Egypt was delightful as was the genuine astonishment they evinced with the parting of the Red Sea, and that did much to make up for the indifference with which the same scenes left me. Most enjoyable was watching the movie seated next to Sheila. No emotion, trite or exquisite, was wasted upon her. She responded with great sympathy to everything and said to me when it was over and we were caught in the crowd at the lobby, "Do you see that it was no mere coincidence that that movie was playing just now? They were showing it just for us, you know. Can't you see that Don was Moses?"

The enormously imposing, fair and gentile-looking Charlton Heston did bear a superficial resemblance to McCoy, I'd admit that. There was no use pointing out to Sheila that Gottlieb was more likely the true heir of that semitic partriarch. Also Sheila had strongly implied once before that Don had been Jesus. I later came to know that one of the characteristics of this amazing lady's superbly active imagination was to always claim the best and most significant roles for herself and Don. Accuracy of any sort, historical or ethnic, was unimportant with the empathetic compulsion that caused her, and indeed all of us, to feel and liken each other with biblical and ancient archetypes.

We stopped on Park Street at Trinca's, which passed for a nightclub with the modern and would-be-sinful set of Calcutta. Here the mobile, western-oriented children of the Indian upper crust felt very sophisticated and risqué as they listened to rock and roll and cast about devilishly come-hither looks, all the while sipping soft drinks. The band wore matching suits with a few sequins sewn to the jackets. All of the Indian couples were dressed elegantly, some of the ladies in gold sarees and wearing their family fortune about their necks and arms, but they swept out of the way as if to accommodate royalty when we entered the tiny dance floor. In dress we were shabby by comparison, to say the least, but none seemed to notice that as they looked upon us with admiration and biting envy. I'm hardly a very good dancer, but my most spastic movement that night could put any of the Indians to shame. We were, after all, by birth and instinct the genuine article which they so sorely imitated.

It was a taxi after that, and as we rode to the Ballygunge apartment, I couldn't help but reflect, with a slightly nervous note of anticipation, how suddenly India had changed and was beginning to accommodate rather than deny us what we wanted, perhaps even romance. Maybe part of her exit procedure, I thought, is to place you a bit back into the person and ego she shattered as part of her entrance initiation.

"This is the best place I've seen yet," Shotsy exclaimed as we entered Ken's flat. "Refreshingly decent! Why, it's like a penthouse."

Mary had gone to bed, but the others were still up practicing some music. They presented us with a brief but most satisfying and illuminating concert. Josh's fingers beat out quick mad rhythms on the tablas . . . ta, ta, ticky-ticky ta, ta ta ta tay. Ken sensitively bowed the ishraj. He was rested upon his knees and threw his whole body into the strokes and counted in between with a happy and innocent expression about his youthful face. Gayle was serious and intent upon her more monotonous but nonetheless essential task as she over and over again plucked in the same order and sequence the strings of the tamboura. No doubt their music suffered Peter's absence. Gone was a good bit of the melodic strength, but I didn't notice because I could feel so much the dedication and love they had for the music. I began to hear again that strange pitch and tone that I had heard when I had first entered that vacant apartment, only now I could identify it. It was the drone, melting perfectly with the highest and lowest notes of the tamboura as it announced and defined the range. That room seemed to vibrate itself within the register and format that had held the attention and commanded the efforts

of these Canadian musical aspirants. The dogs outside continued to yelp, and I could hear the trains as they passed, but
somehow it all seemed part of the harmony and blended perfectly with the music. Either they have learned to control the
environment, I thought of Ken and Josh, or they have surrendered and entered perfectly themselves into the atmosphere of
this place. I knew in that instant that India had called them as
certainly as she had me and that she was filling them with a
craft, a sensibility, a knowledge perhaps which she intended to
transmit through them. That was somehow a reassuring and
truly pleasant realization, and the dreamy reflection of it continued to make me feel good long after the musicians had retired
to their rooms.

The trance coursing through us, wafting within; enveloping
us, holding without – internal motions merging, external borders defining: this static spell that held our forms still but anxious did not cease with the music. Rather it became more certain and palpable, intense and viable as the dhuni tightened,
the energy concentrated, and we four forms strove to understand the moment. Easy to comprehend what is was not. Silently but unanimously we discarded the possibility that the
force that drew us was sexual or an inspiration in any way
relievable or consummative by physical application. The urge
we at that moment felt for union accelerated quickly any individual translation and fast exceeded conventional notions of
coupling.

Sheila's form, especially her face, began to subtly but pro-
nouncedly transmutate to my vision. I quickly beheld my
mother there, my own flesh and blood mother, looking at me,
using the many forms of Sheila to contact me – her fears al-
layed, nodding quick approval, and more than that, with love
substantiated, prompting me on. I could not look for long at
Sheila thus or through her so, and my eyes turned towards an
alert and strident Shotsy. Just as the same energy had the effect
in Sheila of dissolution, multiplication, and generally creating
the impression of universality, so in Shotsy's form it seemed to
emphasize the complementary properties of consolidation, uni-
fication, and a specific and individual particularity. In the grip

of this power what John and I shared was a tendency towards contemplation and passivity, and conversely what Sheila and Shotsy had in common was an impulse and reflex towards action.

Shotsy was on her feet and in motion and claiming that she wished, indeed it was imperative and necessary, to be out in the streets that very instant. More than restless, she felt compelled to make a swift exit and be about her mysterious business. John was a bit miffed at seeing the energy of another sacred dhuni scatter. It not only offended the propriety and sanctity in which he regarded the form of dhuni, but it was also counterproductive to the meditation that alone could invoke more of the coveted mudra and greater illumination. Shotsy was totally unimpressed by his intended persuasions, careless, callous even, to the orthodoxy of his views and feelings. She merely muttered that it was "the hour of the wolf," and nothing could stop her from going abroad.

I was concerned for the psychic safety of this girl should she actually go out and find herself stumbling over sleeping bodies, should she come down from this obsession in back alleys and the company of some of India's prolific cripples and precocious degenerates. Also I was curious as to what could tempt or drive this seemingly well-bred young lady to such a diversion at what must have been near five in the morning. John and I joined efforts to try and stop her.

Sheila interceded. "You must know that Shotsy knows perfectly at all times perfectly well what she is doing. She's thinking much faster than she can possibly speak."

Shotsy halted a moment. She became aware of us again and, attempting to address herself to our inquiries and solicitude, began to babble.

"...period between darkness and light...seizing me again...that how dark when...very dark! There is no light whatsoever...that one hour of no moon, no sun...black! That's the feeling...the void...finite...It's walking the..." She hesitated for longer than the frequent punctuating pauses, and she seemed to search her mind and the universe for the right word. "It's like walking the treadmill..." and she paused again neither certain nor pleased that she had found the right term.

We all leapt to assist her.

"Thin line," John suggested.

"Razor's edge," I offered.

"Tight rope," Sheila authoritatively interjected.

Shotsy settled for "tight rope" and went on. "... the tight rope of existence, walking the tight rope between mortality and immortality, death and life. God, the creepiness of India, really!... the hate and bitterness, the end of the world around..."

At last I thought I began to understand her somewhat.

"Do you feel that India is showing you a kind of death or hell?" I asked.

"Oh, yes."

"And do you feel that you are personally to redeem a part of the world from that?"

"Definitely, I do."

"Do you feel that by going out into the streets of Calcutta and facing that death, walking that tight rope, you will absorb and neutralize some of the chaos and death?" I had become a bit carried away with what I thought I understood in her. As usual I was assuming too much kinship between our feelings. She stunned me with her answer.

"No, that is not the feeling at all. It has nothing to do with the streets of Calcutta. I don't so much wish to be out there as not here. It is like claustrophobia." And then she added with calm finality: "It has to do with the revelation coming into my form and being blocked by an environment."

This precise expression of her feeling seemed to calm it, and she no longer appeared anxious to leave us. What remained of the night, though sleepless, was passed pleasantly with a feeling between us of peace and a respect approaching reverence.

I spent the morning from just after sunrise to near noon engaged in a long, intimate, confessional-type conversation with Sheila. I told her much about myself, my marriage and children, the pressures and heartaches that caused me to leave that life, talked to her about brother Rich and how I had come to

India, and what had happened to me here, and how it seemed that my atheistic philosophical persuasion had turned to love and trust in God. She was not only sympathetic as she listened but seemed to know all of it in advance. If she did not know exactly what I was thinking as Father seemed to, she nonetheless was in possession of an extraordinary intuitive and empathetic faculty that invited me with the assurance of understanding to confide more and more in her.

"You remind me so much of my brother Bill," she said. "He and I shared everything. We used to spend hours and even days telling each other stories and acting out movies. He could imitate anyone perfectly though he was always shy outside of my company, and he would feed me situations and characters that he would make up which always ended with some variation of how we were royal children who had been stolen by gypsies, and we would create these incredibly dramatic scenes where we realized our true identities. Usually I'd discover who I was by singing some song I suddenly remembered from my childhood, and it would turn out that that song was the key to our family identity. I always sang, and he encouraged me. For years he was the only audience I had the nerve to really sing my heart to. Oh, Bill was everything, but he got scared or something somewhere along, and he kind of went into a silent hiding. I haven't heard from him in a really long time, but I know he's there just waiting for the world to get soft and easy enough so his sweet sensitive nature and strong imagination can come out. Can you imagine how many people there must be all over the world just waiting to be sure that truth and goodness will not be signs of weakness or invitation to be hurt, just waiting for the time to come out and resume their true life again? Imagine how many people there must be hiding behind insurance jobs and nine-to-five routines, nodding in front of t.v.'s at night, afraid to be tender or show affection to anyone but their own families just because the world got so heavy that it scared them!

"Give me your timid, the doubting, and insecure, your darkened angels yearning to fly free," she paraphrased that famous quotation and held her right arm aloft. "It used to be liberty that man cried for, political and religious liberty and the freedom to have a good life with all of the good things like t.v. But now the real cry is for liberation, and I think I'd like them to build a monument to me and call it the statue of liberation. I know all the drudgery and complications that hold people back. I've stood for hours with my arms in dishwater, and I've scrimped and saved to send my husband through law school, and I've braided my daughters' hair, and put mercurochrome and bandages on my son's skinned knee. I've done it all so I can show everyone how to do it joyously. I want everyone to be able to say 'I love God and therefore I don't mind doing dishes or housework because "cleanliness is next to Godliness." ' Everyone should be able to say and believe that God loves them so no sacrifice is difficult or hard because God will reward them. It's only the joy of karma yoga. I could do a series, 'Karmic Yoga for the Week' in which I could show the ease of doing various chores now thought drudgery. I can find a song for any occasion to illustrate it, and I know I can make everyone feel it too. I am, after all, the first American housewife to reach Enlightenment."

A little abashed by the certainty of her cosmic mission and the relish with which she indulged her public and media-readied personality, I returned to the earlier point of the communication between herself and her brother.

"My brother Rich and I never lost that closeness, thank God. We were always inseparable, and it seemed that we were able to enjoy a common perspective on things. It started with laughing at adult relatives and others who had seemed to sacrifice their sense to what to us was a boring shallowness. We used to wonder if certain uncles and aunts remembered anything of their childhood or had left in them any vestige of spontaneity or original thought or feelings. After awhile, it just seemed that together we could step out of the action and find ourselves off in another room, a safety zone, a time-out place where we could discuss and comment and usually get hysterical with laughter over just what went on or was going on. Most other brothers were sworn enemies or at least in competition with each other as we were growing up – you know the expected and much touted sibling rivalry of middle class America – Our closeness made us unique. It was an energy and force that attracted other people to us as we grew up, and of course, together, having been so long practiced, we could out-humor anyone and play off against each other and ad-lib in the most incredible ways. We knew each other so well, it was easy.

"There was only a small period when we weren't that close. As I got bogged down in my marriage worries and thought I was going through everything alone and that no one understood me, I even came for a short time to think tht Rich didn't understand me, and then I really lost it. That was only a few years, however, and then our lives merged again, and we picked up that communication here in India. In fact we came so close that a lot of people, especially stoned-out Frenchmen, didn't know if we weren't one and the same and that they weren't undergoing some hashish or morphine-induced optical illusion that made us seem two."

"Well you see," Sheila interposed, "you were raised right. Your mother was probably responsible for instilling in you the importance of the love and closeness between you brothers. How could competition be better than cooperation or criticism more fun than support?"

It is funny but as Sheila spoke this, she again began to look like my mother. This was a "by the clear light of day" confirmation of what I had experienced and sensed during that pre-dawn episode. It was mostly her eyes and a look around her nose that seemed identical in my present memory with my mother. She embodied my mother's love and confidence in her sons, but she was an aggressive and certain expression of it whereas my own mother was easily confused and relied mostly on silent communication of her feelings. The greatest thing for me about talking with Sheila was thus feeling my mother's unarticulated support housed in a highly verbal contemporary who would, I was sure, if the need arose, champion my cause.

"I'm a Jewish mother myself," she went on, "so I can appreciate all those positive traits, like concern for the family feeling without becoming overbearing. I know. My mother Beverly is quite a character. She left us when we were young to go after a career in show business – I inherit my singing and presence from her – and we were raised by a new Jewish mother, Lillian, and from her example I became a perfect homemaker – so I know what that background is like. Oh, I can identify with everyone. It seems my own upbringing and exposure was so diverse just to prepare me to be able to identify with all of America. 'House-wives of America, this is your fairy-godmother Sheila coming to you to tell you that I know how you feel and what you wish for, and I am brought to you by your ultimate Cosmic Sponsor to show you how easy it is to fulfill all those wishes.' And then I'll sing a song or two, and without even knowing how or why, people all over America will start to feel good again."

Sheila moved gracefully about the roof which was at once our terrace and her stage. I sat on the ledge that formed a low wall and looked out over the park where were herded some water buffalo and listened to the silence between the birds' chatter and thought I heard somewhere near the whine and squeak of a solitary cart making its way through the neighborhood. The air was slightly crisp and moist as though the morning had left some mist, unseen but pervasive, lingering about the nearby lakes.

"What happened here in India, it seems to me," I began haltingly, pensive somewhat but mostly alert to and grateful for the pastoral permanence that endured so easily the pretense of metropolitan modernity, "what happened here is that Rich and I began to live our childhood again . . . not the events, of course, nor the emotions really, but the essence of it. We began to sort and sift reality anew as it presented itself through some magical revitalization of our primary impressions . . . an unsought resur-rection of innocence. We didn't plan it, but we knew it was happening. It was palpable and thrilling, and we relished, nur-tured, and indulged it excessively. What I mean is we com-municated so incessantly about the very process of our percep-tions, and we took no responsibility whatsoever for the content. I mean it was a whole new world, and we weren't going to get any older than twelve-year old kids in it. You'd have to know Rich to really understand it, know his connoisseur-like ability to draw out and languish in the most slight-seeming sensation. He had felt lucky in his previous solitude in India just to feel it all and incredibly blessed with my coming to be able to share and communicate it, and there was no way that he was going to get caught this time in anyone else's direction, not the Peace Crops' nor that of the tiresome induction notices that hounded him. Nor would he let me get stuck in worry about purpose. Process was purpose enough, and I surrendered to him – first time in my life I surrendered to him, my younger brother – trusting that somehow by reversing habit and by my following him that delight would not be lost this round."

"Process and purpose," I mused to myself, and the theme inspired me. "It's so easy to see in review," I said, "that in order for the process to be complete I would again have to experience and examine life after twelve years old, relive the adult feelings and portions as well . . . so would Rich, but we couldn't somehow do that together.

"Also, the divine force that was guiding us, and we had come to see it as such, felt guided by divinity as the overseer or purpose, if you like, to it all . . . well, that force, I feel, dislikes redundancy as much as nature abhors a vacuum. It just came to the point where so similar and compatibly close a consciousness just couldn't reside in two forms in the same place at the same time . . . so it became clear that either Rich and I take that giant step of ultimate and final merger and become truly one or that we separate and start having experiences on our own again and build up once more the illusions of our separate identities. Well, we could never stand the loneliness that merging would create, the loss of the ultimate confidante, so circumstance, never mind how, arranged our separation."

As I spoke with Sheila, I felt these well-worn insights with renewed vigor and a fresh clarity of understanding. I had spent so much time in India, alone, thinking over the meaning of all that had and was happening to me, that though it never degenerated in my mind to routine and repetitious analysis, neither could it stun me as fresh self-discovery. But the articulation of any understanding always has its unique and fascinating aspects, and the intensity of Sheila's empathy bathed the communication with an earnestness and the importance of truth.

"What acid had taught me before India," I continued, "was that there were other people privy to that special room Rich and I shared, but it did not tell me who they were. I forgot about it for a long time, and as long as I had Rich, the room, life itself for the moment, felt complete.

"Not that Rich and I forgot that there were others in the game – how could we? Our paths began to cross more frequently with other travellers and pilgrims of understanding. When we met Marc in the V. T. Station, Bombay, we knew immediately that he was one of us, a brother, another frequenter of 'the room,' as it turned out. Not that he or I ever discussed at first the room or what it was like – it's different for everyone, I guess, a different image for the specialness of it, but you know automatically when you meet someone else who has been there.

"For the next months Marc replaced Rich as partner to the next stage of my cosmic journey. It was with him, or rather it was by watching him get involved with other people in the road community, watching him fall in and out of love with Gina, that I had a chance to relive, even if vicariously, the over-twelve, more adult moments of life. Another world to explore, sensations, power, and hesitancy to analyze and communicate. Marc and I had our own way, more academic, less poetic, but equally intense and real as with Rich – our own way to mutually share and forge understanding. Many a night we talked the contradictions of existence out to a single thread, a self-caused moment, a tickle, a lump in the throat – anything and nothing – but we could neither stop nor start it. We could only hope to comprehend and express it.

"God," I burst out, "you must think I'm the world's most incredible egotist to go on like this!"

Sheila's answer was to grab my hand and kiss it. "Don't stop," she said. "You have my full attention."

"Well, listen to this: Marc and I were both bedridden and sick with hepatitis. It was in Kashmir last summer. There's an annual pilgrimage that takes place there, and it was just building up, and we were hoping to recover enough to take part in it. Fortunately, we had a good house there and a fine situation and lots of friends who were looking after us, and they would come to sit by our beds and talk to us. Being an invalid, you know, is sort of like being a yogi – you can't chase the world so the world comes and reveals itself to you. Marc and I had these experiences separately, but we shared notes and later came to the same conclusions. Our friends had come and had actually confessed themselves to us, their innermost aspirations, fears – you know, all that stuff that they were usually too cool to admit. Well, the way it seemed to me was that the whole world as I had come to know it came and confessed itself to me. What I discovered was that everyone, junkie and scam and rip-off artists as well as the would-be saints, had the same urge and dream . . . urge for transcendence, to know and feel themselves as divine. Only they had no way to comprehend it, the direction was blind. Everyone seemed suddenly so young and inexperienced to me. I didn't feel old, for God's sake, but I had had a family and everything . . . like you, you know. Well, I saw that no one knew how or to whom, what or where to pray. We had forgotten how to ask for things, guidance ultimately.

"Marc and I agreed to use the pilgrimage, if we could make it, as our effort to get a message to the gods. We talked all night about it and for two days following – how to get a message to the gods? And then – it flashed us – vice versa, how to receive their message to us! We came damn near – or, more appropriately, blessedly close – to figuring it out that time."

"Figuring what out?" Sheila asked more to inspire than test me. It had the effect, however, of silencing me completely.

"Don't be embarrassed," she said. "Just answer it. You know you figured it out long ago."

"All I know is that there is no way outside of yourself . . . no system, teaching or even effort that can give it to you."

"I always knew that," Sheila said. "I say that not in pride but simply and truthfully. What else or where else would it be but in that voice that most people spend the best part of their lives trying to hush or turn off?"

"I don't know . . . living in India you get into some pretty crazy ideas," I said. "Wrapping your legs around your neck, drinking piss, vows of silence . . . some poor bastards have even cut chords and ducts to their penis. There's a guy in Europe I heard about here who's becoming famous for talking people into drilling a hole in their forehead – trepanning, it's called. Can you imagine that they've legitimized it enough to have a name for it!

"Personally, I could never mutilate any part of my body – no tattoos or pierced ears for me. I guess that's a vestige of Jewish conservatism toward the flesh, circumcision notwithstanding. And God knows, we've even heard it argued that only the circumcised can find it, or can not find it due to the circumcision. I tell you, it can drive you nuts just to think about it.

"Twice I took a vow of silence myself. The last time was just the other night, but here I am, talking as usual, as though there is no tomorrow or my very soul depended on talk and not the other way around as I had thought."

"Doesn't it?" Sheila asked. "I like the way you talk. You speak the truth and that makes my soul soar and swell."

"Well, I thought I wouldn't talk because I know myself so damned well – what could I learn by talking? I could only repeat what I already know. But then I'd find myself talking anyway – to myself if no one else were around. And I've been there too, when the talk and thought ran out for a moment. I've been there, and the strangest thing is that I'm there now even though I'm talking. So why quarrel with what you're doing, why talk and then be arguing with yourself for talking? Why not realize that it is not you that's talking anyway? Doesn't that make all the difference – whether you talk for your ego or talk for God?"

"It sure does," Sheila said emphatically. "It makes *all* the difference. You really did figure it out, didn't you?"

Over and over again she stroked my hand, and she began to hum and then sing softly, "you figured it out . . . my wonderful son . . . you figured it out."

"All those things," she said and nodded her head, flared her nostrils, and gazed intently into my eyes, " . . . all those things that we were compelled to do before, we shall continue to do. Only now we know that we are doing them for God. You're a born talker and teacher – do it for God. I sing for God. Wait until Uncle Lou Gottlieb finds out that he's going to go right on singing and entertaining – not for money, or ego, or prestige, but for God! Don't you see that we were born to do it?''

Father came to see us that afternoon. How he knew where to find us is something of a mystery to me, but I never questioned it at the time, accepting his apparent omniscience as a matter of course, just as I had accepted the ubiquity of his certain and precise appearance at the very rooms Don had engaged at the Grand. Our present location, "the penthouse," as it turned out, lay no more than a block from one of the few private residences in Calcutta that Father would frequently visit. He was coming from there now, from "Śakti's house," as he called it.

"You remember Śakti, Śaktindranarayan Deb. I told you about him," he said, mostly it seemed to Sheila. "A number of years ago I was able to help him in his business. You know I am a chemist amongst other things, don't you? Well, I was able to synthesize some substance no longer available in India but essential to an order that his business had undertaken. I accepted no money at the time, but he has paid me much more since by listening to me, and his house is one of only two or three where the door has stood open to me since the awakening.

"Hurry, please, if you can. I brought with me Śakti's dad. He was feeling enlivened and strong today so he has walked over to see you. He cannot manage these stairs though, so you just come down please so he can see that you have come."

Śakti, when I later met him, turned out to be a man twenty years Father's junior and only about ten years older than I. A sensitive poet, he had put aside his literary studies to assume the eldest son's duties and began to help his father in the pharmaceutical firm he had started. His father fell ill and soon all of the business became Śakti's to manage. Through some routine commercial association he had met Ciranjiva Roy, who by an ingenious chemical feat saved Śakti's business from almost certain ruin. Śakti was grateful enough that, when years later the same man presented himself to him not as a businessman or a chemist but "with a shaved head and speaking as a *pundit*,[1]" he

[1]scholar, teacher (derogatory connotation is "pedagogue"; respectfully, one versed in the Vedas).

could not help but feel that through this person he would again receive some benefit. In the last years he had encouraged Father's visits to his house, and though he, still burdened by business, was limited in the time he could give Father, he nonetheless insisted that his family, otherwise shy and a bit startled by the beggar's presence, bestow upon Father all the courtesy and respect due a true Brahmin.

As we approached the door, Father told us briefly of Śakti's dad and the elder Deb's condition, which had grown worse. In the last year, his eyesight had begun to fail, and fear of blindness caused panic to the old man, who was in years barely older than Father himself.

"But you are healing him, aren't you, Father?" Sheila asked just as we passed through the door. This caused Father to pause at the top of the stairway. He turned to Sheila but addressed us all.

"I can heal no one. God alone heals. Really, I cannot even heal myself, but I can let myself be healed by God. I was healed, it is true, and therefore I know others can be healed. Early in '67 perhaps, before Śiva Kalpa was even one year old, Sudhir Mandal, my landlord, drunk as always, came at me with thunder in his eyes and anger in his heart, and he broke my jaw. I offered him no resistance. I went to the doctors, but I had no money for treatment or medicines so they could do nothing. For eight or nine months I endured constant pain. I developed osteomylitis. My teeth and jaws were clenched. I couldn't eat, not to mention speak. But knowledge of God had already seized me so it was only a matter of time before my form was restored . . . by that same knowledge in application of will, the will to which I had become permanently surrendered. I became an example of the power of that knowledge to heal, not my power as an individual.

"When those same doctors saw me after I had been cured, they nearly freaked out. 'How could it be?' They didn't understand. They were afraid too that it would render all of their supposed knowledge useless . . . because I was healed without the use of any medicine . . . only the benefit of time."

We began to descend the stairs.

"But you are trying to help Śakti's father," Sheila tried again.

"Of course," Father said. "I try to help everybody. I am talking to him lots."

"And does he listen?" Sheila asked.

"Well, let us say that he does not break my jaw for talking." Father paused a moment and then offered, "It is true that he has difficulty listening. His mind is full of concern and worry, but I think seeing you and knowing that you have come will help him a lot."

On the second flight of stairs down Sheila asked after everyone in the village, Don in particular. She wished to know how they were all doing.

Father seemed to have some difficulty recollecting of whom she spoke. He was, as always, totally immersed in the moment. "Oh they are fine," he finally answered. "How should they be?"

Old Deb was seated on the bottom stairs with his hands folded and chin resting upon a polished walking stick. He was clean-shaven, and his white hair was close-cropped upon his head. The pouches under his eyes sagged as did the girth about his middle, which probably a few years back had been a pleasing rotundity, a portly boast of having managed well through this life.

John and I stayed back upon the stairs while Father motioned Sheila and Shotsy to the lobby floor in front of the old man. It was the "goddesses," as he referred to them, that he seemed most concerned to present before the old gentleman. John and I, in the conversation that followed, were referred to as "the others" or used by inference to imply that many more were also witness and testament to the fact that "it had happened."

Father spoke Bengali but broke into occasional English as he presented the ladies. Referring to Shotsy, I was certain that he said "Gauri" in Sanskrit which elicited a long sigh from the old man, and then, after some more Bengali, he dropped into English with the phrase "a very big family in America . . . like Tata and Birla you know."

"My dear, come closer please," the old man said in a very clear English but in a falling cadence approximating a whine. All of his sentences, no matter the content, wound up in tone suggestive of pity or complaint.

When Shotsy approached, the old man began to run his hands over her face. Obviously restraining a reflex to draw back, she looked towards Sheila as if to say "What am I to do now, I'd like to know." Sheila, when her turn came, reacted just opposite. She took the old man's hands in hers and guided them over her own face, head, and hair.

"You see, Baba," she said, "I am live and real, and I want to serve you because you are Father's friend."

The old man let out a moan of "maaaa" which sounded almost like bleating. He began to sob lightly, barely perceptibly, but the effect was nonetheless electrifying to us. Then, swallowing hard and rising to his feet, he clearly pronounced, "It is just as you have said, Ciranjiva. May we all be the better for it."

I stood at the front door and watched them pass out the gate and down the turn of the lane on Lake Street feeding into the long circular passage of Raja Bashanta Roy Road where they disappeared in a courtyard off to the left. Up until this moment Father had been to me primarily a voice, an articulate and verbal form of Knowledge. Now I began to comprehend that his physicality as well, the way he moved, the scenes he presented before us were, if properly perceived and reflected upon, equally illuminating, pregnant and powerful vignettes, emblems and ikons fraught with knowledge. In the play of his bare shoulders, the length of his stride, the manner in which his thin arms seemed both relaxed and taut as they hung by his side, the way his hands, almost clench-fisted, seemed perpetually prepared for action, I saw an athletic and exuberant adolescence about to break forth in the afternoon of its agility and give the lie to his superficial ancientness, betray the thin disguise of his white beard and hair and his balding brow and pate. He would jut forward absently in a kind of natural saunter and then collecting himself, stop short to await or assist his hobbling companion. Father seemed weightless as he bounded down the street while the other appeared burdened by the gravity of years and mass, slowed and earthbound by a pitiless entropy as he dragged himself through the three-legged evening of his life. As these two forms disappeared down the avenue to exit stage left, I realized in an instant with an unarguable completeness that in the drama of aging the tacit consent of the actors is required.

Shotsy seemed to get on pretty well with Ken. They shared an enthusiasm and a humor regarding the fate and future of American rock music. Both were innocent and ambitious in similar ways and could appear equally spoiled and pampered. They jested and teased with each other like brother and sister. The world was their playground in which a very silly game called life was conducted, and India seemed a movie matinee that they were watching with disbelief and lots of chuckling.

They both came in from the balcony that evening doubled over with laughter.

"Did you see that bundle of pomposity?" asked Shotsy. "He looked like an aspic, or better yet a can of spam gift-wrapped. Impassive pontificator!"

"They are Ruskies, those folks over there," Ken pointed out. "I believe they work at the Russian Consulate, probably K.G.B. spies. Either that or M.C.A. talent scouts," he laughed.

"You can bet that they're now watching events here with quite a keen interest," Shotsy said, not at all in jest.

Her tone caught my interest. They were speaking of some white business-type people that occupied a flat a few doors down. By Indian standards this was, after all, quite a decent residential area. I had ignored the straight westerners in India for almost a year now, keeping my visits to consulates and the American Express to a minimum. On the whole, we western sadhus were as bewildered and embarrassed to encounter these corporation-types in "our India" as they were no doubt startled and ashamed to behold such examples of western youth wandering across their terrain in rags and robes. There persisted a feeling amongst those of us who were getting stoned in India, a suspicion, that "we" were being watched by "them." It was not a paranoid feeling that we were under surveillance for any punitive purpose but rather that we were being watched to see what we would come up with, learn, or find through our self-abusive experiments. Usually we were caught in the dichotomy that commonly separates the realms of the spiritual from the material, and so we dismissed the feeling, not understanding how what we found for our soul could in any way interest their politics. Nonetheless, the feeling would return, and in several scenes I had shared around this country, I had heard this theme variously pondered or elaborated. I sensed this to be such an occasion.

"Do you really think that anyone cares at all what we do out here or what happens to us?" I asked, but the question was not even out before that overwhelming messianic impulse assured me that the entire world was in fact very attentive and interested, guardedly waiting, anxiously waiting, desperately waiting for the outcome of all of this.

"I know that they're watching what becomes of me!" Shotsy replied.

"Whether you know it or not, I am a person with . . . international implications."

In the conversation that followed I was surprised to find out that Shotsy made visits to the American Consulate almost daily.

"Why in heaven's name would you do a thing like that?" I wondered aloud.

"To see if there is any mail there for me," was her simple reply. "I make frequent runs to the Grand Hotel as well. I'm quite eager to receive a response to a rather scattered post card I did manage to write. They're beginning to look at me at the Consulate as if I'm on some trip or something, but they'll be getting wires from Washington soon enough, and just wait until cousin Patty hits the States and I'm not with her! Mother and Daddy will issue an all-points bulletin, I swear.

"I was afraid," she continued, shrug-shouldered and gesturing with her hands, palms upwards, "afraid they'd start getting some frightening advance reports from people on the tour that I'd dropped out in Calcutta, so I tried as hard as I could to write so they wouldn't worry. Really I did. But how do you write any of this to your family? I'd thought I'd really done miraculously to get that one post card off, but I'm afraid its effect will not be reassuring as I'd intended but rather the opposite . . . in effect, you know . . . convincing them that I've really blown it this time."

Shotsy was self-assured and possessed, but she seemed a bit indecisive, weighing, I thought, whether or not to lend herself more to the moment of self-confession. Sheila gathered in close signalling her support should Shotsy need it. What I loved were the stories of how these various star-struck wanderers happened to penetrate the borders of the subcontinent in the first place. We all shared an astonishment to find ourselves awake or still dreaming in this alien antechamber, this lotus-lapped shore, this veiled and vaporish peninsula of consciousness called India. I encouraged her with a silent attentiveness, knowing that interrogation at this moment would hamper rather than hasten revelation.

"I did try to get to Kathmandu to rejoin the tour," Shotsy continued in a half-hearted litany of self-justification, knowing that we were not the ones in need of convincing, "but then I gave up and quit trying . . . and stayed. I seemed held . . . but not against my will . . . far from that. So I went instead with Don and Sheila to Pondicherry. At least I knew with them that we were in it sort of together . . . I mean we knew that the same thing was happening. I worried for Mother and Daddy because I'd like them to understand, of course . . . they are not hard to please . . . rebels both in their own time . . . and always teaching me too to persevere in that which I believed, found to be true . . . but I knew they wouldn't be happy to think of me in such company . . . such outrageous ungentle hippies like Don and Sheila . . . it makes me laugh! After all, the whole idea had come about to get me away from much milder influence than that. I'd spent last summer motorcycling through Canada. And Patty, cousin Patty, was going so they thought it'd be a good idea if I joined her.

"We met up in Boston, and it was pleasant enough . . . meeting up with that wing of the family and all, going on this spiritual mission . . . not that I'd have chosen it, but it didn't seem a bad idea. To me there just seemed no place for the world to go except into further fighting, everything was so . . . and the people were so miserable . . . and the Temple of Understanding, that's a chance . . . there's a chance. I didn't hold that . . . It was really more for the pleasure of the trip and the enjoyment of seeing the foreign sights...I didn't have a particular feeling...I knew something interesting was going to happen...I didn't know what...I knew in the back of my mind...my feeling...it was going to be an exceptional trip and exciting and fun. But...the Temple of Understanding, I thought, 'well this is a perfectly good vehicle to end this mess the world's in.' It was very much in the spirit of hoping...at the time...and then, reaching Calcutta, I knew immediately that here was another round of blasphemy. I'd heard this talk, and I'd felt this before ...so many times...the same drudgery...in school and things...that same old heavy, self-serious...Well, you can't bring unity with people through drudgery."

A long pause and then just as we thought she had finished, she continued with "So there comes..." followed by a hesitation rather than a pause.

"Father," Sheila prompted. In those early days, Shotsy was exceptional amongst us in the difficulty she had calling him Father. When she spoke with him, she addressed him as Ciran-jiva, but when she spoke of him, she was invariably at a loss for words. She generally settled for the non-commital, impersonal pronoun.

"So there he comes, the second day, with a light feeling, very fluent, very easy to communicate, and...decisively separate from the entity of the Temple of Understanding."

She stopped abruptly, and it became clear that she was fin-ished with the subject for the moment. Moving towards the phonograph, she put on a Janis Joplin record, and turning to Ken, she said, "Won't it be fun when we get back and give them all a real reason to laugh and crack-up. I mean the Blues really have to go this time."

The four of us together took the tram downtown. We all alighted at Shakespeare Sarani, and Shotsy walked from there over to the U.S. Consulate on Harrington Road. John, Sheila, and I decided to wait for her and camped ourselves on a nice stretch of grass on the Maidan, Calcutta's vast and central stretch of park. The Victoria Memorial, standing marble white and prominent, dominated that particular landscape and lent it an appearance of unearthly, aristocratic splendour, an impression which could not stand too close a scrutiny since the cornerstones were cracking and the grounds around were unkempt. Yet it still commanded an atmosphere of leisure and luxury now long gone from that city, and it afforded a space of welcome silence all too rare and also departing quickly from contemporary Calcutta. We found a large banyan tree under which to enjoy the shade as we talked lightly or vacantly stared ahead, absently plucking at blades of mostly parched grass. A spirit of playfulness came upon us, and we rolled around a bit and made a few half-hearted efforts to climb that tree.

Sheila brought out from her little handbag a small cloth bean bag.

"Catch," she said and tossed it to John. We began to throw it gently to each other. "Not so fast," Sheila warned. "Take time with it. Hold it, feel it, caress it even. Go on. That's what we do at Olompali, the kids and grown-ups alike. Fondle it. Relax, it's good for you. Just let all of your tenseness flow out into the soft furry beanbag and absorb its cuddlyness."

I felt a bit silly at first, but for all the world I certainly had nothing else to do. I could afford to experiment, accept and follow all that Sheila said rather than hold back, weigh, and judge it. I saw that upon the blue cloth Sheila had stitched with yellow thread a heart with wings to both sides.

"I make the beanbags myself," she said. "I'm very good at it. I can make one for each of you in a very short time, while we sit here and talk – only I left the beans and cloth back in my tote bag. I always carry a needle and thread, however. Do you have any loose buttons or torn spots at knees or elbows in need of mending? Oh well, I'll make some bean bags for you later. You'll both have your very own and you can carry them in your pockets or in your travel things and just squeeze them whenever you feel uptight or anxious."

She burst out laughing, "The Sufi heart and wings are optional, of course. But it conveys real magic, I tell you. I'm a true Sufi, you know."

John and I looked at each other quizzically. How far would

we permit her to take us on this never-never land tour of spirituality, we wondered. No harm in it, we silently decided and cautiously considered sailing further on these waves with her as long as they did not break too close or perilously upon our shores of sadhu manhood.

"What actually is a Sufi?" I asked. I knew from having spoken with her and Buz before that one Hazrat Inayat Khan had written books on the subject and that his son Pir Vilayat Khan had attended the Spiritual Summit Conference where they all had met Father, but I was totally ignorant of the doctrine, philosophy, history, or general feeling of the religion, if it were a religion.

"What's a Sufi?" she repeated. "Oh, that's very simple. I'm a Sufi. I sing and dance about God, and as I wander through life, I bring everyone to celebrate and praise Him. Oh, there are arguments and endless discussions sometimes about food and order of priorities, and all that usual stuff that everybody's always fighting about, but we Sufis know who we are, and we don't bother with all that. Just love life and serve God, that's the essence of everything. I've been everything, you know: Jew, Christian, Moslem – the Sufis are Muslims, Allah, Allah, Allah – and everything you can be really points to just loving life and serving God. I've passed from teacher to teacher, and I'm an excellent disciple, you know. I have absorbed totally what each teacher has had to give me, and I've blown all their minds that it comes so naturally and easily with me. I always knew I'd be a star and I am – I'm a constellation in myself.

"It's really amazing," she continued, after dropping the bean-bag into her lap. "More than that, it's nothing less than divine how I have become free to float from teacher to teacher and lend them all a unity they might not see by themselves. That's what God tells me He wants me to do. 'Go on, Sheila, you're free now.' I told you how I was the first American mom and housewife to reach Enlightenment, right? For years I attended the P.T.A., worried, sent my husband through law school, and then, bit by bit, it all began to be taken care of for me. Don came along first and settled us at Olompali, and now my husband and children are all being taken care of, and I am free to do His work.

"One teacher just passed me on to another, and with all of them I just floated to the head of the class. And so Sam Lewis, Sufi Sam we call him, sent me to represent him and the Sufis at the Spiritual Summit Conference. He sent me with letters of introduction, and when Don didn't want to go, Buz popped up magically as an escort to take care of me, but I knew Don would show up. He couldn't let it all go on without him. Not Don! He was just testing us. He's his own man. He never cared much for Sufi Sam or any other teacher. Funny thing is that Sufi Sam sent me off with hugs and blessings to do it for him, and the craziest thing is that his last words to me were 'Watch out for the beggars, Sheila.' He had given me instructions what to tell Pir Vilayat and other things, but I never paid any mind to that. What really struck me, though I didn't know why, was his saying, 'Sheila, watch out for the beggars.'"

Sheila not only looked directly in our eyes as she spoke, but she nodded her head as well, lulling us along in a compelling assumption of agreement. Often she'd clasp our hands and stroke them gently. Her voice inflections were sweet and soothing. No doubt she had practiced these gestures in front of mirrors since childhood, and I'm just as sure she had rehearsed her voice often and indulged frequently in the persuasive rhetoric of talking to herself. Yet there was nothing insincere or artificial about it. Rather her voice vibrated and her person shook in the ecstatic timbre of conviction and certainty. It was impossible to give Sheila a minute and not be seduced into an hour, difficult to check or in any way limit our reception of her. She gave herself totally to every communication with such fervor and energy that I for one felt a bit crotchety or mean if I tried to deny or contradict any of it. It was far easier to suspend all disbelief, relax the censure of logic or impulse to criticize, and just luxuriate and wallow in the certainty of conviction, the childlike faith and wondrous assent that made all things possible.

"If I were to think of all the children," her eyes narrowed and her nostrils flared as she continued, "all the children out there, sleeping on the pavements at nights, with flies in their eyes at noon, dirty faces and snotty noses – if I thought of that without knowing that we were going to take care of them, that we'll cover them at night, tuck them in, wash those faces, and scrub the ears . . . I'm like that, you know. I find fulfillment in cleaning up. Don's like that too. Peanut butter and honey for all the children! He'll see to it. If I didn't know that everyone would be warmed and loved, how could I stand the anguish of what I've already seen here? You couldn't either, neither of you, I know it. So I knew my job immediately when I heard Father call me 'Mother.'

"There he was, the ultimate beggar, the prince or millionaire or magician disguised as beggar, telling me he was less than three years old and asking me to take care of him. Well, I knew immediately. I made them make room for him when the tour bus was leaving the Birla Academy for the buffet, and I saw to it that he got plenty to eat at the reception. He told me he was hungry, so I made sure he ate. He's my baby too, and so's Sufi Sam, even though he's my teacher, and, of course, it is easy for me to see that you are my sons. I must see that everyone is taken care of.

"I never lacked confidence or nerve, even at the beginning of Olompali when I knew everyone thought I was crazy. Well, I don't understand timidity. How could I? God's been whispering to me 'go ahead' for a long time now, so whenever I have to do something that might seem outrageous or daring, I don't stop to think about it. I just close my eyes a moment and get all cozy and comfy with the loving energy He gives me, and I just go into a kind of trance and let It all come through me. So I never doubted, but I didn't know how soon it could happen until that beggar that I did not watch out for but who watched out for me called me 'Mother' – and then I knew the time was right and ripe, and I could just trudge ahead. You see, I know I was born for this job. I'm the one who is going to tell America that the New Age has dawned – and I'll do it by singing to them over all the media at once."

Sheila began to hum "When You Wish Upon a Star" and almost squealed mad comments about how easily America would come to love Father, how they had already been prepared by the media to love him, how he looked like Bugs Bunny and therefore fulfilled the prophecy in Revelations that He would

show a countenance that no man could turn from, and in between each comment she returned to her humming, ending up
by singing aloud the line "your dreams come true." John and I
sat there transfixed and astonished. The sun, clearing the trees
above where the crows suddenly became still, sent its rays full
upon the alabaster brilliance of the Victoria Memorial, which
seemed to sparkle and glisten in response. John and I knew in
unison that one of those special moments was upon us, and we
did not at all resist but let each other become children again
there on the timeless lawn, and we prepared to listen further as
Sheila spread her skirt about her upon the square of burnt grass
which seemed somehow a shimmering green carpet.

"So when we went back down to Auroville in Pondicherry, I
couldn't believe that they had become so rude to us. Why did
they deny who we were or what we were going to do? I had no
hard feelings toward them. In fact, I appreciate everything they
have done. Everything is nice and clean there. Really, it's very
ordered and a good model of how the world should be. Everyone
is gentle there, and there's no hunger or violence, and there are
no children sleeping on the sidewalks. They have worshipped
the Mother there, and really they've done a good job, but like all
insititutions, they've let the wax grow in their ears, and they
can't hear anything. I wondered that they could worship the
Mother and not see Her in me. I was sure that the Mother herself
would recognize us, but they refused to let us see her. But I saw
her, you know. I saw her anyway.

"The first night we were down there, the Mother crept into
my room. I saw that she was worn and tired so I began to play
with her. I tossed a beanbag to her – honest to God I did, and she
became young and happy, and we played and giggled and whispered like sisters. And do you know what? I realized that the
Mother was about to depart from Madame Richard's thin and
frail and all too tired form... and She passed into my form.
That's all there is to it. It's such a joke you know because there
they are worshipping that poor old tired Frenchwoman, and the
Mother has already done Her work through her and now has left
her, and those poor uninspired monks couldn't even see that I
am now She. Yes, I am the Cosmic Mother now, and I tried to

tell them but only Govinda would listen, and that's why he left and came up here with us. It's our turn now, and we've got such a lot to do. We must make sure that everyone is comfortable and happy so they can listen to Father. The sooner they are all relieved of their worries and hardships the sooner the New Age can begin."

"Did you see Her really?" I asked, surprised to find that my eyes had begun to water but reassured when I looked at John and saw the beginnings of tears in the orbs of that ex-marine as well.

"Yes, I saw Her really, but I never did see Madame Richard. I was always Mother anyway. Some of Sam Lewis's disciples used to call me 'mataji' in private. Now the whole world will know. And I want everyone to have everything, beginning with Father. I want everyone to have Father, and I want him to have everything to make everyone happy."

It turned out to be a long afternoon as we sat there until Shotsy finally joined us. The trees and shrubs glowed amber-tipped, suffused with the sun's penultimate and slanting rays as the lengthening shadow of the Victoria Memorial threatened to engulf them. We stood up to head back towards Ballygunge, but we could hardly walk, so overcome were we with the ecstatic communion we had shared. All sorts of thoughts and visions sprung up within me. I felt and then almost saw the world being covered with an ebullient and self-perpetuating trance of welcome and acceptance and hosannas, and I imagined our triumphant exit from India and return to the West occurring as a sort of contagious dance where each of us, joining hands with our brothers and sisters, literally hugged and kissed our way out of the subcontinent, across the Arab world, through Europe, and somehow transmigrated the oceans to cover the western hemisphere, the new world, with love and truth, blessing and embracing the whole of existant humanity.

Later that night John O'Shea told me, "You know, it was the strangest thing, but as Sheila spoke to us this afternoon, she even began to look like my mother. No, I mean it. Her features are actually identical with my mom's, only smaller, of course."

I joined Shotsy on the balcony at Ballygunge. She spent a lot of time there.

"That lake must be somewhere near here," Shotsy said, stretching and thrilling with a particularly pleasant night breeze that passed. "There was a lake right across from the Birla Academy of Arts and Culture where they had the Spiritual Summit Conference."

"I know where that is," I said. "Over that way," I pointed to the right, "but you can't see it from here. It's across Southern Avenue." I knew that area slightly, and I could picture the lake from walks I would take after my visits to Ray's house the year before. It is odd how clear I was on Calcutta geography. Rich and I both were masters of direction when it came to cities.

"I took a very beautiful walk around that lake . . . very beautiful!" she went on in a quiet and lilting voice. "Oh, I couldn't stand it any more because the Temple of Understanding was beating around the bush so much, and there was so much mundanity at that point . . . the conversations between the . . . all of it, it was just . . . it was a great big paperwork, and the feeling was very sketchy. Really I wanted . . . I asked him if he would go with me . . . to get out of there because I was just getting oppressed by the dogmatism that was being displayed . . . and I wanted to hear some pure knowledge. I wanted to hear some beautiful conversation . . . and something more to the point than who was . . . where it was all supposed to be happening . . . each religion describing itself, and that's why I turned to him and said, 'Let's get out of here!' And so we walked around that lake, and I talked a blue streak about everything I could think of . . . just getting out all of my feelings about where America is at . . . and how he's needed to go to America to save America . . . so the rest of the world can follow. It was just one of those wonderful conversations that you'd wish to continue forever, you'd care to perpetuate . . ."

"Do you mean you asked Father to go to America?" I asked her incredulously.

"Of course, I did. And, you know what, I think he was just

waiting for someone to ask him."

When Father came late the next morning, he brought with him his wife Mishtu and their son Udit. In the soft Bengali they spoke, they referred to the youth as "Koka," which to my understanding indicated an only or eldest son and to my ears implied the affection and expectations invested in the future progenitor of the family's reputation, fortune, or, in this case, the honor of their sense of purpose and respect for truth. At age sixteen, Koka stood about a head taller than Father which made him about that much taller than myself as well. He stooped a little at the shoulders out of what seemed to me a kind of adolescent reticence and shyness. His face was sensitive and intelligent-looking, and no matter how poorly garbed, he could not be taken for a member of any but the most refined caste, nor did his humble bearing (he had been raised in an abject poverty of which I came to learn later and to experience in some degree) disguise in any way an unmistakably aristocratic nature. The same was true of the mother, Mishtu, only the impression was stronger since its embodiment was more mature and self-possessed. The few lines in her face and the misssing front tooth, which offered a hint to the severe physical neglect and hardship to which life had subjected her, did more to emphasize and affirm than mar a sense of regal identity within her. She did not half hide her face in her saree edge as did so many Indian women when they were introduced, but she looked at me and everyone and everything else with an open, intent, and full gaze. In height she stood only a little over my shoulder, but her bearing made her seem almost tall. The strong line of her cheekbones and the straightness of her nose, softened by a slightly receding chin, suggested to my eyes the very portrait of timeless, enduring, silent, and compassionate Mother India. Mishtu and Udit were very quiet and spoke hardly a word to us, but the impression was one of monumental strength and force. Though Father had spoken of his family, I had continued to conceive of him alone, a single solitary voice of truth that existed only to reveal to us. Now with the appearance of these biological relations, I began to glimpse, but only barely, the human possibilities and implications of the situation.

Father came with the hope that we would accompany them back and take up residence with them in their village. He caught very few of us at home, however. John O'Shea had taken off, I knew not where, to attend some of the numerous Calcutta associations he maintained. Shotsy had left earlier with Ken to "play" with him as he undertook some complicated procedural details preparent to his elaborate subcontinental departure, which would include transporting a large and cumbersome collection of musical instruments. Ken welcomed feats of physical and pragmatic challenge that would overwhelm, frustrate, and immobilize a person like me. As though the crating and packing and bureaucratic hassle over forms and fees involved in the shipping of a veritable museum of ancient instruments were not enough, Ken was also arranging, with a kind of conspiratorial dedication and delight, for the purchase and export of five thousand chillums. Shotsy's own hyperkinetic energy was drawn easily to his fever of material activities, and she accompanied him readily, anticipating, no doubt, what mischief or havoc she could stir in the puppet world of Calcutta business. Josh, I believe, had gone off to accompany David Bray to the British Consulate pursuant to the latter's repatriation. Mary also was somewhere else, perhaps at her dance class. That left only Gayle of their household, and Sheila and myself, to receive this seminal unit of the Roy family.

Sheila had met both Mishtu and Udit before, on the famous night that Father had taken them from the Birla Academy of Arts and Culture to his mud hut in Gorkhara, and she crinkled her nose and her eyes danced with warmth as she embraced them and stroked their hands. These were the first Indians I had met who did not recoil instinctively or become embarrassed by physical contact with us westerners. Gayle, by temper and disposition, is a kind person and a natural hostess, and she offered them all she had on hand or could easily acquire. Mishtu and Udit, gently tossing their heads in polite assent, accepted tea which was prepared in the British and American manner of adding sugar afterwards and offering a choice of lemon or milk.

Father leapt at the opportunity to have coffee. Gayle sweetened it heavily and was also generous in the proportion of milk. Father smacked his lips in enjoyment and made a great fuss about its excellence. Frequently in the years that followed, whenever Father would again meet her, usually after long periods, he would seldom fail to recall "that fine cup of coffee you prepared for me, Gayle," and he would look upon her with eyes full of gratitude as though that simple act of kindness were ever present to him.

Father spoke directly to Sheila when he finished with the coffee. "I'm sorry Shotsy isn't here. You both are needed at Gorkhara."

There followed the story of how in the days that had transpired since their move to the village, the attention of the Americans had become scattered and dispersed. They were so caught up in the reactions to all that they were feeling as a result of Father's revelations and the novelty of their new environment that it had become increasingly difficult for them to listen to anything Father had to say. He spoke of them as though they were spoiled and uncooperative children, and he showed increasing signs of frustration, and possibly anger, the longer he spoke of it. Lou in particular was annoying to him with his inadvertent but persistent lack of consideration and respect. Father's face grew ashen as he recounted Lou's frequent interruptions and inappropriate schemes and theories.

"Now look at your face," Sheila babied him. "It's all grey and worried-looking. Is that any way for a three-year-old to feel? I like to see your face all rosy and pink, and you should always be smiling, Father. You look like Bugs Bunny when you smile, and that's the face that makes us all feel happy."

Father fell silent a moment and his head fell upon his chest as he sat there. When he looked up again his complexion was in fact rosy, and he was sweet and smiling. "Now isn't that better?" Sheila asked, giving his knee a condescending pat.

"It is how I always feel, Sheila, just like an infant in the pleasant womb of this existence," Father answered. "But don't you know I maintain this aged form so it can act with the expressions of an adult as well? I only reflect you, you know. If you are sweet and loving then that is how I appear to you. If you are naughty then it is my duty and a natural reflex to turn towards you a stern and seeming disapproving visage. I assume that you are secure enough in the love I feel for you to know that I am really never displeased or disappointed in you. I know that it is all a part of the game. But it is also a part of the game that we grow up a bit and not simply bask in this mutual love but allow the adult work to flow through us so the love can spread into a greater universality. This is the third time, Sheila, that you have reduced me to an egg. Please don't abuse the power that you have over me by doing it again. It is great to enjoy your children, but don't stifle them and always keep them children, and don't allow your affection to postpone the natural perform- ance of the duties which responsible manhood shall demand. If you do not permit me to grow up, how will you grow up, and how will Śiva Kalpa come of age? I cannot change your diapers forever."

Sheila conceded the point as she always would, quickly and laughingly. She was never hurt or affronted in any way by being "told off" by Father as it turned out the rest of us often were. Father went on to appeal to her to help him stabilize order and receptiveness in the Gorkhara crew. Sheila responded immedi- ately with acquiescence and a speedy willingness to depart that moment for the village. More than motivated, she was abso- lutely inspired by direct assignment. Soldier-like, she was ready for anything that divine duty might require.

I too without any hesitation went to gather my things. After my rooftop talk of the other morning, I was ready to again take possession of my staff and responsibility for my bag of identity. I had come to accept what I always knew, that no one but myself could pick up for me, and that I was the only one who could play out the particular hand that had been dealt me; and so, more than resigned, I was quite content to resume my role and play each card as it now God-blessedly came toward ever-increasing odds of a happy and fortunate conclusion. We left word with Gayle for Shotsy and John to follow, and it was almost as one unit that the five of us made a prompt and easy exit.

A new phase was beginning, another cycle initiated. I thrilled with excitement and wonder at the potentially infinite extent, the adventuresome and unknown perimeters that would be touched by this moment of rebirth, and each step we traversed together was made light and buoyant in the enthusiastic reflection and anticipation of it all. As we flowed along and merged with the streams of human traffic on those Ballygunge streets, increasingly inundated with pedestrian floods, we fell, by natural energy, into the following formation: Father and I preceded the others, with Mishtu and Sheila next, and Udit at the rear. Sheila was as engrossed in all that she had to tell Mishtu as I was in all that Father was telling me. Udit was silent in the temporary isolation of his adolescent shyness.

I had walked these streets before with increasing degrees of familiarity, ease, and comfort. I had sauntered along them in my youth, it seemed, with my brother Rich beside me, and we had spoken ceaselessly about the nature and mystery of this strange world which was becoming our companionable home; I had stalked them alone in the solitary manhood of my spiritual quest, and now I strolled them in childlike security, wrapped in the protection and confidence of the love and care of my growing family.

I had not been quite this far south in my Calcutta expeditions, but I could easily guess by the increasing frequency of cluttered stalls and the haste and business of the rapidly multiplying brigades of foot travellers, as well as the invasion of lorries and trams into this otherwise relatively quiet residential district, that we were nearing Ballygunge Station. We seemed completely invisible and not at all a part of those other portions of humanity that had this same station as their objective. I was totally absorbed, not so much in the content of what Father was telling me in that moment but more with the feeling of love and familiarity that was emitted from him towards me, and I revelled in this mobile moment of communion in which I was the sole object and recipient of his attention.

"And so you see, . . ." he said, and paused where would naturally fall my name. Never on the four preceding occasions that we had been together, twice in the Astoria, once in the Grand Hotel, and once at Ken's flat, had Father asked or had I volunteered my name. Nonetheless, I felt that Father knew me intimately and individually and he, no doubt feeling the same only more, was momentarily taken aback to find that for all this love and familiarity, he did not know what to call me.

We stopped a moment in our tracks, and Father asked smilingly, "By the way, my son, what is your name?"

How many times since then have I thanked the providence that inspired my reply!

"I don't know, Father. If you are my Father, and I feel that you are, you shall name me."

I have relived that moment often, and of the multiflux of emotions that passed through me, I am aware of three distinct vital impulses or reflexes that prompted me to respond in that manner. One was that Father's "what is your name?" reverberated very quickly through me, each time becoming more sing-song and taking on the exaggerated cliché Indian accent with which I had so often been interrogated by the unfailing trinity of the catechism: "What is your name?" to be followed by the inane sounding "You are coming from?" almost invariably to climax with the befuddling "What is your mission?" Suddenly these questions assumed their cosmic importance. Surely it was not too much for those other illuminati to expect that I could now answer these three simple questions! If I were to become one with their company, enter at last that ever-bounteous room which is itself but a mere vestibule to all the cosmic corridors of mystery, the spiritual hallways and wondrous mansions of Self-knowing, certainly the answer then to these questions would be child's play. No doubt I had been attentive enough to the priviledge of conscious witness to so many of my past and future lives which had unveiled themselves so prolifically during this Indian stage and process of illumination and initiation, attentive enough to have finally learnt something. The answer was on the tip of my tongue, of course, but where I was coming from and my mission got jumbled in my head, appeared one and the same but elusively so, and because I could not answer these latter two, it seemed I had no right to answer the other one, as simple and self-evident as it might seem. What emerged inside was a gigantic but humble "I don't know."

Another thing that flashed instantly when Father asked me to identify myself was a power I had felt early in my journey when I had travelled so closely and compatibly with my brother Rich, a power that we had come to enjoy in direct proportion with our anonymity. Though many knew us personally and individually, we were generally spoken of as "those brothers," and something about that made them all readily confide in us a lot. I became appreciative of the freedom and ease with which almost everyone would volunteer their stories to us. For a long period I listened to others tell their tale and spoke little of myself. I enjoyed a power during that period, the power to enjoy and appreciate others, almost indiscriminately, without the need to explain, justify, or project myself. It did not pass with Rich's departure, for there was my communication with Marc to prolong it, but it did diminish in time, and I perceived that I was hearing less from others and more holding forth about my own experiences and what I thought I knew myself. My meeting Father was definitely a hearkening back to that other, more original and innocent state. I hesitated a moment before I should in any way delineate myself prematurely to Father and thereby risk the loss of his delightful free association of thought with me, and so I heard myself utter a cautious, "I don't know."

Also Father's question returned me to the recent resolve of being quit at last of the few remaining remnants of my legitimate identity. I could recall the feelings I had upon returning to Ken's flat during my late hours of acid and seeing my Tibetan bag and staff abandoned there. The insight of that moment was that I had but one short birth more to take, only a slight veil to remove, and I would stand tall and straight, take my rightful place amongst my illuminated peers, to become heir to my eternal share of understanding, and I had wished to hasten the process by denying and negating my most recent past association with myself. Although I had come since to accept the necessary resumption of my identity and things, I hoped it would not have the result of limiting me or weighing me down. So too there was something of proud determination and perhaps a suggestion of challenge as well in the answer that came out, "I don't know."

"I don't know, Father. If you are my Father, and I feel that you are, you shall name me."

We paused long enough to bring Sheila and Mishtu beside us. Sheila had heard my remark and said to Father, "Oh, yes. This is my little nameless child. You must name him, Father, so he'll no longer be our child without a name."

I felt a momentary tinge of annoyance. My gratitude to Sheila, for how much she had helped me to understand about Father and myself, paled slightly in the discomfort I felt with her intercession. If she were to play Mother to all or indeed any of us, then she must be sensitive not to become overly protective or ambitious for us. If as a mother she had helped lead me towards the great patriarch, then she must be content that she had done well by me and leave me to grow into my own manhood. Let me breathe, mother! I instantly empathized with Father's insistence that Sheila not "reduce him to an egg" again.

Father, however, paid her no mind at all, nor Mishtu nor Udit either as they surrounded him. He was totally absorbed in what I had requested of him.

"All right, my son," he answered, looking directly at me with eyes filled with warmth and affection. "Not now. When it comes to me." We proceeded on.

It was not upon the next morning, but I believe the one after that, that the communication was completed. I was returning from a bath, feeling very much at home and pleased with the entire existence, as I entered the dark but cozy room of the mud hut in which I knew Father and the rest of my family were enjoying morning revelations. Father stopped speaking upon my entering and looking full upon me said, "It came to me last night, son. I saw you . . ." He paused what seemed an interminably long time to me, though I am certain it was really no longer than a moderate swallow, before he finished with "Hari."

Almost three months later and two houses removed from our original residence in that mud hut, there came a sequel to this revelation of identity. We had moved from the Gorkhara to the Sonarpur side of the railroad tracks, and we lived up the road in a cement dwelling across from the District 24 Parganas power station. We always referred later to that stage of our life with Father and the Indian family as the one by the "power house." The family had grown considerably. For some time our inablity to handle our own things had been obvious. Any valuable possessions like cameras disappeared quickly as their owners became more stoned on dope or spaced out by Father's revelations. It got so that even worthless items like old worn sandals and occasionally even lungis carelessly placed while bathing had a way of getting lost or stolen. We had decided therefore to leave our real valuables, our passports or any money someone might have, in the trust of Father's eldest daughter Ruma, Vishnu's mother.

She, it seemed, was being trained to keep track and be responsible to the most minute and insignificant seeming bits of matter as well as to somehow miraculously manage the food and finances for an indeterminate growing number of people. This she did not only with competence but an awesome and truly worship-worthy equanimity which never shattered no matter how inconvenient or impossible seemed the demand. Often I would hear her and the other female members of Father's family (Udit seldom indulged in this particular game) babbling softly and giggling as they fingered through our passports. What delighted them was the contrast of the photo therein attached with the individual as he now presented himself as part of their household. Many a clean-shaven and callow youth pictured there had come to them as a scraggly and wizened sadhu. The young girls whose portraits showed them to have once been conventional in their employment of cosmetics and tutored smiles had come to them as world-weary and mature earth mothers, heroic in determination but a touch joyless in expression. To us our passports revealed a past shallowness which almost embarassed our sense of present purpose and achievement.

One afternoon I came upon Father himself chuckling over the passports and making funny comments in Bengali to Mishtu. To my surprise I saw that the passport that commanded his attention was my own. I too looked at the photo and was amazed at the enormous change between the person then and now, though in my case the change was not so much physical as in the attitude portrayed. I was bearded in the passport photo as I was standing there by the "power house." My beard was shorter before, more trimmed. What was striking was the earnestness and seriousness of expression of the face that stared out at me; it seemed much older than I presently felt. But it was not so much the photo that Father noticed as he learned for the first time the name that had been my legitimate nomenclature and tag to my communicable identity for nearly twenty-nine years. "H-a-r-v-e-y-space-M-e-y-e-r-s" it spelled, and Father read it aloud, "Harvey Meyers."

"So, Harvey Meyers," he said and laughed, and though his laughter seemed to me excessive, I joined since the name now sounded strangely distant to me and that somehow felt humorous. "Well, Harvey Meyers," Father continued, "you were pretty thinly disguised to yourself even in the ignorance. Did you really need me to tell you who you are?" He paused for what I was certain was indeed a long moment and no mere swallow and then ended in the most rhapsodic and pleasing tone imaginable – "Hari, master of maya."

This concludes Part One of
The Hariyana
in which is given the example of one person who
through
the Yoga of Dejection
is brought into reunion with
his Father.

May all beings, mental and sentient, find heart in the moments
of critical departure from truth which so overwhelm and con-
fuse on the mortal plane and in the human trance of existence.

AUM  TAT  SAT

ॐ

# सत्यम् शिवम् सुन्दरम्

## Śiva Kalpa
*Prathama Brāhmaṇa*

Seized by the divine will of self revelation the world is being consciously evolved by the immortal self awareness of Çirañjıva beginning ŚIVA KALPA on the nineteenth day of September One thousand nine hundred and sixty-six years after death of Jesus Christ.

ॐ

*Pranava, the* absolute movement of the PRIMAL SOUND of creation upholding manifestation in the eternal moment of existence by the indestructible presence of *omkāra* in perpetual evolution within the destructive silence of *mahākāla*.

सत्यम्

Truth of the real and vast Knowledge realizing the power of *satyam rtam vrhat*, the real and vast TRUTH by *rt çıt*, the Truth Consciousness.

शिवम्

*Çaitanya*, CONSCIOUSNESS experiencing all forms and forces as the luminous movement of ITS knowledge manifesting within the static subjectivity of ITS absolute existence beyond time and space.

सुन्दरम्

BEAUTY of the harmonious existence of Truth Consciousness revealing the power of ITS fulfillment and freedom in the phenomenal world of mind, life and matter.

The Truth of Existence is Beauty of Consciousness. Consciousness is the Truth of Beautiful Existence.

ABSOLUTE EXISTENCE
IS BEAUTY OF TRUTH CONSCIOUSNESS

TRUTH IS THE BEGINNING

TRUTH IS THE MIDDLE AND TRUTH IS THE END

Because

GOD IS TRUTH ● TRUTH IS LIGHT ● LIGHT IS LIFE

Because

Truth is Knowledge, Knowledge is Light, Light is Power,
Power is Existence, Existence is Life, Life is Beauty,
Beauty is Love, Love is Man, THE MENTAL BEING.

Because

Mental Being is Self Consciousness, Self Consciousness is Self Respect and
SELF RESPECT IS THE WAY TO THE LIFE OF TRUTH, KNOWL-
EDGE, POWER AND LOVE.


## KNOWLEDGE

ŚIVA KALPA is the Truth of infinite Knowledge manifesting the power of self realization in all Its forms and forces.

Within the absolute freedom of Its formless existence Knowledge is consciously apprehending the limitations of all forms of human knowledge infinitely exceeding them all at once effectuating their mutual harmony by the inevitable synthesis of the individual contradictions of their imperfect existences in the limitations of individual formations.

Beginning with the subtlest forms of spiritual and supra physical experience It is moving through all forms of knowledge including the grossest forms of material pragmatism embracing both *avidyā* and *vidyā*, ignorance and knowledge in the universal and unanimous synthesis of Matter and Spirit in the vast comprehensiveness of Its higher order of existence.

## LIGHT

Luminous quanta of divine intelligence thrilling out in infinite vibrations of accordance breaking joyously into the rhythm of greater and higher waves of illumination intensifying towards the growing light of a self-existent Knowledge spontaneously awaking to Itself as the SUN OF TRUTH receiving the world from the murky depth of an obscure physical bondage into the enlightened height of spiritual freedom by the transforming radiation of ITS glorious *jyoti*.

## POWER

The Power of infinite knowledge is evolved by the unique method of live expressions accelerating into infinite co-ordinations of illimitable forms and forces of human experience growing into the intended synthesis of subjective illumination of the divine will of self revelation by progressive transformation of the fevers of a deliriously hilarious existence groaning under the darkness of mounting pressures of mechanical wants and necessities of the seeming victory of an analytical form of material knowledge into the thrills of awakening in the dawn of a beautifully harmonious world of fulfilment and freedom evolving out of an apparent defeat of the synthetic knowledge of LOVE AND MANLINESS.

## EXISTENCE

The world has dawned in the light of its existence as an infinite consciousness realizing itself in the individual being of its infinitesimal forms, forces and movements by the liberation of human perfection in the ecstasy of self expression in the boundless form of its Knowledge and Power revealing the TRANSCENDENT in ITS supra cosmic conception of a static evolution of Consciousness cognising Itself as the Existence of Conscious Blissfulness translating Itself into the substance, force and form of a cosmic manifestation objectivised by a terrestrial consciousness of a mental, vital and physical form involving the self into the relativity of phenomenal existence of cosmic multiplicity by exclusive concentration on formal and material limitations by negation of the very essence of existence until the critical departure from TRUTH touches off the recoil of a spontaneous reawakening in the divine light of *Saççıdānanda*.

## YOGA

The Truth of *Tapas*, the creative omnipotence of *yoga* is revealed by the individual ascension of *Prakṛtı*, the Nature of *Çaıtanya*, the conscious being by the instrumentality of *ātma śaktı*, the self power of human force into the *jyotı* of absolute existence of Çaitanya manifesting the power of Çit, the will of Her being in *Puruṣa* enjoying the *līla* of *mahāmılana* with His willing *Prakṛtı* diverging out and converging in into infinite harmony of multiple existence of the same power of nature in the phenomenal expression of ŚANKARA, ecstatically dancing the rhythm of *pralaya* in the evolutionary publications of ŚIVA KALPA within the absolute silence beyond the conceptual opposites of existence and non-existence of *Çırañjıva*.

## PERFECTION

Awakened by *Śiva Śakti* from absorption in the constructions of *aparā prakṛti* into the native omniscience of *paramaṃ padaṃ*, the supreme status of absolute knowledge and power, *Bhagavāna Śankara* is blissfully witnessing the beauty of His *Prakṛti*, manifesting the power of upholding the creation of phenomenal existence by infinite divisions of His indivisible *vīrya* that is spirit into cosmic multiplicity of ego, breathlessly persuing the futile charms of *avidyā* obviously intensifying the agony of a critical existence until the divine is roused in the luminous synthesis of a physical, vital and mental form in perfect accord with thought, speech and action liberating the world from inertia of its formation by the subjective transformation of His cosmic multiplicity with an active objectivity of His individual expression of *paramaṃ padaṃ*, the supreme status of Mental Being in cognizable form and force of *Śankara*, evolving the Self in all His forms by the supra mental power of *Yoga*.

## EVOLUTION

Within the delirious experience of the intensifying apprehension of the age running headlong for its inevitable cataclysm, the world has evolved into the most thrilling and interesting stage of its existence by the fulfillment of the highest and the noblest urge of *Prakṛti* by the successful birth of human perfection in possession of the Truth and Knowledge of practical omnipotence.

These spiritual and supra physical experiences are not merely the inspired revelations of an individual, unseizable by thought and incommunicable by speech but the most simple and logical conclusion of a vast accumulation of Knowledge of illimitable forms and forces of human experience spreading out in boundless space and time by an absolute concentration of experience of illimitable forms and forces of human knowledge of infinite space and time into an individual form of Knowledge of an individual force of human experience in an individual point of space in an individual moment of time working out the individual events of its collective existence by the self conscious will of evolution constituting the RHYTHM OF THE ECSTATIC PERIOD of Śiva Kalpa.

# RE EVOLUTION

The journey that never was made
Amid hopes and perils the trail was laid
    Through adventures that never took place.

Mission lost in passions transient
Seeking pleasures always in pain
    Desire-moments fettered time thru' space

Path blazed by desires in flame
Journey awakes to its joyous game
Guided in darkness, now in light
Motion becomes its own delight

The end is ever in the source inscribed
Around the circle never described
Time and space and Motion sublime
Rhythm of Stillness signs the hymn

All is yet an intense Reality
A moment in Conscious luminosity.

ॐ तत् सत् ।

Published by His will in Nirmalya, Gorkhara, P.O. Kamrabad, Dist. 24-Parganas welcoming the world for personal experience of evolution.

This book was set by Eileen Ostrow in 10-point Pilgrim and was printed at the West Coast Print Center, Berkeley, Ca. 94703